DRIVERS, START YOUR ENGINES

Jaycee focused on her salad and did her best not to remember the way Rory had looked when he'd taken a bite of her carrot. More importantly, the way he'd looked at her as if he'd wanted to sink his teeth into her and nibble away.

As if.

Rory Canyon didn't like her like that. Not then. Not now.

It's a game, she told herself. *He knows you're gunning for his spot and he wants to distract you.*

But as much as she wanted to think he was a low-down, dirty, conniving snake-in-the-grass, a man willing to use his sex appeal to weaken the competition, she couldn't quite believe it. Any more than she could forget the hunger that simmered in his gaze whenever he glanced at her.

Maybe he really and truly wanted her.

Maybe . . .

KIMBERLY RAYE

Slippery When Wet

LOVE SPELL NEW YORK CITY

For all of my loyal and dedicated readers who wrote to
me wanting more love and laughter and NASCAR,
This one's for you . . .

LOVE SPELL®

December 2008

Published by

Dorchester Publishing Co., Inc.
200 Madison Avenue
New York, NY 10016

ISBN 10: 0-505-52773-1
ISBN 13: 978-0-505-52773-8

The name "Love Spell" and its logo are trademarks of Dorchester
Publishing Co., Inc.

Printed in the United States of America.

10 9 8 7 6 5 4 3 2 1

Visit us on the web at www.dorchesterpub.com.

Slippery When Wet

Chapter One

The place reeked of testosterone.

This was Riley Vaughn's first big clue that something was desperately wrong. Clue two came when she stared across the massive warehouse that housed the set for the day's magazine shoot.

Her breath caught as she eyed the individuals who emerged from the dressing rooms and took center stage in front of the white backdrop and blazing lights. They were the best of the best when it came to stock-car racing. They all looked hot and hunky and totally *GQ* in black Armani tuxedos.

The problem?

This was a photo shoot for *Vogue*, showcasing the new women's line. More importantly, one of the "Fab Four" was a woman. A stubborn, unreasonable, irrational woman. Wearing a tux.

Riley frowned and started toward the quartet. She'd barely made it two steps when a wail split open the busy hum of people working and bounced off the twenty-foot walls.

"No, no, no!" A fiftyish woman rushed toward the group, a camera in her hand. She wore an NYU sweatshirt, a long, flowing, flower-print skirt, flip-flops and a thunderous expression. "What *is* this?" Her narrowed gaze swept the Fab Four before shifting back to the eager young assistant who carried her camera bag. "She's supposed to be wearing The Dress," she growled, before shifting her attention to the frazzled-looking costume designer. "Rochelle!" she wailed at the woman. "Where's The Dress?"

"Dwayne!" Rochelle yelled, her frantic gaze searching the surrounding group. "Justice wants The Dress!"

A man rushed from the sidelines. He was short and trim, his spiked blond hair barely visible behind the pile of fuchsia taffeta and silk he carried. "Don't get your panties in a wad," he said in the familiar southern accent that had made Riley feel at home for the first time since she'd arrived in the Big Apple just a few short days ago.

Of course, everyone she'd met, from the reporters to the sports anchors, had been pleasant and cordial. But they'd all been more interested in firing off as many questions as possible, rather than making her feel less homesick. She couldn't blame them. They had their livelihoods to think of, just as she had hers.

Her fingers tightened on the Revved & Ready energy drink in her hand, the label emblazoned with a hot pink RACE CHICKS, INC. R & R was the main—the only— sponsor for Riley's racing team. Which was why she'd singlehandedly given away hundreds of cans of the stuff over the past few days, along with coupons for free music downloads at RandR.com, caps, T-shirts, koozies and even hot-pink condoms. She'd been a walking promo machine, hitting everything and everyone in sight.

Then she'd entered the studio a few hours ago and met Dwayne Mulligan, wardrobe assistant. He hadn't asked for one freebie—not even the bubble gum–flavored condoms. Rather, he'd offered her a glass of sweet tea, a smooth, twangy *Aren't you just a pretty little thing?* and a smile, and she'd actually forgotten that she was about as far out of her element as any born-and-bred Texas girl could get.

We're talking New York City and *Vogue* magazine.

That was also when she'd started to entertain the possibility that maybe this whole media blitz wasn't a waste of time. Maybe, just *maybe*, the exposure might help garner a few more desperately needed sponsors and boost her racing team's image.

Their *new* image.

"We need The Dress," the photographer bellowed. "Get her in The Dress. *Now*."

Fat friggin' chance.

Too much refined sugar had obviously created a false sense of euphoria, during which Riley had forgotten one all-important fact—Jaycee Anderson.

Twenty-six-year-old Jaycee had finished fourth in the final race for the Nextel Cup this past November. She was the first woman ever to place in the top five and a major contender for the upcoming race season scheduled to start in mid-February, just six short weeks from now. Jaycee was the only driver for Riley's newly organized team, Race Chicks, Inc., and a major pain in the ass.

Oh, and she was also Riley's younger sister. Half sister.

"Honey," Dwayne said as he walked over to where Jaycee stood on the set, "I already told you—nothing gets past Justice. She's a major bee-yotch when it comes to her photo shoots."

Dwayne—bless him—gripped Jaycee's arm and tugged her toward the dressing area. The stubborn blonde tried digging in her heels, but Dwayne was strong for such a petite guy. "Come along now, before you get us both booted out on our toned and tucked assets."

"Sounds good to me," Jaycee muttered.

"Now, now, you don't mean that. Every woman wants a spotlight in *Vogue*."

Which was the problem in a nutshell.

Jaycee wasn't every woman. Far from it, in fact. She was a tomboy, from her unkempt ponytail to the tips of her scuffed black biker boots. She didn't know her mousse from her hairspray. She didn't wear makeup or do her nails. She didn't even watch *Grey's Anatomy*.

Dwayne held up a dress. "You're putting it on, sugar. If I have to stuff you into it myself."

"Make one move toward me with that thing and I'll shove my foot so far up your ass, you'll look like a Popsicle."

"You just described my last date. Now move." Dwayne kept pulling, Jaycee kept tugging, but eventually they disappeared down the hallway.

"Hurry it up," the bee-yotch called after them. "We're wasting money, not to mention time. I've got two more shoots today and I need to wrap this up ASAP. Models," the woman huffed as she turned to hand her camera to her assistant. "So damned temperamental."

"She's not a model," Rochelle told her boss. "She's a driver. They're all drivers." She motioned to the three men, who lingered on the set. A smile tugged at her lips. "NASCAR drivers. Don't you know who they *are*?"

"I'm a fashion photographer. Why would I know them from Adam?"

She wouldn't, which was why NASCAR, in conjunction with several of the various team sponsors, had set this up in the first place. It was a prime chance to beef up the sport's image with its fastest-growing fan base—women.

The three male members of the Fab Four had been all too happy to oblige. Riley hadn't seen one frown, nor had she heard one complaint since they'd arrived that morning with their PR and sponsor reps. Even Rory Canyon of the notorious Canyon brothers was behaving himself.

Jaycee was a different story.

Riley's sister had been difficult from the get-go, despite the fact that Race Chicks desperately needed the exposure to lure a few more sponsors or, at the very least, keep the one they had. Thus, Riley wasn't the happiest camper in the RV park.

An all-female racing team plus a new female-targeted energy drink equaled a match made in marketing heaven, right? In a perfect world. But Riley's world had been screwed up since the day her father, the late Ace Anderson, had walked out the door and abandoned her at six years old. While he'd been one hell of a driver, he'd sucked as a father.

At least, he'd sucked as Riley's dad.

He'd actually stuck around for Jaycee.

A hell of a lot of good it had done her. While Jaycee hadn't spent years worrying and wondering and hating Ace for all the things he hadn't done, she'd still had her own problems to deal with. She'd lost her mother in a car accident and had then been stuck with Ace, who was nothing short of a selfish jerk/SOB/insert your favorite synonym for *certifiable asshole*. She'd had no time for dolls or tea parties or anything remotely resembling a normal childhood. He'd made sure of that. Instead, he'd had her following him around the garage, learning the ins and outs of an engine.

Which explained the current predicament.

Jaycee had learned too well. She'd followed in Ace's footsteps, from the very way she dressed—her hair stuffed up under one of his old ball caps and her curves hidden beneath one of his trademark "Ace in the Hole" T-shirts and a pair of baggy jeans—to her behavior: forceful, demanding, overly cocky. She could chug a can of Bubba Beer faster than most of the men in her field, and burp even louder. But while she could hang with the guys—she'd gained the admiration of NASCAR's loyal male audience—she hadn't scored any brownie points with the women.

Yet.

"Who cares about drivers?" Justice took the bottled water that her assistant handed her. "This is a fashion magazine. We need the latest Donatellini Borishka."

"I'm sure Dwayne will get her into it as fast as possible," Rochelle assured her boss.

Only if Dwayne's a miracle worker.

Riley ignored that depressing thought and focused on the one and only positive thing in the entire situation: for the first time in the six months since Ace had died and left her in charge of his failing team, she didn't have to be the one to deal with Jaycee.

She smiled and stepped toward the disgruntled photographer. "They, um, might be awhile. How about a can of Revved & Ready in the meantime?"

"You have to loosen up," Dwayne told Jaycee a good half hour later. "It's like you're the one with something shoved up your ass."

"I'm loose already," Jaycee said from beneath a pile of taffeta. She blew out an exasperated breath and tried to ease the pounding of her heart. "I put the damned thing on, didn't I? I'm fine."

"I mean literally." Dwayne stood behind Jaycee and tugged at the garment's edges. "Relax your shoulders so I can get the buttons fastened."

"Oh." Jaycee let her arms fall to her sides and tried to fight down the panic rising in her throat.

It was just a dress. No big deal. It wasn't like she was buying the thing and wearing it during the next race. She could handle being uncomfortable for, say, ten minutes. Fifteen, tops.

"I got it," Dwayne finally said. He worked at the buttons, one after the other, until he slid the last into place. "How does it feel?"

"I can't move my arms."

"You don't have to move. Just look sexy and thoughtful, and Justice will work her magic with the camera."

"I can't breathe, either." Jaycee fought for a deep breath, but there just wasn't enough room inside the dress. The fitted bodice tightened and the air stalled. The plunging neckline caught and lifted her breasts that much higher, until her nipples threatened to spill over. "I think I might be in serious need of an oxygen tank." She eyed her chest. "And a net. Just in case anything decides to dive over the neckline and swim for the nearest exit."

"They won't make it far. Justice is a shark." Dwayne turned her and gave her a push toward the door. "Now scat before she comes looking for you. Trust me. You don't want to piss her off any more than she already is."

"Yeah," Jaycee grumbled as she stepped forward. "I'm shaking in my shoes."

"Ohmigod!" He caught one shoulder and spun her

back around. Taffeta flounced and swished and Jaycee's head spun. "I can't believe I almost forgot." He dug through a mound of boxes before pulling out a pair of silver snakeskin heels. "Here. Put these on."

Jaycee shook away the lightheaded feeling courtesy of the too-tight dress and trained her gaze on the three-inch heels. She shook her head. "You must be smoking some heavy-duty stuff if you think those things are getting anywhere near my feet."

"You *have* to."

"The last time I looked, this was America. Death and taxes. That's it."

"Exactly. Justice will *kill* you if you go out there without these," he told her, his voice twangy and overly dramatic.

"Don't you think you're taking this a little too seriously?"

"Okay, she'll kill *me*." He gave her a level stare. "Do you know how long it took me to get this internship? I've been at NYU the past six years just praying for a chance like this. You have to put them on." As if on cue, Justice's voice carried down the hallway.

"Duh-wayne! I'm waiting!"

"We're on our way." He turned back to Jaycee. "Come on, sister. Time is money."

Jaycee stared at the high-heeled shoes and a memory fought its way into her brain of a similar pair of flashy shoes and an even flashier dress.

Her first. And her last.

She shook her head. "Forget it. I'm not doing it."

"You're not?" He eyed her and realization dawned in his gaze. "Or you can't?"

Jaycee frowned. "Kiss my ass."

"I can't believe this. Rough and tough Jaycee Anderson is afraid of an itty-bitty high heel."

She glared. "Give me the damned things, already." She dropped them to the floor and shoved one foot into the narrow toe. "It doesn't fit," she declared after several tries. Relief swept through her and a smile tugged her lips. "It's the wrong size."

"We have more," Dwayne told her as he turned toward a stash of boxes. "Just give me a sec—"

"Time is money." She threw his words back at him, turned on her heel and traded the dressing room for the hallway.

The tulle swished and tangled around her legs with each step. A dress was bad enough. But no way was she going to wobble around in front of God, a bunch of magazine people and the other drivers.

Especially the drivers.

She was halfway to the set when a door opened to her left and suddenly she collided with a solid shoulder and massive bicep. She stumbled, and strong hands came up to catch her arms and keep her from pitching backward.

Her gaze met Rory Canyon's, and awareness sizzled through her. His fingers burned into her bare skin, upping her already-soaring body temperature. Her heart pitched forward.

For a split second, she forgot about the tight bodice of the dress and the material smothering her legs, and her bare toes peeking from beneath the hem. Instead, she found herself thinking about how blue his eyes were and how she would really, really like to see him naked.

Chapter Two

"You look really . . ."

Pretty, hot, sexy?

". . . pink," Rory finally finished. His deep voice shattered the moment and jerked Jaycee back to reality and the all-important fact that she couldn't stand him. Even if he did have great eyes and a really dynamite smile, and the best body she'd ever seen.

"The same pink as that race car of yours," he added with a wink. "You're missing your true calling, sugar. You'd make a great hood ornament," he said in typical Canyon fashion.

Rory's dad was one of the founding members of Men On Top, a group of good ole boys who longed for a return to the past when men were men and women weren't. Like his father and his brothers and every other card-carrying MOT, Rory liked a woman he could intimidate.

At least, that's the conclusion Jaycee had come to after she'd offered herself to him that fateful night so long ago and he'd turned her down cold.

"Such charm." She gave him a fake smile despite her heart, which chugged like a freight train. "The women must swoon."

"You know it, darlin'."

"Confidence," she quipped. "That's good. You'll need all you can get to make up for the lack of talent." His gaze darkened for a split second, but his smile didn't waver. *Score one.* "I could practically feel my arteries hardening when I watched you at the last track test at Bristol," she added. "It wasn't much of a speed exhibition, but you could definitely use it as an audition tape for the remake of *Driving Miss Daisy*."

He didn't so much as flinch. Instead, his grin spread wider.

Her thighs actually started to quiver. Bad, *bad* thighs.

"I knew beneath those big, sloppy T-shirts lurked the heart of a stalker," he murmured, his voice raw and sexy.

She cleared her suddenly dry throat. "I wasn't stalking. I was observing."

His eyes gleamed, hot and knowing. "That's what they all say, sugar."

She focused on the anger stirring in her gut rather than her buzzing hormones, and frowned. "You know good and well I wasn't *watching* you. It was strictly for competition's sake. I wanted to see you in action."

"That's what they all say, too." His smile faded and something hot and bright sparked in his gaze.

Jaycee's breath caught and her nipples tightened. She drew a deep breath, steeled herself and held tight to her irritation. "Can you and your ego move out of the way? I've got people waiting."

He grinned, slow and easy, and her heart stuttered a few beats. After a long, unmoving moment, he finally stepped aside. "Ladies first." He gestured.

"You're a jackass," she muttered, and sauntered past. At least, she tried to saunter past, but her feet kept tangling in the hem of the dress and she stumbled again.

She *so* wasn't good at this stuff. Riley could pull it off with her long legs and big boobs and perfect figure. But Jaycee . . .

No, she'd never been comfortable wearing anything even remotely girly, no matter how hard she'd tried. She'd always been too short and stocky to look good in dresses, too awkward to wear sandals or heels, too self-conscious to wear shorts and tank tops, too . . . wrong.

Her father had recognized it right away, so he'd steered her clear of the whole girl experience and let her take refuge in the garage.

At least that's what she'd always thought. That Ace had really and truly loved her. That he'd focused on her attributes rather than her flaws when he'd given her a future behind the wheel of a race car—a reputable, no-nonsense, get-the-job-done black Ford, just for the record.

But then Ace died, Riley had stepped into the picture and Anderson Racing had become history. Her older sister had renamed the small team, wangled a new sponsor, and just like that, Jaycee had found herself behind the wheel of a Pepto-Bismol–pink Chevy.

Even more, she'd found herself rethinking her entire life.

A lie.

It had all been a lie.

She drew a deep breath and tried to calm her pounding heart. She could do this. It was one little photo shoot. A blip on the radar of her career. The last thing she needed to worry over. Rather, she had bigger problems. Three of them, to be exact.

She emerged from the hallway to a round of collective sighs, and her eyes turned to the two men who stood near a lavish table spread with food. One munched on finger sandwiches while the other scarfed down raw vegetables and ranch dip. Trey Calloway and Mackenzie Briggs.

The two men sat in the first and second spots, respectively. They were good. Determined. But she knew she could beat them. Eventually.

First things first . . .

Her attention shifted to the hallway where she'd left Rory. As if her mind had conjured him, he appeared, striding through the doorway in his crisp black suit.

He had short, dark hair and the kind of good looks that made every father nervous and every mother hopeful. Brilliant blue eyes fringed with incredibly long lashes. A strong, shadow-stubbled jaw. Perfect nose. Sensuous lips. He was tall compared to most of the other drivers, well over six feet, with broad shoulders and a trim waist.

His gaze collided with hers for a brief moment and an easy smile curved his sinful mouth. Jaycee's heart stuttered and she had the sudden urge to smack him. Or hump his brains out.

She ignored the strange push-pull of emotion and focused on the fact that Rory Canyon was sitting in third place.

Her spot.

One she fully intended to claim this next season.

She was good enough. She just needed a faster car. A better engine. A Schilling engine.

Martin Schilling was the best engineer in the industry. His designs had won five out of the past five championships. He was brilliant. Creative. Intuitive. Insightful. And incredibly expensive.

But Jaycee didn't need him to design a complete engine for her. She already had her own design. What she needed was for him to take a look at what she'd come up with and offer some suggestions. In fact, she'd already contacted him and asked for his help, despite the fact that Riley had vetoed the idea.

Jaycee shifted her attention to her sister, who stood on the sidelines handing out Revved & Ready items. The tall blonde spared her a sweeping glance. Disapproval sparked in her vivid green eyes when she spotted Jaycee's bare feet peeking from beneath the hem of the dress.

The car is adequate, Riley's voice echoed in Jaycee's head. *What we need is enough sponsors to get us through the coming season.*

Making it. That's all Riley cared about. Fulfilling the requirements of Ace's last will and testament. He'd specified that his oldest daughter had to serve as team owner for a full race season—from start to finish—in order to inherit her half of the estate.

Since he'd died in the middle of this past season, the clock didn't officially start until next month in Daytona.

Riley's main concern was getting them to each race, regardless of the outcome. Jaycee wanted more. She wanted to win.

She had to win.

"Let's go, people!" Everyone in the room started to move as Justice called out orders. "Guys, get over here."

Mac and Trey turned from the buffet and their gazes stalled on Jaycee. Surprise sparked in both pairs of eyes, followed by disbelief. Then Trey winked and Mac gave her an amused grin.

"One word," Jaycee told them, "and I'll kick both of your asses. Right here. Right now."

Both men threw up their hands as if to say *Who me?* as Jaycee barreled past.

Just another day, she told herself, doing her best to ignore Rory and his continued shit-eating grin. She fixed her attention on the race car that sat center stage.

This particular sleek, silver model was Chevy's newest version to conform to NASCAR's rigorous specs, from the revamped front end to the controversial spoiler. The "car of tomorrow," as it had originally been called, had debuted the previous year in an attempt to "fair up" the racing experience. It had been mandatory in several of the races and was fast becoming the standard.

Jaycee, like every other driver, still had objections to the design—namely, that it was harder to handle than the typical car—but then, that was the point: to promote equal opportunity on the track and force the drivers to bring their best game.

Game on.

"Let's make this happen," the photographer continued. "You"—she pointed to Trey—"there. You"—her finger whipped to Mac—"prop your hip against that rear fin. You"—she motioned to Rory—"lean up against the driver's side. And you . . ." She eyeballed Jaycee. "You get the hot seat."

Jaycee smiled, reached down and gathered her skirt to climb through the window. She was just giving herself a mental pat on the back for not fitting into the snakeskin heels—she couldn't very well climb into the driver's seat in stilettos—when the photographer's voice stopped her.

"Not there! There!" The irate woman jabbed a finger toward the front of the car. "Climb onto the hood. We need to see The Dress."

Rory's soft chuckle slid into her ears, and Jaycee made her decision.

Forget wanting to kiss him.

She would much rather smack him upside his hand-some head.

She was wearing a friggin' *dress*.

Rory Canyon fought against the frown that tugged at his lips. Not that he had anything against a woman wearing something soft and frilly and flattering.

Unless it was *the* woman.

He had a hard enough time keeping his head on straight whenever Jaycee Anderson popped onto his radar. He sure didn't need to see her like this. So soft and close and pretty and . . . *close*.

Easy, guy. Just slow up and remember to breathe and you'll make it to the finish line.

He drew a deep, calming breath and focused on the positive. Despite the dress, she looked about as ap-proachable as a hissing radiator. A red stain crept up her neck and fired her cheeks. Her pretty pink lips drew into a tight frown. Her eyebrows furrowed together. Her caramel-colored eyes flashed with fury.

Lucky for him. When Jaycee got the notion to smile, the result never failed to stall the oxygen in his lungs, which was why Rory had made it his personal mission over the past five years to make sure she *didn't* smile. Lack of air meant poor focus, and he couldn't afford that.

He had a job to do. Even more, he had an image to uphold. He wasn't driving the Bubba Beer car for nothing. He was the proud representative of Men On Top everywhere, and he wasn't letting them down by letting some woman get under his skin and into his head. Even more, he wasn't letting himself down. He was the closest he'd ever been to winning a cup championship, and he wasn't slipping up now.

"Okay, people, look at me!"

Rory trained his gaze on the photographer and tried to forget the blonde in his peripheral vision. She looked even better than the last time he'd seen her in a dress. A bad sign, because he'd crashed and burned back then in a major way. Temporarily, of course. He'd picked himself back up, climbed back into the driver's seat and punched it ninety to nothing away from Jaycee Anderson. He'd been gunning in the opposite direction ever since.

He drew a deep breath and tried to ignore her soft, shallow breaths. In a few minutes she would shed the dress, pull on her baggy jeans and oversized T-shirt and morph back into the old Jaycee. The Jaycee who, thankfully, kept everything covered.

Out of sight, out of mind. That had been Rory's motto since that fateful year when Jaycee had turned thirteen and left her chubby girlish body behind. He'd been seventeen at the time, and already an upcoming star on the short tracks. He'd also had loads of experience when it came to sex, thanks to the trophy girls who'd been eager to teach him all the particulars in exchange for bragging rights. When he'd suddenly seen Jaycee as more than just a sweet kid, he'd wanted her so much it hurt.

They'd been friends back then.

Not when they'd first met, of course. She'd been only four and he'd been eight, and he'd only seen her at the occasional race.

But when Rory's mother died, he'd started to see a lot more of Jaycee. His dad had been a driver back then, so he'd hauled his boys to the track on a regular basis—much like Jaycee's old man. Rory had been there when she'd busted her knee falling on a crank shaft, and she'd been there when he'd flipped the engine on his first car.

They'd learned the ins and outs of a race car together.

But when things had changed, when *she'd* changed, he'd done the only thing he'd been able to under the circumstances—he'd turned his back on her and walked away. He wasn't throwing his career away for a woman. Not then, and certainly not now.

His mind traveled back and he remembered the way Jaycee had looked the night she'd shown up on his doorstep wearing a pink number much shorter than the one she wore now. She'd never been tall, but damn if her legs hadn't looked long and endless. She'd had curves he'd never noticed before, and a smile that had spun him around and turned him inside out.

And then she'd kissed him, and he'd all but come right there in his jeans.

He'd known then and there that he had to get while the getting was good. He'd had no room in his life for romantic entanglements. Racing after school and on the weekends had taken everything from him—his full attention, his determination, his passion. Even more, Canyon men didn't let women drag them around by their pubes. No, they called the shots. Led the pack. Both on and off the track.

He'd turned her down and turned his back on that delicious body of hers because he couldn't afford any distractions. Translation? When it came to women, he'd take casual flings only. Something temporary and physically gratifying, with zero emotional content.

He allowed himself a quick look. His gaze drank in the curve of her bare shoulders, the creamy expanse of cleavage, the distinctive outline of her nipples beneath the skimpy pink bodice, the narrow tuck of her waist, the tips of her bare toes peeking from beneath the dress. His attention shifted to her face and the soft pout of her full lips.

Lucky for him she wasn't smiling; otherwise, he would have had to gun it for the nearest door.

That, or kiss her.

Yep, he wanted to nibble her lips and plunge his tongue deep and taste her really, *really* bad.

He'd always had a sweet tooth, and she was so damned tempting sitting there like a fluff of cotton candy. His stomach hollowed out and his mouth watered. His dick throbbed.

"You look morose," the photographer called out, her disapproving frown fixed on Jaycee. "You're supposed to be having fun." She waved her arms. "You've got a great outfit. You're surrounded by hot-looking guys with great big packages. Look happy!"

Rory waited for Jaycee to verbally chew the photographer up and spit her back out the way she would have any man who made the mistake of ordering her around. He'd seen it time and time again. While it pissed off his dad and the other "Himanists," it stirred Rory's admiration as much as his lust.

The Himanists, aka Men On Top, was a non-profit group dedicated to the self-preservation of men in a society fast becoming dominated by women. Word Canyon, Rory's dad, was the president and founder of the group and the biggest male chauvinist of them all. Word couldn't stand Jaycee.

Rory fought against the tightening in his groin and tried to calm the frantic beat of his heart.

Fat chance.

Time seemed to stand still for the next few seconds as the entire room paused. Then, from the corner of his eye, he saw Jaycee's lips tighten.

Thank you, thank you, thank you, he sent up the silent prayer. *Let it rip. Just open up your mouth, sugar, and let loose with the ballsy attitude.*

But then those full, pink lips curved and parted and—

Holy shit.

Chapter Three

Jaycee watched Rory hightail it off the set and barely resisted the urge to beat a hasty retreat herself.

She was *not* running after him.

Even if he did look ready to toss his cookies or have a seizure. Maybe he'd eaten something bad. In that case, she should stop angsting over his well-being and start being more concerned with her own. She could have eaten the same thing and sucked down her own share of wicked bugs. Which she couldn't afford. She had a full weekend ahead, starting with a wind-tunnel test on her new engine tomorrow morning. Being sick wasn't on her calendar.

Thankfully, she'd been too worked up over the dress to even touch the buffet set up in the far corner of the warehouse. Her gaze shifted to Mac and Trey. They'd both scarfed enough to feed an entire racing team, but neither looked ready to toss their cookies.

No, they looked as handsome, as fit, as amused as ever.

Amused?

Because poor Rory was sick.

Jaycee stiffened. What a couple of dicks! Why, she ought to give them both a piece of her—

"What the hell is this?" Justice shrieked. "This is the

Fab Four. I can't do the Fab Four with just three. Someone find out what the hell is going on!"

The seconds ticked by as a trio of flunkies rushed after Rory. "He's sick," someone called out almost im-
mediately.

Uh-oh. The air rushed from Jaycee's lungs. Crazy,
right? Considering she was nearly incapable of sucking in a decent breath in the first place, thanks to the
dress.

"Do we have any stand-ins?" Justice demanded.
"Where's Jeremy?"

"But he's an underwear model." Her assistant
stepped forward. "He's not a NASCAR driver."

"Well, get me another driver."

"It's not that easy."

The photographer shook her head. "Forget it. We'll
shoot it as is." She started snapping, and Jaycee found
herself caught in a blinding flash.

"Stop turning your head," Justice ordered. "Look toward the front of the car. You're going to get whiplash
if you keep staring behind you."

"I wasn't staring."

"She was staring," the assistant offered.

"I was not—"

"No talking!" Justice kept snapping, and Jaycee
barely resisted the urge to hop from the car and stomp
off the set herself.

Not because she was worried about Rory, mind
you. So what if he was sick? Maybe it would be something long and lingering and he would miss the race at
Daytona.

A girl could only hope.

At the same time, Jaycee had never been one to color
outside the lines. She kept everything on the up-and-

up. She wanted to beat Rory Canyon fair and square. Which meant she wanted him healthy. Then she would gladly kick his ass sixty ways 'til Sunday.

"You're staring again," Justice snapped, and Jaycee forced her attention straight ahead. The camera flashed and her heart pounded.

A fair race. That's what she told herself a half hour later as she combed the hallway looking for Rory. To see if he needed anything. A glass of water. An antacid. A doctor. Mouth-to-mouth.

She was such a horny toad. But months of intense training—and celibacy—would have the same effect on anyone, man or woman. It wasn't that she lusted after Rory in particular. He was male. Good-looking. Sexy. What woman wouldn't want to have sex with him? He was just the handiest thing with a penis.

Oh, yeah? If it was all a matter of equipment, you'd be panting after Trey and Mac and any other member of the opposite sex.

She ignored the nagging inner voice and continued on with her search.

"What is with you?" Riley asked, when she spotted Jaycee searching the back hallway. "They need you back on the set."

"I thought they were finished." She opened a door to the storage closet. No Rory. She slammed the door shut and moved on.

"With that particular set. They need you for round two."

Jaycee hauled open another door. "Having me on the hood wasn't humiliating enough? What do they want now? To drape me across the rear bumper?"

"They're not going to do that." Riley averted her gaze. "It's the roof this time."

"It figures." She opened yet another door. And another.

"What are you doing?"

"Looking for Canyon."

"He left."

Jaycee came up short. "You saw him? Is he okay?"

"Yes, and I guess so."

"Was he walking or riding on a gurney?"

Her sister gave Jaycee an odd look. "He was walking."

"Between two paramedics or by himself?"

"By himself."

Relief rushed through Jaycee and she managed to take a nice, easy breath despite the tight bodice.

"What is up with you?" Riley repeated. Before Jaycee could reply she added, "No, never mind. I don't want to know. Your personal life is your business. If you actually—"

"I don't," she cut in before Riley could say *like*. "He's egotistical. Domineering. Bossy. A real hard-ass."

"In other words, your soul mate."

Jaycee glared at her half sister. "Very funny."

Riley didn't blink. "I'm serious."

"I'm not egotistical."

"I could argue that, but I don't have the energy, despite all the Revved & Ready I've been sucking down. You're still three for three." When Jaycee didn't argue, Riley added, her voice suddenly softer, "I could make a few calls and see if he's okay."

"Just make sure he's going to be at Daytona. I'm bringing my best game and I don't want anyone saying I won by default." She turned and started down the hallway before Riley could speculate on the situation any further.

It was all about professional concern. Personally,

Jaycee couldn't care less. She had more important things to worry about. Like tomorrow's wind-tunnel test. And next week's track test at Daytona. And the performance of her new engine. She was not—repeat, NOT—going to obsess over Rory.

She'd already made a fool of herself once where he was concerned. A mistake that had cost her a lot more than just her pride.

Never, ever again.

"Take off all your clothes, put this on and I'll be right back."

Rory stared at the paper hospital gown the orderly handed him and wondered how in the hell he'd gotten himself into this mess.

You skipped out, bud, and now it's time to man up.

It had been a full day since he'd walked off the *Vogue* shoot, and he'd spent every moment since trying to convince his dad and his brothers that he wasn't about to bust a kidney or have a heart attack.

If only.

Rory hadn't been able to admit a major case of lust, and so he'd ended up back in Dallas. In an exam room at North Baptist Hospital. With an orderly named Sean.

Correction. He wasn't just an orderly, but a die-hard race fan named Sean, who'd begged Rory to autograph his forehead right before he'd asked for a urine sample.

"I can't do this," Rory told the man.

"I know the feeling, dude. These robes can be tricky. One minute you're keeping it cool and the next, it's a full moon." He let loose a wolf call and waggled his eyebrows. "I'd be more than happy to help you undress. Don't worry," he added when Rory held up a hand. "I'm not gay. At least, not when it comes to NASCAR drivers. Now if you were the lead singer for Nickelback, I might think about it. As it is, I don't want your bod, but I do want the gown once you're done." He snatched up the magazine Rory had abandoned. "I'm going to make a killing on eBay with this stuff." He reached out to help with the gown.

Rory shook his head. "Thanks, but I think I can manage."

Disappointment flashed in the man's gaze. "Really? Because my girlfriend and I have been saving for a new car, and I bet this thing will bring in enough for the down payment."

"It's yours if you'll do me a favor. Can you get my brother in here? He's in the lobby."

"If you'll put on two—one back-to-front and the other front-to-back—I bet I could get enough for custom rims, too." Rory nodded and the orderly grinned. "Righteous." Then he disappeared.

Rory paced the tile floor for the next few minutes until the door swung open and Cody appeared, a concerned look on his face. "What's wrong?"

Cody Canyon was the oldest of the four Canyon brothers. He had short dark hair and the Canyon trademark blue eyes. He wore khaki Dockers and a polo shirt that read XTREME RACING on the pocket. Cody was the only Canyon who didn't make his living behind the wheel of a race car. Sure, he spent his spare time racing the short tracks, but he wasn't an official driver. No sponsors. No crowds screaming his name. No big money car. Nothing, thanks to Word Canyon who'd all but disowned him when he'd violated the Himanist creed and married a headstrong woman. Ever since, Cody had kept his driving low-key (far below Word's radar) and funded the hobby himself via his "real" job—serving as Rory's crew chief. "You're not feeling short of breath, are you? Heart palpitations? High blood pressure? Chest pains—"

"No."

"It's nothing to be ashamed of. Everybody gets sick. You just can't keep it to yourself. No trying to tough it out. This is the best hospital in town. Whatever's up, they can deal with it and you'll be back to normal—"

"There's nothing to deal with."

"Don't say that, bro. They can treat anything these days. No matter how bad. They'll find it. Just drop trou and let these folks do—"

"Cody, stop," Rory cut in. "I mean it. Nothing's wrong." He shook his head. "This is all a big mistake. I don't need to be here. I'm not really sick."

"You walked out on a sponsor commitment," his older brother pointed out. "You've *never* walked out on a sponsor commitment."

Rory shrugged. "There were extenuating circumstances."

"I know. I heard. The PR rep said your face was beet red. You were either ready to blow your top or toss your cookies. Since you didn't jump anyone's ass, I'm assuming it was number two. At least that's what the rep told Dad. And speaking of Dad, he wants you to take some time off. He says you need a vacation."

Because Word Canyon wasn't half as concerned with winning as he was with having his boys carry on the family legacy. Word came from a long line of drivers. His grandfather had driven one of the first stock cars in the sport, and his father had been a driver as well. Word had kept the family tradition going by driving for the past twenty-two years. Now that he'd retired, he'd

passed the buck to his sons—the three who hadn't defied him by marrying a headstrong female, that is. Ian,
who was twenty-two and the youngest, was currently
dominating Busch, while Jared, twenty-five, drove in
the Craftsman Truck Series. Rory was twenty-nine and
drove Nextel—now called the Sprint Cup Series.

Rory had been driving for twelve years now. Twelve
long years spent working his way up from last place
into the third overall spot, where he'd been sitting for
the past six years.

While Word might be satisfied just to have Rory in
the game, Rory himself was extremely *dis*satisfied. He
was through idling. It was time to step on the gas. To
do something.

To win.

"I don't need a vacation."

"No, first we need to find out what's wrong, and then
you can think about a vacation."

"But there *is* nothing wrong."

Cody's frown deepened. "What's up with you?"

My libido.

Over the years, Rory had managed to tolerate the occasional contact with Jaycee because (a) they drove for
different teams; and (b) she always had her long, soft
hair stuffed up under a sponsor's cap, her sweet curves
hidden beneath a driving suit and her vulnerability bar-
ricaded behind a don't-mess-with-me-or-my-car attitude. She had such a big mouth and a rough exterior
that it was easy to forget there was a soft, warm female
beneath it all.

But there was no way—no way in hell—he could tell
that to his Himanist father.

"It was one of those twenty-four-hour things," Rory
blurted.

So much for coming clean.

But admitting that he'd walked off the set because of a woman would worry Cody even more than the possibility of an aneurysm. While his oldest brother didn't share the family's Himanist beliefs, he did share its passion for racing. He wanted Rory to win almost as much as Rory wanted it.

Maybe more.

Rory ignored the crazy thought and focused on the here and now. "It's been twenty-six hours"—he glanced at the stainless-steel Tag Heuer that encircled his wrist—"so I'm fine." Or he would be, once he managed to push the image of Jaycee Anderson, all sweet and curvy in her low-cut pink dress, out of his mind.

He would. He would slam the door. Bury it in the past. Gone.

Eventually.

Rory picked up the hospital gown and steeled his resolve. It was one measly exam. He motioned toward his brother. "I'll have them call you when we're done."

Cody nodded. He'd just pulled open the door when Sean returned, a box of disposable gloves in his hands. "Looks like we're good to go," Cody told him. "Tell Dr. Harrison my dad wants a complete work-up." He reached for the door and started from the room. "From top to bottom."

The orderly smiled. "He's already ordered a full slate of tests."

"Good." Cody nodded at Rory. "I'm here if you need me, bro." He excused himself and the door swung shut.

Sean turned to place his box of gloves on a nearby counter. He tugged off the cardboard opening, pulled two individual gloves free and set them on the counter. At Rory's raised eyebrows he said, "For the physical part of the exam, dude. Dr. Harrison likes to get the invasive stuff out of the way first."

Rory stiffened. "This just keeps getting better and better."

"Look on the bright side. At least he's got small hands."

Chapter Four

"You're *dumping* us?" Riley stared at Aaron Jansen, the president of Revved & Ready, who sprawled in a dark leather chair on the opposite side of her desk.

They sat in the headquarters of Race Chicks, Inc., a huge white building located just north of Dallas. RCI housed the garage/shop area on the first floor and administrative offices on the second.

The place was modest, compared to the huge chrome and glass tower owned by Xtreme Motorsports, or even the tall black structure that had been home to Anderson Racing just six months ago. When all but one sponsor had pulled out, Riley had been forced to move the team to a less pricey facility.

"We're not dumping you," Aaron told her. He wore Nike jogging pants, a white tank top that showed off his sculpted biceps and a look of pity that made her want to pull out the box of cupcakes stuffed in her bottom desk drawer and eat her way into a sugar coma. "We're just *thinking* about dumping you. Seriously thinking about it."

"But why?"

"It's all right here in black and white." He motioned to the stack of newspapers fanned out across the top of Riley's desk. They were from all parts of the country, but they had one thing in common—they all featured Jaycee Anderson.

Jaycee getting down and dirty in the pit. Jaycee behind the wheel of her race car at Talladega. Jaycee doing donuts in Victory Lane at Sonoma. Jaycee in the pit with her crew. Jaycee flat on her back on a creeper in her Fort Worth garage.

"She's just not a good representative for our product."

"Because she's a woman?"

"The fact that she's a female is the only reason we've held on this long. We admire her. And we admire you. You came into this situation with absolutely no background in NASCAR. You had to deal with a lot of crew members who weren't particularly keen on working for a woman."

"I had three quarters of the team walk."

"Exactly, but instead of feeling defeated, you took the chance to do something no one else has done—you put together a predominantly female racing team. It's ingenious really, and the perfect marketing vehicle for our new product."

"So what's the problem, then?"

"We need our customers to relate to Jaycee, and right now they just don't. We want young women to see her and think that if they downed a few cans of Revved & Ready every day, they, too, could be like Jaycee Anderson. But what woman wants to be covered in grease twenty-four/seven?" He stared at one picture in particular, then at another. "I swear she lives in that driving suit."

Riley leaned forward, riffled through the stack and slid a particular article toward the CEO. "Here's one where she's not in the suit."

Aaron glanced at the picture. "She's wearing baggy jeans and a sweatshirt. A grease-stained sweatshirt."

He shook his head. "You can't even tell she's a woman. She looks androgynous." His gaze met Riley's. "How can female customers relate to her if they're not even sure she's a woman?"

Riley leaned back in her chair and pointed out, "She put on a dress for the *Vogue* shoot."

"Which is the only reason we're willing to give you one more chance. I saw the preliminary pictures. They're good." He tapped one of the papers. "We need her to look good every day. Granted, she can't walk around in a floor-length designer dress, but she can certainly be more in tune with today's woman. Hip. Trendy."

All of the things that Jaycee wasn't.

"When she's not behind the wheel," he went on, "we want her looking like our target demographic. And we want her acting like it. We aren't just appealing to the tomboys out there. We're going after a broader market. We're aiming at the non-tomboy female sports-loving crowd. Everyday women who enjoy a good football game or a NASCAR race as much as they enjoy a good chick flick. We're going for women who care about their health and their appearance." He pulled free one of the papers and slid it across the desk. "Jaycee's got a wrench in one hand and a Big Mac in the other." He looked closer. "And I'd be willing to bet that cup sitting on the sidelines contains a vanilla shake."

"I'm sure it's chocolate. Chocolate's her favorite."

Aaron gave her an outraged look. "Do you know how many fat calories are in a shake? Just thinking about it makes me feel sick." He shook his head. "Jaycee needs to be in better shape. Do you have any idea what her muscle mass–to–body fat ratio is?"

Riley had no idea what her own muscle-to-fat ratio

was, nor did she care, but she wasn't about to point that out to Aaron. Not with a hefty sponsorship on the line and no other prospects on the horizon. "Jaycee is an athlete. She's in great shape, regardless of the occasional fast-food indulgence. She works out every day."

"Where?"

"Home gym during her off times. During the season, she catches a workout in her RV. She's got a treadmill and a weight set. And there's also the motor-coach facilities. Like the other drivers, she heads for the motor-coach gym when her schedule permits."

"That's all good, but it's all done away from the public eye." He leaned forward. "The public at large doesn't actually see her exercise. What they see are pictures of her with Big Macs and vanilla shakes."

"Chocolate," Riley corrected.

"Whatever. The point is, she doesn't race for Hershey's or McDonald's. She races for us. We know she's a good athlete, but that isn't necessarily the picture she's presenting to the public."

"So?"

"So, Revved & Ready is more than just a product. It's a way of life. We want Jaycee to look the part. To *be* the average well-rounded, non-tomboy, sports-loving woman. These people can help." He pulled a white business card from his pants pocket and set it on Riley's desk. "They're not just into extreme makeovers. They're image specialists. We don't just want Jaycee to drive our car. We want her to embrace her femininity and represent our product on and off the track. And we want her smiling while she's doing it. She looks perpetually pissed off."

Riley glanced at the dozens of images and not one depicted a happy Jaycee. She looked everything from busy to focused to annoyed. But not happy. Since Riley had walked in and taken charge (thanks to Ace's last will and testament), Jaycee had been sullen and miserable.

Then again, maybe she'd been that way before Ace had passed away and Riley had waltzed onto the scene. Riley wouldn't know, because she'd had zero contact with her sister. They'd never dished over boys or fixed each other's hair or opened Christmas presents together.

Riley had never had much of a Christmas, actually. Her mother had been sick with emphysema, which had taken what little she'd made as a waitress and most of the monthly child support she'd received from Ace, so Riley had done without the new Baby Alive and the latest My Little Pony. But she'd had her mother's love, and for that she'd been thankful.

Jaycee, on the other hand, had only had Ace. Her own mother had died in a tragic car accident when she'd been two, and she'd been raised by her father. He hadn't turned her out or turned his back.

Not that Riley cared. She'd stopped wanting Ace in her life a long, long time ago.

"If you'll work with Image Nation," Aaron went on, "then we're willing to give Race Chicks another chance. If not, we'll have no other choice but to terminate our contract."

Riley mentally weighed the likelihood of getting Jaycee to go along with Aaron's plan.

Not happening.

That's what her gut told her. Jaycee could very well kiss off Revved & Ready and walk over to another team. The thing was, any other team would want the same— to take advantage of the fact that Jaycee was different— and she had to know that. While she was as stubborn as they come, she was also smart. Enough to realize that any other team would want to capitalize on the fact that she wasn't just one of the few female NASCAR drivers in the history of the sport, she was the first to make it into the top four. A trailblazer for womankind.

That meant milking the PR angle for all it was worth. NASCAR's fastest-growing fan demographic consisted of women. Women who loved the sport. Women who respected the sport. Women who could easily share a common hero—Jaycee Anderson. Talented. Determined. Destined to win the NASCAR Sprint Cup championship.

Not that Riley gave a fig about winning.

She simply needed to stay in the game a full race season. From start to finish. It was all about the money, she told herself.

No, the desperation burning deep down inside certainly had nothing to do with the fact that she wanted to prove Ace wrong. That she wasn't weak or lazy or useless like her mother.

That's what he'd said on the day he'd left. What he'd believed right up until he'd taken his own life six months ago, after discovering he had prostate cancer. While he'd handed over a check every month to help with Riley's care, he'd given nothing else to his firstborn.

Not his time.

Nor his attention.

Nor his love.

You're weak, Arnette. And lazy. And I've had enough.

Arnette Vaughn had been all of those things. She'd been a cocktail waitress/cashier/shampoo girl who'd latched onto the first good, solid thing to come her way—up-and-coming race-car driver Ace Anderson. He'd been interested in her long blonde hair and killer body, and she'd been looking for someone to take care of her. She'd gotten pregnant on purpose and trapped him into marriage, and he'd hated her for it.

Riley would have felt for him, if he hadn't done the inexcusable—held his daughter responsible for the situation—and so she'd grown up knowing she was better off without him in her life.

At least that's what she'd been telling herself for the past twenty years.

She knew the money was his way of having the last word. A final test to nail home the truth—that he'd been right to leave his wife and a loveless marriage, and justified in abandoning Riley. Because she was just as lazy, as worthless, as incapable of real work as her mother had been.

Riley intended to prove him wrong.

"I'll make it happen," she told Aaron.

He nodded. "You've got six weeks until Daytona. More than enough time to introduce the new Jaycee to the world slowly, carefully, so that it doesn't seem like a huge PR ploy. That's what we don't want. Jaycee must seem real and genuine. We want people to believe in her. We want them to believe in our product."

Riley gave him her most confident smile. "Consider it done."

Once Aaron left, Riley locked her office door and gave instructions for her receptionist to hold all calls. Settling into her chair, she reached for the box of cupcakes in her bottom desk drawer.

It was the worst way to deal with stress. She knew that. She should pull out her yoga mat and meditate. Meditation was good for a nail-biter like this.

At the same time, meditation didn't really clear her head and help her think. And it certainly didn't taste so damned good.

Mmm . . . She closed her eyes and savored the sugary-sweet chocolate and cream. For a long, delicious moment, her senses buzzed and her worries slipped away. No more Aaron. No Jaycee. No past-due rent notices sitting on the corner of her desk.

She swallowed.

Three notices to be exact.

Sunny Side Up, the tanning salon she'd started a little over a year ago, wasn't faring so well without its CEO—Riley—to steer the ship. She had one full-time employee for the day and two teenagers who handled the evening shifts. But without Riley there on a regular basis, things were slowly falling apart. Profits were down. Bills were piling up.

She needed cash. Now.

But if she left Race Chicks and went back to Houston, she would leave with nothing. Since the past six months had been eating away at her modest savings, she'd almost hit rock bottom. She didn't have enough money to bail herself out. Instead, she would be struggling, starting over from scratch to build a business that those six months had all but killed.

No, the only thing she could do was see this thing through. She could eke out enough money by way of a minimal owner's salary to cover things until the end of the race season, and then she would be set. She could sell her half of the race team to the highest bidder. There would be enough money to pay off her bills, and even franchise. Not to mention, she could finally buy herself a real house.

If she could persuade Jaycee to get with the program.

Her mind traveled back to the previous week. It had

taken a full plane ride filled with threats and lectures and promises, followed by several hours of the same, to get Jaycee into a dress (minus the shoes) for fifteen measly minutes.

Her anxiety stirred and she scarfed another bite of cupcake. Her taste buds hummed and her nerves tingled, and all was right with the world again.

So Jaycee was stubborn? Riley was pretty damned stubborn herself when she wanted to be. Like now.

Another bite and she nodded.

Damn straight she was stubborn, and she wasn't taking no for an answer. Jaycee was going to get with the program.

But how?

She wasn't sure, and since the cupcakes weren't sparking anything brilliant, she reached for her makeup bag.

"You've got your work cut out for you," Savannah Calloway said a half hour later when Riley called her in and explained their predicament with Revved & Ready. Savannah was the Race Chicks crew chief and Jaycee's best friend. She was also married to Mackenzie Briggs, who'd placed second overall last year in the race for the cup. "What are you going to do?"

Buy a new tube of Sparkling Pink Perfection, a small voice cried, reminding Riley of the empty tube now sitting in her trash can. She'd applied and reapplied, but the only thing that had struck was a sinking feeling when she'd worn out her favorite lipstick. "I'm going to talk to her. Explain things. She's smart. She'll get on board." Hey, it sounded good.

"And if she doesn't?"

"I go to Plan B. I plead for her cooperation." It

wasn't as dignified as Plan A, but Riley had exactly two dollars and eighty-seven cents of discretionary income left in her bank account—not nearly enough for her favorite lipstick—and she was desperate.

"Jaycee's never been very sympathetic. Sure, she helps out at that camp for sick kids and she's always making charity appearances, but we're talking *you*." The crew chief's expression grew somber. "Don't take this personally, but she really doesn't like you."

"What if I beg?" Okay, now she was grasping. But the clock was ticking.

Savannah shrugged. "If I were you, I think I'd be leaning toward something a little more harsh."

"You think I should threaten her?"

"Hog-tie her, stuff a shop rag into her mouth and then threaten. That way she can't interrupt."

Jaycee speechless? Talk about a gift from God.

"And if that doesn't work, you can always call in a hypnotist," Savannah went on. "My brother Trey did that last year when he was trying to quit smoking. It didn't work at first, but after a few persistent suggestions, he started chewing gum instead. Now he's smoke free."

"You think that would work with my sister?"

Savannah seemed to think. "We could always hire more than one hypnotist. Maybe a double, or even a triple whammy. Oh, and we should have a back-up team, too. In case the first group passes out from exhaustion. And it might not hurt to bring a Tazer along. Just in case things get really ugly."

Riley shook her head. "This is crazy. Jaycee is a normal, sane human being. Even she can't be that difficult."

Savannah shrugged. "We're talking the woman who

skips shaving her legs in the winter in lieu of wearing socks."

Riley blew out a deep breath and pushed to her feet. "I'll get a rope and meet you downstairs in five minutes."

Chapter Five

Jaycee had just stretched out on a creeper and slid beneath the front end of the race car when she heard the whoosh of the garage door. Heels clicked across the concrete floor.

Riley. Undoubtedly with paperwork to sign or pictures to autograph or something. There was always something.

"There's a reason I taped up that keep-out sign," she called out. "We're track testing at the end of this week and I've still got a dozen adjustments to— Yikes!"

Hands closed around her ankles. Before she could grab for the undercarriage, she found herself yanked out from beneath the car. In the blink of an eye, two crew members flanked her, pinning her arms into place.

"What the—"

"Just shut up and listen." Riley loomed over her and slapped a piece of tape over her mouth.

No, really.

"I know you're not happy with the current situation— me in charge, and you not—but neither am I," her half sister rushed on. "I've got my own business to run, not to mention I would rather be anywhere but here. But I *am* here and so are you, and we have to make the best of the situation."

Jaycee struggled to move her arms, but the two men—her jackman and one of the tire specialists—held tight.

Men. Traitors. The whole friggin' bunch.

"We're on the same team," Riley went on. "We both want the same thing—to make it through this next season. You want it. I want it. This whole team wants it. The thing is, we can't do it without a sponsor, and we're this close to losing ours." Riley's gaze zeroed in on Jaycee's. "I met with Revved & Ready today and they're ready to back out. Right now," she added. "Today."

What?

As if Riley heard the frantic question ping-ponging in Jaycee's brain, she added, "That's right. They want to pull the plug. They're not reaching their current demographic with the way things are—with the way *you* are—and they're ready to bolt. No sponsor means no money, which means no car, which means no season. No hope of a season. Nothing." She paused to let her words sink in. "We're all going to wind up with zilch, unless . . ." Riley turned away, as if thinking of the best way to verbalize whatever was swimming around in her pretty little head.

Jaycee flexed her mouth and the tape popped off. "Unless what?" At the sound of her voice, Riley whirled and Jaycee shrugged. "You should have used electrical. Masking tape has zero grip." She arched an eyebrow. "*Unless?*" she prompted again.

"Unless we make some major changes."

"We've already made changes."

"To the team." Her gaze met Jaycee's. "I'm talking about you. They want a spokesperson, not just a driver for their car."

"I am a spokesperson. I drink gallons of the stuff, don't I?"

At Riley's pointed stare, she shrugged. "Okay, so I don't drink that much. But it tastes terrible."

"You have to get used to it. Which you should be by now. The fact that you aren't speaks volumes as to why we're in this predicament. I can't believe Ace never made an issue of this before."

"He was all about the driving. If you bring it on the track, the sponsors will come."

"Not in this case."

"I'm sure once the season starts—"

"There won't be a season, Jaycee. Don't you get that? We've got one sponsor. *One*. That's barely enough to keep us in the game. If they back out, and they will, we're shit out of luck in a major way."

"We'll find a new sponsor."

"There's no time. We have six weeks until Daytona, and there isn't anyone beating down our door for the opportunity to write out a megacheck. We're an untried commodity."

"I've been racing for years."

"For Ace. He made this team."

And now he was destroying it, just the way he'd destroyed himself. With no thought to anyone else.

Jaycee's eyes burned and she forced them wide, determined not to shed even one tear. She didn't cry. Not ever. Not since her father had told her what a ridiculous waste of energy it was. And that she'd never make it, if she wept like a girl every time something bad happened.

She had to be strong.

Tough.

Ace.

"Revved & Ready is not just a product," Riley went on. "It's a lifestyle, and yours doesn't fit. Your clothes don't fit. Your food choices don't fit. And your attitude . . ." Riley shook her head. "Can't you smile once in a while?"

"I've got two traitors holding my arms and masking tape dangling from my chin. What the hell do I have to smile about?"

Riley motioned to the two men. They mumbled their apologies and let go of Jaycee's arms. "We can make this happen. R & R is willing to give us one last shot. We only have six weeks, but if we put our minds to it and give it our all—"

"Give what our all?" Jaycee cut in, snatching the tape off her chin and wadding it into a ball. She flicked the wad and nailed Riley in the side of the head.

Her sister didn't miss a beat. "The makeover." When Jaycee narrowed her gaze, Riley added, "You're a woman. It's time you started looking and acting like one." She pulled out a white business card and handed it over.

Jaycee trailed her grease-covered fingers across the raised silver script. IMAGE NATION. She lifted questioning eyes to Riley. "What's this?"

"The group that's going to turn you from a grease monkey into a goddess in time for the season opener."

A *goddess*. The word stuck in Jaycee's head and stirred a sudden vision of a pink dress and high heels and an entire night spent crying herself to sleep. Her heart pounded and she felt a trickle of sweat slide between her shoulder blades. "By 'goddess' you mean someone that is massively popular and worshipped by every NASCAR fan the world over?"

"I mean 'goddess' as in the pinnacle of all that is

feminine. You're going to embrace your femininity and then, if we're lucky, the massive popularity and worship will follow."

"If I say no?" she asked after several seconds.

Riley pulled a Tazer from her small purse. "Then you'll be saying it to my little friend."

"You wouldn't have zapped me," Jaycee told Riley the next morning as they sat idling in front of a large glass building in the heart of downtown Dallas. Sunlight sliced between the towers of chrome and steel that surrounded them and spattered the street in brilliant yellow streaks. Jaycee shoved her Oakleys more firmly into place and eyed her sister. "You were just bluffing."

"Says you."

"You're the devil, you know that?"

"Careful with the compliments. I might get a big head."

"To go with your big, bossy mouth."

"You don't like me very much, do you?"

"Nah, you think?"

Riley pulled out a gold tube of lipstick, stared into the rearview mirror and dabbed at her bottom lip. "You're making too big a deal about this." She pressed her lips together and recapped the tube. "You wear a little makeup and some trendy clothes, fix your hair and watch what you eat. No big deal. Women do it every day."

Women like Riley.

But Jaycee wasn't like Riley.

She'd wanted to be, once. What little girl didn't envision being pretty and perfect at some point in her life? But then she'd come to her senses and realized that some girls looked good in frilly dresses and lace socks, and some looked better in a baseball jersey and jeans. Jaycee had learned that truth the hard way, but her father had always known. During her moment of ultimate humiliation, he'd been the one to tell her to straighten up. He'd tossed the pink dress into the trash, bought her a set of tools and taught her how to change the oil on his car.

He'd saved her from even more humiliation.

That's what she told herself as her gaze roamed over Riley. From her shiny hair that streamed down around her shoulders, to her elegant brown dress cinched with a rhinestone belt, to her brown snakeskin pumps. There wasn't a flaw visible to the naked eye. She was totally put together.

Perfect.

Jaycee caught her own reflection in the windshield. She wore her hair in its usual sloppy ponytail, her face free of makeup. She had on faded overalls and a white sleeveless T-shirt. A scratch from the rear underbelly of the car cut across one of her biceps. She looked rough. Unkempt.

*Im*perfect.

"It's not that bad." Riley's voice slid into Jaycee's ears before she could speculate any more. Thankfully. "Flaunting your femininity," she added when Jaycee turned toward her. "It has its perks."

"Like?"

"Well, you can usually get away with just a warning if you get pulled over by the police."

"I get that anyway." Most cops figured if she made her living going one-eighty, she could handle a car well enough at seventy-five to avoid a pileup.

"You get attention. Men notice you."

"Men already notice me. I race for NASCAR."

"I'm not talking about men who'd kill for a ride in your car. I'm talking about men who'd kill to ride you. And don't tell me you already get that. I've been around for the past few months and I haven't seen you go on a single date or even have a measly one-night stand."

"I was right in the middle of a race season when you decided to stick your nose into my business. I didn't have time to date."

"And the one-night stand?"

"I need my sleep."

Riley gave her a knowing look. "Besides, I didn't stick my nose in. I was sucked in, and stop trying to change the subject. You have no social life."

Jaycee shrugged. "I'm busy with sponsor commitments and race prep."

"You won't have any sponsor commitments if you don't do this." Riley's voice lowered and her green eyes darkened. "This is serious, Jaycee. They're really going to pull out, and then we're screwed."

"You mean you're screwed. You'll walk away with nothing."

"And so will you. Granted, this piddly race team isn't much, but you still want it."

"I wanted Anderson Racing."

"Change the name back, paint the car, hire a bunch of bozos who'll sit around and suck down Bubba Beer with you—you can do whatever you want after you buy me out. The thing is, it doesn't belong to either one of us until we make it through *this* season. So however much you hate it"—*however much you hate me*, her gaze seemed to say—"we're in this together."

Thanks to Ace.

Why?

The thought popped into Jaycee's head for the zil-lionth time since she'd walked into the law offices of Bickford, Morgan & Stern six months ago and spotted Riley for the first time.

Her sister.

She hadn't even known that Ace had been married before, much less that he'd had a child. He'd never said a word. Not about Riley, nor anything else for that matter. He'd never been much of a talker. A hard-ass. That's what most people had called him, and they'd been right. He'd lived and breathed the competitive world of stock-car racing. He'd been determined, driven, tough.

He'd had to be.

But to turn his back on his daughter . . . That went beyond the typical nerves of steel. We're talking a man who'd been cold. Callous. Selfish.

It explained so much. Why he'd pushed his youngest into the garage and cut out every other aspect of her life, and why he was now trying—even from the grave—to take the very thing she'd worked for her entire life. Because Ace had been all about control. That's why he'd stopped driving and started his own team. He'd liked calling the shots and controlling everyone.

Then. And now.

"You're stuck with me," Riley added. "And I'm—"

"I get the point," Jaycee cut in.

"Do you?" Riley slid off her sunglasses and eyed Jaycee. "Because I got a phone call from Schilling's people yesterday, and I distinctly remember telling you not to contact him."

Jaycee perked up. "He called?"

"His assistant. She wanted to set up an official meeting to discuss our engine."

"No shit?" Jaycee smiled for the first time since climbing into Riley's Taurus earlier that morning. "That's great."

"I told her to forget it."

"I can't believe he actually agreed to work with me—you *what?*" Her gaze swiveled toward her sister.

Riley shook her head. "Your car is more than adequate as is. We just have to make it through the season. It doesn't matter if we win a race or not."

But it did.

This was all that Jaycee had, now that Ace was gone. She had her reputation and her stats. Her wins.

"Do you know how difficult it is to get a call from Schilling? The man is busy. And selective. He doesn't work with just anyone."

"He won't be working with us."

"You're an idiot, you know that?"

"I'm practical, and I'm the boss. We can't afford it. End of story."

"You're right."

Riley looked relieved. "It's about time you started to see reason."

"About the fact that I don't like you? I don't."

Not that Riley topped her "People I'd Like to Smear Across the Pavement" list. She sat somewhere in the middle. The numero uno spot belonged to one Rory Canyon. A healthy Rory Canyon.

Riley had called the PR rep for Xtreme, who'd assured her that he'd suffered a temporary stomach flu and would be back to normal in no time. Which meant Jaycee had stopped worrying and started disliking him again.

He was a jerk. Worse than a jerk. He was an insensitive jerk, a truth she'd had the good fortune to learn early on.

Her mind raced back to the night she'd opened the door to Rory, wearing a stupid outfit she'd picked out at the local mall. A mall, of all places. She'd been nursing a crush on him for ages and finally, with the help of the *Seventeen* magazine she'd found in Sue Ellen Watson's desk, she'd decided to clue him in. She'd been thirteen, after all.

Sue Ellen had been the prettiest girl at Grapeland Intermediate School and, therefore, an authority when it came to boys. Since Sue Ellen swore by *Seventeen*, Jaycee had decided to give it a try. She'd swiped it when no one had been looking, and had read the entire "What's Hot in Fashion" section. She'd needed something scorching to get her noticed by one Rory Canyon. Granted, he'd been a few years older, but that didn't matter in the face of true love.

She'd thought so.

But then she'd poured out her feelings and he hadn't returned them, and that had been that. The beginning and the end of her social life, and the death of their friendship. She wasn't about to make a fool of herself again.

Even as the stubborn thought registered, another one pushed its way in: It wasn't her heart hanging in the balance this time. It was the success of her racing team. The livelihood of the few loyal team members who'd stayed on after Ace had passed away and Riley had taken charge. They'd ridden out the past six months on faith alone, nursing the hope that Riley would succeed and the team wouldn't be dismantled and sold. They believed in Jaycee and the team's future.

A future that would be nonexistent, if they lost their biggest sponsor.

Jaycee unhooked her seat belt and reached for the door handle. "Let's do this before I change my mind."

Chapter Six

A few minutes later, Jaycee followed Riley into the lobby of Image Nation.

The offices, located in the penthouse suite, had floor-to-ceiling windows that gave a spectacular view of the city. Early-morning light streamed through the glass and reflected off the chrome end tables. The decorating theme? White. White leather furniture. White carpeting. White stucco walls. A white blonde receptionist in a white tailored suit.

"Ms. Savoy will be with you momentarily," the receptionist said as she motioned Jaycee into a nearby chair. "Can I interest you in a glass of wine while you wait?"

"Wine?" Jaycee wiggled for a comfortable position and tried to calm the pounding of her heart.

Some new clothes. A little makeup. No big deal.

"We have spritzers and flavored coffees as well," the receptionist went on. "But I usually offer something alcoholic first." Her voice lowered several decibels. "It takes the edge off for our serenity-challenged clients."

"Excuse me?"

"The nervous ones." She smiled. "Red or white?"

"If it doesn't come in a keg, I don't drink it."

The receptionist's smile faltered and Riley piped in, "She's kidding. We're not really thirsty. But thank you."

The woman shrugged. "If you change your mind, just let me know." She walked back and perched behind her desk. The phone buzzed and her attention shifted from Jaycee to the caller on line one.

Jaycee grabbed a magazine and flipped through. A dozen images of women twisted this way and that stared back at her.

"It's yoga," Riley said. "It's healthy."

"I know what yoga is." She'd heard of it, of course. Who hadn't? But—and she would never admit this to Riley—she'd never actually twisted or stretched herself.

She studied the glossy pages a few minutes. It didn't look so hard. Complicated, maybe. But difficult? Not for an athlete such as herself, who could lift a cylinder head without even breaking a sweat.

She slapped the magazine closed and glanced at her watch. She should be under the hood by this time, picking over the engine with Savannah. They had a track test this weekend and she intended to be ready. "How much longer do you think we'll have to wait?"

"We've been waiting all of thirty seconds."

"I don't like waiting." Jaycee reached for another magazine and riffled through several pages of Oscar dresses. "I've got things to do."

"Right now, this is first on your priority list."

"So sayeth the woman who knows absolutely zip about stock-car racing."

"I know enough to know that it's all about money and sponsors. It's business, like everything else." Riley cast a sideways glance at Jaycee. "You're nervous."

"Why would I be nervous? We're talking a make-over. Not a root canal or a mammogram or an audit. I'm irritated. Big difference."

Before Riley could challenge her, a distinctly southern, distinctly feminine voice echoed through the room. "Good morning!"

Jaycee's gaze swiveled.

One word came to mind when she saw the woman standing in the office doorway: *perky*. From the high-pitched exuberance of her voice and her excited smile, to the double Ds pressing against her ivory silk blouse, the woman was a walking poster girl for the Big P.

She looked to be in her midtwenties, with long blonde hair and big blue eyes. Her makeup was immaculate, and she walked as if she were vying for the Miss Texas crown with each and every step.

"You must be Danielle Savoy." Riley pushed to her feet and stepped forward, her hand extended. "Thanks for seeing us on such short notice."

"No problem. We're more than happy to accommodate in any way we can."

Of course they were. For what they were probably charging, Jaycee figured, Danielle Savoy would be happy to stand on her head and sing "The Yellow Rose of Texas," if it meant tacking on an extra few dollars.

The woman's blue Barbie doll–like eyes shifted to Jaycee. A single frown line wrinkled her forehead as her gaze swept head to toe. "I can see why you said it was an emergency."

"Nice to meet you, too."

Danielle smiled. "Don't you fret, hon. We've all been there. You don't think I was born looking like this, do you?" Before Jaycee could reply, Danielle rushed on. "Okay, so maybe I was. But the point is, 99.9 percent of the population isn't. They're born with flaws, from the inside to the outside, which is why I'm here. To note those flaws, to shape and mold and twist them into one great big asset."

"My asset is already big enough."

"At the same time," Danielle went on, ignoring Jaycee's comment, "it's going to take more than just my commitment. It's going to take dedication on your part, as well."

"We're ready to do whatever is necessary to see this thing through as smoothly as possible," Riley chimed in. "Aren't we, Jaycee?"

"Ten-four."

Danielle cast a questioning glance at Riley. "That's car talk, right?" When Riley nodded, she smiled. "Too cute. Anyhow . . ." She nailed Jaycee with a piercing blue stare. "It's all about being committed. About saying no to that next slice of pizza when you'd rather give up your first-born child, or doing an extra set of sit-ups when you'd much rather curl up on the couch and watch Dr. Phil. It's a belief in yourself. One that says, 'I'm great. I'm worth it.'" She held out her hands. "'I'm totally and completely wonderful!'" She sighed and folded her hands. "Here at Image Nation, we're all about wonderful, and before we're done you'll be totally and completely wonderful, as well. A bright, shiny, well-dressed, wonderful example of today's woman."

"We'd settle for just the woman part," Riley said.

Danielle laughed. "A sense of humor. I like that. Come with me." She led Riley and Jaycee into a plush inner office and motioned them into a pair of white brocade chairs.

"I've been briefed on all the specifics by Revved & Ready," she said as she rounded a large glass desk and sank into a white leather chair. "I have copies of their demographics, their advertising campaign for the new drink and their expected results as far as Miss Anderson is concerned. I've also spoken to their board of directors myself, just to make sure we're all on the same page." Carefully manicured fingers flipped open the manila folder sitting in front of her.

"Revved & Ready is interested in a complete image makeover, which means that we're going to address the three major aspects that serve as the foundation for any image: appearance, lifestyle and attitude. I've got a great beauty consultant who'll be in charge of the first one. Number two will require a 'big sister.' She's an Image Nation lifestyle coordinator. What she'll do is construct an ideal lifestyle chart based on your needs. Then she'll spend forty-eight hours with you, document your current habits and compare them with the ideal we're hoping to achieve. She'll eliminate any and all activities that don't fit with the image we're trying to create. After that, it's just a matter of engaging in the appropriate activities and following the chart. The attitude seems to adjust itself, changing and morphing as the image is shaped and molded."

"What if it doesn't?" Jaycee voiced one of the many doubts swimming in her head.

"In that case we usually opt for a lobotomy." When Jaycee's mouth dropped open, Danielle smiled. "Just a little Image Nation humor. I wouldn't worry about the attitude. I know a wonderful team of psychologists—I call them The Reinforcers—who'll meet with you toward the end of the makeover. They're specially trained to help individuals embrace and revel in new behaviors."

"Like shaving your legs," Riley spoke up.

Jaycee made a face. "You're too funny."

"We'll start first thing tomorrow with a complete

salon workup—hair, makeup, manicure, pedicure, waxing."

"Waxing?"

"You know, your eyebrows, bikini line, that sort of thing. If there are any difficult areas you'd like the waxing specialist to concentrate on, just mark it on here." She slid a small booklet across the desk toward Jaycee. DIARY OF A GODDESS gleamed in pink metallic script.

"What's this?" Jaycee took the book and started to flip through.

"Your bible during the process. It's got various forms for you to evaluate your own appearance so that we can try to integrate your personal likes and dislikes into our plan. It has sections for food, activities and hobbies, in addition to a daily record where you record the new rules you're learning throughout the process. Things like what wardrobe colors to wear and when and what foods to avoid, and the like. You'll want to keep it with you at all times." She smiled and turned back to her file. "The salon is tomorrow, the appointment with your very own personal shopper the day after that, and the lifestyle rep the day after that, which is Friday—"

"I'll be in Daytona on Friday," Jaycee cut in. "A track test."

"Oh." Danielle frowned. "That is a problem. Our lifestyle coordinators are highly trained and, therefore, in demand. If I don't have a client ready when Angela is ready, then she'll take the next person in line from one of the other agencies that she services. I don't suppose you could postpone it?"

"No." Jaycee shook her head. "There's no way in hell, heaven or the in-between that we're canceling a track test."

"How about first thing Monday?" Riley asked. "We'll be back on Sunday."

"Hmm . . ." Danielle turned toward the computer setup to her left. Her fingers clicked away. "It looks like we might be able to get Ruth Anne on Monday. She's really wonderful. You'll love her." Danielle tapped at her keyboard. "There. Done." She beamed at Jaycee. "By the time we're finished, you'll be every woman's icon. No more grease under the fingernails or limp ponytails. You'll be completely in tune with today's female."

"Sounds great," Riley said. "Doesn't it, Jaycee?"

Jaycee stared down at the white leather-bound book and barely resisted the urge to bolt for the door. She had too much on the line to chicken out now. It was time to man up. Or, in this case, woman up.

She gathered her courage.

Goddess, here I come. . .

"For the last time," Riley said into the phone later that afternoon, "Jaycee's too busy to give you guys an interview right now." She barely ignored the urge to stab the off button. "She's neck-deep in prerace prep."

"Track tests and performance evaluations?" asked the woman from *Life in the Fast Lane*, a wildly popular talk show hosted by ex–NASCAR driver Trick Donovan.

After the meeting at Image Nation, Riley had returned to her office to find eight messages from Donovan's assistant. She'd just tossed them in her drawer to give herself time to cook up a good excuse, when the ninth call had come through. She'd unwittingly answered because Gail, her receptionist, had gone to lunch.

"Miss Vaughn? Care to comment on what Jaycee's up to?" the woman prodded.

Riley sighed. Ready or not, now seemed as good a time as any to start working on Jaycee's new image. "Jaycee's a very complex, multidimensional woman. While she's completely and totally dedicated to the sport, she does have other interests, as well. Shoe shopping. Cooking. Yoga."

Okay, so Riley had just described her own interests. But she'd never been a quick thinker. She liked to sit. To muddle. To worry.

"Yoga? Jaycee Anderson doesn't do yoga. And how long does it take to buy a pair of sneakers or pay for a Big Mac?"

"She's not buying sneakers. She's busy putting together a new wardrobe for the upcoming race season."

"She wears a racing suit."

"On the track. I'm talking about when she's off track. For interviews. Press conferences. That sort of thing."

"Like I said, she wears a racing suit."

"Usually, but she wants people to see her softer side. She's a woman, and she's proud of that fact. And she's given up Big Macs." Riley chose her words carefully. "She wants people to see her healthier side."

"Or maybe she's undergoing a drastic makeover to boost her ratings with the fans. My boss heard a rumor that Revved & Ready is launching a new energy drink geared toward women. Is that true?"

"How did he hear that?"

"He's a sports anchor. It's his job to know what's going on. So is it true that the people over at Image Nation are in charge of Jaycee's makeover?"

"No comment."

"That would be an unofficial yes. So when are we

going to see the new and improved Jaycee? In time for Daytona?"

"Jaycee is in tip-top shape for each and every race."

"That would be another unofficial yes. What about Jaycee? How's she taking all of this? Is she pissed?"

"Jaycee is being as cooperative as expected."

"That would be a big, fat, unofficial yes—"

"Stop." Riley drew a deep breath. "I know there's more to this phone call than verifying rumors. What do you really want?"

"My boss wants an exclusive."

"I can't promise that right now. Revved & Ready has their own PR campaign in place. They'll want her to talk to everyone, from local women's groups to the Speed Channel. I can't guarantee an exclusive."

"Then my boss has instructed me to post Jaycee's Image Nation makeover as the hot news topic on our Web site first thing tomorrow."

"Your boss is an ass."

"Now, now, watch your language, Miss Vaughn," a deep male voice rumbled over the line, and Riley realized all too late that she'd been on speakerphone. "Otherwise I might be inclined to think that you're not head-over-heels crazy for me like the rest of my female viewers."

"If the ass fits . . ."

"I want an exclusive," the voice of Trick said, his charm fading in a wave of determination that was almost palpable. "You let me unveil the new Jaycee and I'll make sure that the motivating factors—namely, the threat of losing your main sponsor—don't go beyond this conversation."

"I can't do that." Her mind raced for a plausible excuse and came up short. What the hell? The man was already onto them. "Revved & Ready wants the new Jaycee to be believable. They want things subtle and slow."

"But in time for Daytona, right?" When Riley agreed, he added, "We'll play it up as a glimpse into the private life of one of NASCAR's hottest drivers, rather than a bald-faced PR move aimed at gaining fans. While there's a lot of press out there on her, it's a relatively small amount compared to most of the other drivers. Fans don't really *know* her. This will give them a chance."

"If you've heard the real reason behind what's going on, what makes you so sure other people haven't?"

"Maybe some have, but they don't have the ability to broadcast it to over two million viewers. I do, which means you want me on your side. If you're cooperative and we do the interview, I'll make sure Jaycee looks authentic, rather than fake and money hungry."

"In other words, you'll only play nice if I give you an exclusive."

"Something like that," the deep voice rumbled ominously over the line. "So, what do you say?"

"I don't really have a choice, do I?"

"There's always a choice, Slick."

But there wasn't, not if Riley meant to see this thing through.

"So you're really going to do it?" Savannah finished installing the last spark plug and leaned back to eye Jaycee.

"Absolutely." They were alone in the monstrous garage with the hot pink race car, the Revved & Ready slogan emblazoned across the side. It was noon and the other team members had left for lunch.

Savannah wiped her hands on a shop rag. "No digging in your heels or acting like an overgrown baby?"

"I don't act like a baby! When it comes to taking orders, I act just like any of the male drivers out there."

"That's what I said." Savannah grinned. "A big baby."

Jaycee smiled before the expression faltered. "I know I have to do this, Van. I *will* do it." The sooner the better, in fact.

Jaycee eyed the bean-sprout sandwich that sat on the counter a few feet away, between her new goddess diary and a box of spark plugs. She'd ordered from Veggies-R-Us the moment she and Riley had returned after the Image Nation appointment. Jaycee was determined to get herself on track before the lifestyle specialist stepped in. She wasn't stupid. She'd had the half-hour drive from downtown to mentally tick off all the things she needed to change. The quicker she started, the less time she would have to waste meeting with expert after expert.

Rather, she could use that time to perfect her engine and think of a way to get to Martin Schilling. One that didn't include her interfering sister Riley.

"All I have to say is, I'm glad it's not me." Savannah walked over to her own lunch—a burger, extra-large fries and a large Diet Coke. "I don't think I could do it."

"You already do it." Jaycee stared at Savannah's blonde hair, which had been swept back into a chic clip. Though she wore jeans and a Race Chicks T-shirt now, Jaycee knew her crew chief had a closet full of designer dresses and trendy shoes. Once upon a time, Savannah had been the marketing rep for her own family's racing team. Her father owned Calloway Motorsports and her brothers drove for him. She'd handled the PR for her brothers and played the typical girly-girl for her father. Long story short, she'd married Mackenzie Briggs and traded her high heels for a pair of work boots.

"I bet you know every shade of pink there is."

"I do. In fact, I have every shade of pink shoe known to Nordstrom's. But I'm talking about the lifestyle part." She scooped up ketchup with one fry and motioned toward Jaycee's sandwich. "That looks like grass."

"Thanks. Now I'm really hungry."

Savannah smiled. "You know what I mean."

"The diet thing is only temporary. I just have to buckle down and then it'll all be over."

"In nine months. Nine long months."

"Aren't you supposed to be encouraging me?"

"Nine is nothing." She stuffed a fry into her mouth. "Now, ten . . ." She picked up another fry and wagged it. "There's an impossible length of time." She popped the ketchup-drenched goodie into her mouth and reached for her hamburger.

Jaycee's stomach grumbled and she reached for her sandwich.

"What are you doing?" Savannah asked as Jaycee rewrapped her lunch and stuffed it back into the brown paper sack.

"Getting out of here." She grabbed her goddess diary and stuffed it under her arm. "Before I wrestle you for a bite."

Savannah's voice followed Jaycee to the door. "I guess I should count my blessings that I ordered a soda instead of a chocolate shake."

And how.

Otherwise . . .

Jaycee shook away the thought, gripped the door handle and left the delectable smells behind. She headed upstairs and took refuge in an empty office.

You are a goddess. She silently chanted the opening line of her goddess diary as she pulled out the sandwich. *You walk like a goddess.* She took a bite. *You talk like a goddess.* She chewed. *And now, you eat like one.* She swallowed.

There. That wasn't so bad.

She flipped open the goddess diary and turned to the section titled "Food." She penciled in the date and the day's lunch choice—omitting, of course, the two Krispy Kremes she'd scarfed down that morning before committing herself—and smiled.

As she stared at the endless blank pages of entries to come, the expression died. Nine months of this. Was she crazy?

Chapter Seven

Rory glanced up from the disassembled motorcycle engine spread out on the counter in his shop. "Hand me that wrench, would you?" He motioned to his oldest brother, who'd just appeared in the doorway.

Cody Canyon set aside his black duffel bag, XTREME RACING emblazoned on the side in electric-blue letters, and walked over to Rory's work area. "Quarter inch or half inch?"

"The quarter. You headed home?" It was late Tuesday evening and the sun had long since set.

Cody shook his head. "Already been there for dinner. I'm headed back to Xtreme to make sure everything's ready for tomorrow." Cody handed over the tool and eyed the scatter of parts. "What's the problem?"

"No problem. I'm just replacing a few of the screws with these new titanium ones. It should help with the acceleration when you open her up."

Her referred to the custom-built chopper, its frame sitting up on blocks in the middle of Rory's garage. It was the current project he'd been working on with the kids from one of the local YMCA groups. They'd started building the bike from the ground up months ago. Once completed, it would be auctioned off, and the proceeds would be used to purchase playground equipment and fund various activities for the kids.

"Did you take a look at the clips from last year?" Cody asked.

"Haven't had a chance."

"You're feeling okay, aren't you?"

"I'm fine."

"Maybe the doctor missed something—"

"He didn't. I'm healthy. I feel great."

"Good. We leave in twenty-four hours for a two-day test session, and I want you to be ready."

"I am. You just make sure the car is ready for a win this time." He'd managed to run a decent third at Daytona last year, but he'd wanted better. Two laps shy of the finish, he'd gone for a slingshot to slow down the leader, Linc Adams, and push himself into second, but it hadn't worked. Rory had finished in the number-three spot. As usual.

Cody had determined that his younger brother simply needed to work harder. Better driving. More focus. More prep. "You really should drag your carcass inside and watch the films."

But Rory didn't need to watch them. He'd been there and he knew what was up. While his driving had been off, it had been off because the car simply wasn't fast enough for the superspeedways. His proof? He'd kicked butt on the short and intermediate tracks and racked up several impressive first-place wins, including his first at Martinsville. His skill level was exactly where it should be.

No, it was definitely the car. Which was why Rory needed Martin Schilling. The man was one of the best engineers in the business and a surefire ticket into first place.

Finally.

A wave of restlessness washed over him and he raked a hand through his hair. "Did Schilling come through?"

Cody nodded. "The new engine was delivered last night. The crew is going over it, checking the specs as we speak." Cody watched Rory change one of the pins. "Listen, I know you think this new design is going to make all the difference, but you need to be in top form as well."

"Meaning?"

"You should be getting psyched for the track test instead of messing with this bike. Play some video games. Take your Mustang out for a spin. Do something to pump yourself up and get the adrenaline flowing."

"Watching this thing come together gets me going."

"Yeah. You look about as excited as Darla at an all-you-can-eat steak buffet."

Darla was Cody's oldest daughter. She'd just turned fourteen and had announced this past Thanksgiving—before the bird—that she was becoming a vegetarian. In the months since, she'd managed to convert her eleven-year-old sister and Cody's wife, Cheryl, an airline pilot. Despite his long love affair with beef, Cody had finally buckled under the pressure—aka nagging.

He was always buckling for the women in his life, but then Cody didn't follow the Himanist doctrine like the rest of them. Instead of despising bold, headstrong women, he'd done the unthinkable and married one. And Word Canyon had yet to forgive him for it.

That was why, truth be told, the old man had never given Cody a chance to drive for the team. Sure, he'd given him a job behind the scenes, but it was more an insult than anything else. Cody hadn't let it bother him. He loved racing and was willing to take whatever he could get just to make a living in the sport. And while Rory couldn't really understand why Cody would let any woman lead him around by the nose hairs, he had to give his older bro props for having the courage to stand up for what he believed in.

"No pot roast for dinner?"

"I had a bean and egg-substitute omelet."

Rory let loose a low whistle. "That explains why you're so cranky."

"I'm not cranky." At Rory's pointed look, he added, "All right, I'm a little on edge. But it isn't because of this damned eating lifestyle—that's what Cheryl and the girls are calling it. I'm more worried about the next few days. Daytona sets the pace for the season," Cody went on, launching into his traditional prerace spiel as if Rory hadn't said a word. "You've never won at Daytona before. If you could pull it off, it might give us the momentum we need to actually move up this season."

Rory had been thinking the same thing himself. He needed this win. He needed it big-time.

"The race is yours," Cody went on. "I know it. Everyone knows it. But you have to know it. In here." He tapped his temple. "And in here." He tapped his chest.

"If you start singing 'I Believe I Can Fly,' I'm going to lay you out."

Cody frowned. "I'm serious."

"So am I. Look, bro, I've got it covered."

"I hope so, because Linc Adams will be gunning for you just the way he did last year. You really should watch how he blocks the slingshot. He keeps it tight, but you could have gotten around him if you would have hit all your points right up until that moment. You didn't, so you were about two seconds shy of being in the right position." When Rory arched an eyebrow at him, he shrugged. "What can I say? *I* watch the race films."

"Just make sure the new car meets spec and leave the driving to me."

But Rory knew that was easier said than done for Cody. While he wasn't a driver, he had as much passion for the sport as anyone who'd ever climbed behind the wheel. A passion he'd inherited not from their father, but their mother.

She'd been just as passionate about motorcycles. So much so that she'd been out racing the motocross circuit, despite the fact that she had four boys at home who needed her. She'd died doing wheelies on a dirt track down in Florida. That's when his father had bottled up his grief and turned it into self-righteous anger. He'd decided that a woman's place was in the kitchen and started Men On Top.

Cody had been a teenager at the time. Old enough to remember her. Rory had been, too. He could remember the soft feel of her hands when she'd tucked him into bed at night and the way she smelled—a combination of motor oil and determination.

Even more, he could remember a time when his father had loved her. Her spirit. Her courage. *Her.*

Sometimes it felt like just a dream, since his old man had turned into such a die-hard chauvinist, but when he thought really hard he could remember the happy man that Word Canyon had been.

Then again, he was starting to think that those times were just wishful thinking on his part. Particularly since Word had done such a complete one-eighty and turned his back on his own flesh and blood.

"Just watch the films before we leave," Cody told him, drawing Rory away from the dangerous thought.

"As a personal favor to me. I'm nervous enough with Cheryl on my back all the time now."

"I could sneak you a couple of sirloins."

"It's not just the diet." He rubbed a hand over his tired eyes. "She wants to send Darla and Denise to the Montgomery Girls' Academy. One year's tuition costs more than she and I both make in six months."

Which meant that Cody needed a win just as much as Rory did. Maybe more.

"I'll watch the films," Rory heard himself say. "Consider it done."

"Good. I'll pick you up tomorrow evening after you finish the radio spot for Dynamite Auto Parts."

"I'll be ready."

"Now put your left foot behind your head and relax."

Jaycee grasped her ankle, tugged her leg up and managed—after a lot of heaving and panting and praying—to hook her heel behind her neck. It was the *relax* part she was having trouble with.

Not so much because her body was twisted into the shape of a pretzel. It was the fact that said body was stuffed into black Lycra leggings and a matching tank top that had her nerves on edge.

We're talking *Lycra*.

While Jaycee had never been overweight, she was far from the perfect body shape. Her hips were a little too wide and she had more than her share of junk in the trunk (despite the bean-sprout sandwich yesterday). And she had volleyball ankles. Not that she'd ever served a ball in her life. Her afterschool activities had consisted of following her father around the garage. Still, she had them. Thick, athletic-looking joints that led to a pair of even thicker calves—the trademark of every girl on the Grapeland volleyball team. Hence, the name.

Jaycee glanced down at the white athletic socks stretched to their limit, the Nike at least twice its normal size. A sight that was even more conspicuous, thanks to the white toilet-paper dots freckling both calves.

First note to goddess: do not shave for the first time in six months a half hour before wearing knee-length leggings.

She'd thought about tugging on her usual gray sweats when she'd hauled herself out of bed that morning and bypassed the coffee maker in favor of—what else?—a can of Revved & Ready. But the Powers That Be wanted ultrafemme. While Jaycee wasn't an expert when it came to the subject, she was savvy enough to realize that a cover-everything-up sweatshirt that read MANNY'S MEAT MARKET did not qualify.

Since the makeover shopping extravaganza wasn't scheduled until tomorrow—today was all about hair and makeup—she'd stopped off at the nearest twenty-four-hour Wal-Mart and grabbed the first thing she spotted in the exercise section. It had been this or a pink bodysuit.

Black *was* slimming.

She focused on the thought and fixed her attention on the tall, svelte blonde prancing around in bright red bicycle shorts and a razor-back half-tank. The instructor had long hair and even longer legs, and a wide smile that said she was (a) hyped up on coffee, or (b) insane from too many vitamins. It was too early—barely six A.M.—and she was entirely too happy.

Not that Jaycee was a stranger to early mornings. She followed a very busy, very demanding schedule, so her alarm clock rang ridiculously early. But to be happy about it? Not before her mandatory six cups of java. Black. Extra sugar.

A pang of longing shot through her and she stiffened. She was *not* crazy, she reminded herself.

She was desperate. And determined.

"Now that we're all relaxed, let's focus on our breathing. Breathe in . . ." The instructor drew a deep breath that lifted her massive chest. "Then out. In . . ." *Inhale.* "Out." *Exhale.* "Feel the oxygen sliding into your nostrils and filling your lungs."

Jaycee tried, but the only feeling that made its way to her brain was the burning of her thigh muscles.

Hold up. Burning?

Hardly. She worked out everyday for two to three hours. Thirty minutes of yoga was not going to kick her ass.

She glanced at the large clock on the wall. Ten after six. Wait a second. She'd only been at this ten measly minutes?

"Now imagine that the oxygen isn't just sustaining your body, but your spirit as well. Feel the peace and serenity seeping through your pores, along with fresh, rejuvenating air. Breathe in. Breathe out."

Jaycee's blood rushed and her heart pounded. She felt her cheeks grow hot. The backs of her thigh muscles whimpered.

That's good, she told herself. *Sure, it hurts. But no pain, no gain. Everybody knows that.*

"Imagine you're floating weightless in a deep, blue pool. The water is cool. Soothing. Miss Anderson? Are you all right?"

"Fine," Jaycee managed, as she stared up at the instructor who'd stopped in front of her. "I'm"—she gasped for air—"great."

The instructor, a woman by the name of Dorothea, knelt down and eyed Jaycee. "Your cheeks look pink."

"Too much bottled tan."

Dorothea frowned. "Wouldn't that make you orange?"

Would it? Jaycee didn't know. She'd never bought a self-tanner in her entire life, much less slathered one on. But it had been the only thing that had popped into her head after an entire twenty-four hours spent reading past issues of *Cosmo*. "I'm fine." She gasped for another mouthful of air. "Uh, really. I"—another gasp—"can"—gasp—"do this."

Dorothea's frown deepened. "Yoga is about finding your inner self. It's not a method of torture."

Says you. "Really . . ." Jaycee drank in several deep drafts of air. "I'll make it."

"Why don't you forget the stretch position and just concentrate on the breathing exercises? That's usually what I have all my first-timers do."

First-timer? She could bench press two hundred pounds. Lift a rear tire without so much as straining herself. Jump the concrete wall on pit road—repeatedly—without even a cramp. Granted, she usually had a dozen other things on her mind and an MP3 player that blasted Fuel or Hinder, rather than the sound of trickling water that floated from the room's surround-sound system, but the point was, she *did* it. She was an athlete. She had strength. Stamina. Endurance. And she could certainly handle a few boring stretches.

"I can make it," Jaycee said again. "Really. Don't worry about me." She forced a smile and bit out the words, "I. Feel. *Great*."

Dorothea examined her a full moment more before she finally shrugged. "If you get too taxed, don't be shy about easing up a little."

"I promise I won't bust an artery." A promise she managed to keep for the next twenty minutes, as she twisted her body into a dozen other positions that drew on muscles she never knew existed.

By the time the instructor dismissed the class, she could barely move. She collapsed on her back and closed her eyes as the other students bounced to their feet and filed out of the room. None of the women said good-bye. Or waved. None of them even knew who she was.

Yet.

The only thing remotely good about the past half hour was that she was now too sore to move, much less worry about the Lycra clinging to every inch of her thighs.

That is, until a deep, familiar voice slid into her ears and rumbled along her nerve endings.

"Nice outfit, sugar. You hire someone to paint that on or did you do it yourself?"

Chapter Eight

Her eyes snapped open and she found Rory Canyon looming over her. He wore gray sweatpants that hung low on his hips. A thin line of dark black hair bisected his six-pack abs and funneled to a thin line that disappeared into the waistband of his pants. A crisp white Xtreme Racing T-shirt emphasized his broad chest and heavily muscled arms.

His gaze slid over her body, clear to her toes and back up again, and her heart stalled. His eyes glittered and there was something hot and potent in their depths as he stared down at her.

For a split second, she was thirteen all over again. She felt the spark of attraction, the blazing connection, the pulse-pounding I-want-you-so-bad-I-can't-stand-it desperation.

He smiled and arched an eyebrow. "So which is it, sugar? Professional job or a do-it-yourself?"

The question killed the moment and zapped her back to reality, to the all-important fact that the attraction didn't go in both directions. Rory Canyon didn't like her in that way.

Not then, and certainly not now.

Insecurity whizzed through her, followed by a rush of anger. Her lips parted, and she started to tell him where to go and how to get there the way she always did. But before the words could make it from her brain to her lips, Riley's voice echoed in her head.

It's not just about looking like a woman. You have to learn to act like one. No more arm wrestling in the pit. No more verbal tirades. No more talking first and thinking later.

Jaycee swallowed against the comeback and forced a smile. "It's a little, um, clingy, I know." Another swallow. "But it's perfect for yoga stretches."

Her reply wiped the smile off his face faster than her most colorful comeback, and she gave herself a mental high five. Maybe this whole goddess deal wasn't such a bad thing.

Rory frowned as he glanced around, as if noting the mats spread out across the room for the first time. "*You* just sat through a yoga class?"

"Actually there wasn't much sitting involved." She drew a deep breath and bit back a groan that tickled the back of her throat as she pushed to her feet. "Just lots of bending and breathing." She gave him another smile. "You should try it sometimes. It's totally relaxing."

"I don't do yoga."

"That's what I always said, but it's not only physically beneficial. It's wonderful for the spirit." Even as she said the words, she couldn't believe they were coming out of her mouth. Okay, so it wasn't altogether the truth. But that didn't mean that it wasn't true for the dozens of others in the class. Which meant it wasn't a total pile of horse manure. Besides, it was much better than telling him off. She couldn't let him get to her anymore. She wouldn't.

"I'll take your word for it." His gaze narrowed as he eyed her. "What are you doing here?"

"Heading for the cycle machines." She took a swig of bottled water. "After that, I'm jumping on the treadmill."

"That's not what I meant. I mean *here*. I've never seen you work out here before." He studied her face as if searching for the answer to world peace. "Since when are you a member?"

"As of this morning. I've got a gym at home, but it's so boring for someone like me."

"Like you?"

"A people person." She smiled even wider.

"Since when?"

Since her sponsor had given her an ultimatum.

"I've always been a people person. I'm just so focused that I don't come across as one. But I love to hang out with the girls. Hey, there." She waved at a woman who'd been working out in the row just in front of her. "How's it going?"

The woman gave her a strange look and a nod. "Uh, fine." She turned her Nikes around and hurried from the room.

Jaycee's gaze shifted and collided with Rory's. Sexual awareness rippled through her. She hated how her heart seemed to skip its next beat and she hated the way her insides went all tight and itchy, and she *really* hated him for being the one responsible. At least that's what she told herself.

"Let me get this straight. You're here to hang out?" His voice dripped with disbelief, as if he knew she'd rather *hide* out.

While she'd made up her mind to take the initiative and make the transformation, she hadn't been able to work up her nerve to go to one of the big, commercial facilities like World Muscle & Fitness or Body Perfection—black Lycra could put a damper on the best of intentions. She'd opted for a smaller, more neighborly type of gym located near Race Chicks headquarters.

Unfortunately, Race Chicks was located near the racetrack, right along with three of the other major Texas teams. Rory's included.

"Hang out," she said again. "And work out. Gotta get pumped, you know. Daytona's just around the corner."

"Yeah," he said, as if weighing her words. "I know."

"Speaking of Daytona, I hope you've recovered enough for the race."

"Recovered?"

"From the stomach flu. You're feeling all right, aren't you? Wouldn't want you to miss the fun."

"Oh, I'll be there all right. Guaranteed."

"Good." Relief rushed through her, along with a bolt of excitement. Her nipples pebbled, pushing against the fabric of her shirt as if desperate to break free and make contact with him.

If only.

She squelched the thought and blurted, "I'd better get going. I've got a busy day at the garage." She summoned another smile. "It was really great to see you." And then she gathered her courage, turned and walked away.

"Right back at you, darlin'." His voice followed her, a deep, husky sound that stirred the heat in her belly and made her think that maybe, just maybe, he was telling the truth.

But Jaycee had learned the hard way a long time ago never to listen to her instincts when it came to Rory.

Sure, it might seem like he felt something for her. Something hot and wild and totally inappropriate. But that was just her wishful thinking. He wasn't the least bit attracted to her. Not then and not now.

Why wasn't he? Because Jaycee wasn't half as hot as the women who begged for his attention on a daily basis. Women who didn't need a friggin' diary to get them in touch with their feminine side. They had boobs out to there and legs up to here and they could walk and talk the part with no lessons required. No, she wasn't woman enough for Rory and she wasn't fool enough to think he liked her like that.

Never, *ever* again.

It was really great to see you.

Her words echoed in his head as he watched Jaycee walk away. It took everything he had not to haul butt after her and demand to know just what she was up to. In the past fifteen years, she'd never given him so much as a kind word. And she'd never smiled at him.

And she'd never, ever shown up *here*.

He'd been working out at Chucky's Muscle and Fitness since the early days. While he had a home gym like most of the drivers on the circuit, old habits died hard. It wasn't the most convenient at times—waking up at 5:30 A.M. on a Monday following race day was tough, to say the least—but he did it anyway. Because Chucky's felt like home.

It was still a small, quaint, old-fashioned setup that didn't rely on chrome-and-mirror pretense. The equipment was old but functional, and Chucky himself still walked around and handed out clean towels.

Even more, Chucky was a card-carrying Himanist

and one of the smaller sponsors for Xtreme, so Rory
had been coming here most every Monday, when his
schedule permitted. Not once had he ever run into
Jaycee Anderson.

A shiver of excitement worked its way up his spine
and he fought it back down.

Focus, buddy. It's all about focus.

Rory headed for the free weights, determined to
push the parting image of her curvaceous backside
completely out his mind.

No sweet, round ass.

No gently swaying hips.

Nothing. Nada. Zip.

He did forty-five minutes of heavy lifting, working
his arms, chest and abdomen. The muscles of his legs
and back screamed from the exertion and sweat dripped
down his face. He breathed through the pain, pushing
himself harder, faster, until he couldn't go anymore.

He hit the showers next, pausing on his way to shoot
the breeze with a couple of the regulars. They were
die-hard race fans and very excited about the upcoming cup season. He talked and laughed, but despite his
best efforts, Jaycee kept creeping back into his head.

A people person?

Yeah, right.

He was the people person. Straight up.

He liked being around his fans, talking race stats or
just chilling down at Jimmy's Grill whenever he could
find the time. And he really liked working the shop
project with the kids down at the Y.

Jaycee was a different story.

She'd been so desperate for her father's attention
while growing up that she'd turned into a female version

of Ace. Meaning, she'd lived and breathed her driving to the point that she had no room left over for anything else.

Which had worked to Rory's advantage the past thirteen years. He'd never had to worry about running into her socially. While he took every NASCAR promo opportunity that came his way, she'd always been a lot more picky, doing only what she *had* to do. Sure, she had friends. She and Savannah Calloway, her crew chief and the daughter of the great Will Calloway, who owned one of the biggest racing teams on the Sprint Cup circuit, were extremely tight. But Rory rarely worried about running into either of them while judging the local barbecue cook-off or attending the grand opening of a new auto-parts store. Savannah was as committed to winning a championship as Jaycee was, so their get-togethers usually took place in the garage.

On top of that, Savannah had recently tied the knot with hotshot driver Mackenzie Briggs. In other words, she and Jaycee didn't spend much time tossing down beers at the nearest sports bar. Or cosmos. Or whatever women drank these days. Savannah had Mac, and Jaycee had her driving.

And Rory had . . . ?

He had his driving, too, and his chopper project with the kids from the Y and . . . and that was pretty much it.

But it was enough.

It was more than enough.

After hitting the shower, Rory wrapped a towel around his waist and headed for the dressing room. He pulled on jeans and a T-shirt and stuffed his feet into worn black biker boots. Shoving his dirty clothes into a duffel bag, he tugged at the zipper and reached into his pocket for his keys.

On his way out, he passed the yoga room and glanced toward the open doorway before he could stop himself. Not that he expected to see her, but he looked anyway, so that she didn't catch him off guard again. It was all in the interest of self-preservation. He was going over Schilling's handiwork this afternoon and he needed a clear head.

He walked the short distance to the parking lot and found his black Harley leaning on its stand where he'd left it. Bright red metallic flames glittered from the black gas tank. After spending hours on end with his foot to the floorboard of a stock car, driving something as tame as an SUV or even a Mustang held little appeal. The bike was the only thing that provided even a third of the adrenaline rush he got from racing.

That, and his mother had ridden a hog. She'd had three of them locked away in the garage. Old, beat-up models that she'd worked on whenever she wasn't messing with her dirt bikes. Rory had been helping her piece together the parts for a late-sixties model when the accident had happened.

After her death, Cody had stepped up to take her place as best he could and help the other boys. Ian and Jared had been too young to really understand what had happened. Word had retreated to the garage, and Rory had been stuck trying to cope with his grief.

He'd done a piss-poor job.

It's going to be all right, he'd told himself over and over and over. But he'd never really believed it until Jaycee had sneaked over to his house late one night when he'd been sitting in the garage, staring at the half-finished

Harley. He'd wanted to keep going on the bike, but he hadn't been able to bring himself to touch it. On that particular night, she'd tiptoed across the concrete and sat down next to him. She'd been seven years old and she'd worn her Speed Racer pajamas. She'd slipped her hand into his and had given him a squeeze.

"Don't be sad," she'd whispered. "It's going to be all right."

His eyes had blurred as he'd stared at the pile of metal.

That had been the first time he'd cried since the funeral.

And the last.

The memory lingered in Rory's head as he strapped his duffel on the back of his Harley and straddled the black seat. He'd picked up a wrench that night long ago and gone to work on the old bike. He'd been young and inexperienced, and the restoration had taken forever. But he'd finally managed to piece it all together.

And then Word had ripped the whole thing apart with strict instructions to forget the past. To forget his mother. She'd been too big for her britches. A fool who should have been at home with her boys instead of burning up some dirt-bike track. She hadn't been good enough to compete with a bunch of men and it had gotten her killed.

She hadn't been good enough, period.

With the heel of his boot, Rory kicked the starter and fired the engine. The motor roared and the tires ate up pavement as he sped from the parking lot.

Instead of heading for Xtreme headquarters, he hung a left and started for home. Before he went into the garage, he had to finish watching the test tapes Cody had dropped off.

Even more, he had to forget Jaycee and her pleasantries and the way she'd looked in her skin-tight yoga outfit. He had more important things to worry about. Rory was through coming in third place.

He was going all the way this time.

Lycra or no Lycra.

Chapter Nine

"Just relax and breathe deeply."

Soft, cool fingers brushed a strand of hair away from Jaycee's face. She opened her eyes to see a woman looming over her. The woman wore a white fitted top and white slacks. She wore her brown hair pulled back into a neat bun and an air of tranquility that eased the pounding of Jaycee's heart.

Jaycee let her eyes drift closed as the woman dabbed a heated thickness of wax onto Jaycee's left brow bone.

This wasn't so bad. Nothing like she'd imagined when Savannah had told her what was involved. Hot and uncomfortable. That's what her crew chief had said. But this wasn't hot at all. Just nice and warm. And uncomfortable? It did feel a little tight, but nothing she couldn't handle.

In fact, so far the day hadn't been all that horrific. She'd sat through three hours of highlighting, cutting and blow-drying, and all without having a major panic attack. She'd also managed to smile and drink a few cans of Revved & Ready while making small talk with Gwen the stylist.

Gwen, as it turned out, wasn't a race fan. But she'd promised to tune in to the Speed Channel just as soon as the season started. And she'd even asked for Jaycee's autograph. Granted, it had been for her dad. But a girl had to start somewhere.

Correction, a *woman* had to start somewhere.

She was definitely hauling A over the starting line.

"This isn't so bad," she said, easing her grip on the sides of the padded table.

"Of course it isn't." The woman smoothed a fabric strip over the wax and rubbed. "It's all about attitude. If you come in expecting it to hurt, obviously it will. But if you're psyched, then you're home free."

"I'm definitely psyched." And she was also a little sleepy, thanks to the methodical rubbing.

The woman smoothed the strip to the left and then to the right. Back and forth. Over and over. This goddess stuff was a piece of cake.

"Are you ready?"

"Let her rip," Jaycee murmured.

The woman caught the edge and . . . *rrrrip!*

Jaycee arched up off the table. Pain splintered through her and pulsed along her nerve endings. Her eyes burned and her teeth clenched.

"I meant that figuratively!" she finally gasped. Her heart raced pedal to the metal and her brow bone throbbed.

"I didn't hurt you, did I?"

"Not half as bad as I'm going to hurt you."

"You're funny. You've definitely got the right attitude for this," the woman declared, her voice much too happy and pleasant for someone who was *this* close to getting body-slammed. "Time for the other side."

"I'll shave," Jaycee blurted.

"Your eyebrows? You'll have stubble. And what if you slip and whack off half the brow?"

"What if *you* slip? I'll be blinded for life."

"I never slip. Now just relax. The first time is always the worst."

"Really?"

"Definitely." She walked to the opposite side of the table and leaned over Jaycee's head. She smoothed wax onto Jaycee's right brow. "Trust me. This won't seem nearly as intense."

Jaycee grasped at the notion and forced her fingers to relax their grip on the edge of the table. Her left eyebrow throbbed so bad that she felt certain anything else would pale in comparison.

The woman smoothed a strip of cloth over the wax and rubbed this way and that again, and the pain faded into a dull sting.

"Ready?"

"Yes, but go slow this—"

Rrrrrrip!

The air stalled in Jaycee's lungs and her right eyebrow screamed in agony.

"I—I said slow," she gasped.

"Fast is better," the woman replied. She eyeballed Jaycee. "Perfect, as usual."

Jaycee gave her a hopeful smile. "Does that mean we're done?" The woman nodded, and relief rushed through Jaycee like a rookie gunning for pole position. Her eyes closed and she sent up a silent thank-you to The Powers That Be.

"With the face."

Jaycee's eyelids popped back open. "What is that supposed to mean?"

The skin specialist smiled, and her gaze shifted south. "We're moving downtown."

* * *

"For the last time, I did not punch her," Jaycee told Savannah later that afternoon when she finished at the salon and walked outside to the parking lot to find her crew chief waiting to pick her up. "And who told you, anyway?"

"Riley got the phone call right before I left the garage. She was fit to be tied. The salon is threatening to sue."

"But I didn't hit her."

"Technically, you did." Savannah backed her Lincoln Navigator out of the parking space and pulled onto the main road. "You bolted off the table and bopped her with your head, and now she has a black eye. You might as well have hit her. At least as far as Riley is concerned. When I left, she was promising the salon owner free tickets and pit passes, in addition to your firstborn."

"It was an accident."

"Either way, you're in deep."

"I said I was sorry."

"What exactly happened?"

"Bikini wax."

Savannah opened her mouth and then closed it. Enough said.

"While I'm willing to do most anything right now, I've got my limits. I'm not doing it. Not happening. No way. Not for Revved & Ready. Not for Brad Pitt."

"I'm sure Aaron isn't interested in full-body compliance. He's just concerned about the visible parts." Savannah spared Jaycee a glance. "They did a good job. You actually look female." Her gaze dropped to Jaycee's overalls. "From the neck up. When are you meeting with the personal shopper?"

Jaycee smiled. "Right now. Turn left at the corner. I saw a strip mall on the way over here."

"You're kidding, right?"

"The personal shopper can't see me until tomorrow afternoon."

"So?"

"So tomorrow's Thursday and I'm track testing on Saturday."

"*So?*"

"So Rory Canyon is track testing on Friday, and I plan to be there bright and early in the morning when he hits the track. To do that, I have to catch a plane out on Thursday. The latest flight leaves at six, which means I have to skip the afternoon appointment with the shopper."

"I don't know if that's such a good idea."

"The more I see these guys in action on the actual track, the better I can anticipate their moves come race day." And the sooner she could wrangle a meeting with Martin Schilling. If Rory was going to be in Daytona, Martin was sure to be there, as well.

"Right now, I think you should be concentrating 100 percent on this makeover. No sponsor, no car. No car, no race."

"That's why we're here. We'll get the new wardrobe picked out ourselves, then there'll be no need for a personal shopper." Jaycee gave Savannah a pleading look. "You know good and well that all the miniskirts in the world aren't going to help me once I climb behind the wheel of that car. I'm sitting fourth, Van, and I need to move up. I should have finished in the top three this past year, but I blew it. I let myself get distracted."

"Your father died. How you managed to pull yourself together and even finish the last dozen races, I'll never know."

She'd had to finish. To prove to herself that at least

something about her life hadn't been a complete lie. While she'd never measured up as a daughter, she could measure up on the track. That's what she'd told herself, how she'd kept going, when all she wanted to do was curl up and cry.

But she'd fallen short. She'd missed two races because of her father's death and the loss in points had pushed her down the totem pole.

No more.

She might not be the daughter Ace had always wanted, but she was every bit the driver he'd wanted her to be. And every bit as worthy of his love.

She forced aside the ridiculous thought. It was too late to win any brownie points. This wasn't about the past. It was about the here and now. About winning.

"Just hang a left," she told Savannah.

Second note to goddess: never, ever wear Hawaiian-print pants.

Jaycee stared at her reflection in the floor-length mirror and shook her head. "I look like a beach towel." She ignored the urge to reach for a pair of sunglasses and turned toward the curtained doorway leading to the dressing room.

Savannah poked her head through the curtains. "It screams 'Florida chic' to me."

Jaycee turned back toward the mirror. For a second, her gaze riveted on the face staring back at her. Perfectly arched eyebrows. Eyes rimmed with black eyeliner and a thick fringe of eyelashes. Pale pink lips. Prominent cheekbones.

Riley.

The thought struck, but she knew it was just her imagination. Sure, her blonde hair now hung straight and stylish like her older sister's, but that's where the resemblance stopped. Her nose was a little too narrow, her jaw a little too wide. Her eyes much too brown. She was far from the perfect Barbie. She was more like one of the knockoffs. Still blonde. Still so-so pretty. But not as good as the real thing.

She never had been.

She forced aside the thought. She might not be Riley, but she looked good enough for Revved & Ready. Almost.

Her gaze riveted on the flaming-orange tank top and print pants. "Maybe we could go for something a little less busy," she told Savannah.

"I'll be right back." Savannah disappeared for the next few seconds while Jaycee stripped off the hideous outfit. "Try this." She shoved two hangers past the curtains and into Jaycee's waiting hands.

"Now I look like a beach umbrella," Jaycee announced after several tugs and pulls. "Maybe we could try something a little less striped."

"Here." Savannah thrust another outfit at Jaycee. "And if you say you look like a beach ball, I'm going to smack you."

Jaycee eyed the primary-colored miniskirt accented with palm-tree buttons and thrust it back out through the curtains. "Maybe we could try something that doesn't make me look like an extra for *Beach Blanket Bimbo*."

"That's it. I'm smacking you."

"The words *beach ball* never passed my lips. I need something with more material."

"First off, this whole new image thing revolves around you looking feminine—i.e., sexy. Secondly, you're coming out of the closet in Daytona. Aka Florida. Aka beach. Sexy plus beach equals this stuff."

"I feel naked." And she was alone in a dressing room. She could only imagine how she would feel at the race-track. In front of her crew and the other drivers and . . . Rory.

Her mind traveled back and suddenly she saw him in the hallway at *Vogue*. His gaze had been so fierce and blue, and for a split second, she'd been dead certain that he'd wanted to kiss her.

But, of course, that was crazy. She'd been the one desperate to kiss him.

As always.

". . . see why you don't just move the appointment with the personal shopper and do it when you come back."

Jaycee shifted her attention back to Savannah. "I would, but Riley booked me for some PR tour of the Daytona track with one of the local high schools on Friday. It's a field trip for their auto-shop club, and yours truly is going to be the tour guide. I have to have at least one outfit before I board the plane tomorrow night."

"Okay, so you need something tour-guidish."

"Riley's actual words were 'feminine, casual and con-servative.'" Jaycee transferred the beach-ball miniskirt to the pile she'd mentally marked *not in this lifetime or any other.* "Maybe we could try a solid color."

Savannah seemed to ponder. "I think I saw a few solids when we were walking in." She glanced at her watch. "Listen, Jaycee, I hate to cut this short, but I promised Mac I'd meet him at the doctor's office."

"His regular physical?"

"Mine." She smiled. "We're thinking about having a baby."

"A baby? You're having a *baby?*"

"We're just thinking about it. And we want to talk to

the doctor about cycles and vitamins and all that stuff." She gave Jaycee an apologetic smile. "When you said fifteen minutes, I thought you meant, well, fifteen minutes."

And they'd already wasted an entire hour.

"You go on. I can pick something out on my own. I'll catch a cab back to the shop and meet you there."

"You're sure? I'll call him and cancel if you need—"

"Don't you dare. A baby." She eyed Savannah. "Are you sure?"

"No. I'm scared to death, and so is Mac." She beamed. "But it's a good kind of scared. We're in it together, you know?"

But she didn't, because she'd never been *together* with any man. Not that she was a virgin. She'd lost that title years ago with one of the mechanics for a competing team. But it had been quick and not nearly as much fun as she'd imagined. While she'd had sex a time or two since and it had gotten better, it had never been great.

Because there'd been no real connection.

No love.

No togetherness.

A pang of envy shot through her as she looked at her friend, followed by a sliver of longing. She ignored the strange feeling and motioned to Savannah. "You go on. I'll be fine."

"You're sure?"

"I'm a big girl."

"A clueless big girl."

"True, but I'm determined. Besides, it's one measly outfit. How hard can it be?"

Chapter Ten

"You look like Geneva Elmerson," Riley stated the moment she caught up with her sister near pit road at Daytona.

Jaycee arched an eyebrow. "And Geneva Elmerson would be the birth name for a famous supermodel, right?"

Riley shook her head. "Try my ninth-grade algebra teacher."

Her voice was lost in the sudden grumble of an exhaust pipe. It was the third week in January, weeks before the season officially launched in mid-February, but the track already hustled with activity. Several race-car transporters blazed in the midday sun, the big rigs sporting familiar sponsor logos. They stood sentry near the garage, a single-story, steel gray building that sat just beyond a chain-link fence.

A string of individual stalls lined the concrete strip known as pit road. Some were empty, but others housed the familiar setups of the various teams who were track testing. Engines screamed and motors idled. Crew members, headphones hooked securely over their ears, clustered here and there, checking suspension settings for this car, changing tires on that car. There were computer monitors and other high-tech electronics set up on various tables. A handful of guys stared at the data flickering across the large screens. They calculated lap times and corner speeds, and recommended adjustments accordingly.

Jaycee stood near the far end of the strip, near a cluster of Porta-Potties, and prayed for the umpteenth time that no one—repeat, *no one*—noticed her. In particular, the guys working beneath the Calloway Motorsports awning just a few yards away in stall number one.

Not that she actually cared what that particular team thought of her. It's just that they were the closest—much closer than Xtreme Racing, which occupied the stall at the farthest end of the road—and therefore more likely to recognize her. Once that happened, she had no doubt the news would spread like wildfire.

It's the dawn of another race day, folks, and the adrenaline is pumping. Race fans are on the edge of their seats waiting to see what's up next for Jaycee Anderson. Will she defy the odds and go for the blue eye shadow or the purple? Bell bottoms or Capris? Tank tops or turtlenecks?

She wanted people speculating on her performance, not her appearance.

At the same time, she *had* made a commitment. To the team—and herself. She was doing this. No matter how much her skin itched from the awful fabric of her new outfit. Or how her face felt as if it were suffocating from all the makeup she'd slapped on. Or how her scalp practically burned from the ridiculous amount of hair gunk she'd sprayed and splatted on not more than five minutes ago, when she'd morphed from grease monkey to goddess.

Judging by her older sister's frown, the term *goddess* might be a bit premature at this point.

"My *ancient* ninth-grade algebra teacher," Riley added. Her gaze swept Jaycee from head to toe and back up again. "She had a blue suit just like that."

Jaycee glanced down and ignored the disappointment that niggled at her.

Disappointment? Because Riley disapproved? She should be giving herself a mental high five. She'd been searching high and low for ways to piss off Riley since they'd been thrust together six months ago.

"It has pants," she told her older sister, "which says casual. It's also no frills, which smacks of being conservative. You wanted both, you got it."

"Nobody under social-security age wears clothes like this." She rounded Jaycee, eyeing her from all angles. "The legs are too wide, the jacket's too boxy and—oh my God, are those shoulder pads?" Riley touched the shoulder area of the jacket, her mouth drawing into a tight line. "I don't believe this." She reached into her purse for her cell phone.

"What are you doing?"

"I'm calling Image Nation. They're charging us an arm and a leg for *this?*" She punched in several buttons and held the phone to her ear. "I don't know what their personal shopper was thinking—"

"She didn't pick it out," Jaycee confessed.

Riley paused. "Excuse me?"

"I canceled the appointment."

Riley punched the off button, her gaze incredulous as she eyed her younger sister. "You *what?*"

Jaycee shrugged. "I canceled the appointment because I had to catch a plane here. I wanted to be around when Trey and Rory started their track tests this morning." Jaycee motioned to the nearest pit stall. "That means I had to fly in last night instead of early this morning. Since I couldn't be on a plane and make the appointment, I went shopping yesterday before I left."

"But you were at the garage all afternoon."

"I stopped on the way over from the salon. And for the last time, it was an accident," she added when Riley's eyes brightened. "I didn't mean to give that lady a black eye."

"I'll have you know, we had to foot the bill for season race tickets."

"You already told me."

"Otherwise, she was going to press assault charges, and we don't need that kind of publicity." Riley blew out an exasperated breath before nailing Jaycee with a stare. "You can't meet the Sparkies dressed like this. You just can't."

"The who?"

"The auto-shop club from the Pemburton School for Girls. They're the group taking the tour." Her gaze swept Jaycee. "You're supposed to look like their role model. Not their grandmother."

"I thought you said I looked like your algebra teacher."

"Same thing." The seconds ticked by like quick laps around a short track as Riley fell into a thoughtful silence. "You don't have a change of clothes in there, do you?" she finally asked, eyeing Jaycee's duffel bag.

"Just the jeans and T-shirt I took off five minutes ago."

"Hand it over." Riley rummaged inside the bag, her eyes sparking, her brain ticking away. "Maybe we're not totally screwed after all." She motioned Jaycee toward the nearest Porta-Potty. "Get inside and put your old stuff back on. Right now."

"Really?"

"Yes. In," she said, shoving Jaycee inside.

Relief swept Jaycee, and she actually smiled as she shut the door and flipped the latch to OCCUPIED. She peeled off the uncomfortable clothes. "I really think you're making the right decision," she called out. "This whole new image thing really isn't me." She tugged on her old clothes, stuffed the suit into her bag and pushed open the door.

She exited the small cubicle and joined her sister on the asphalt. "I know R & R is a little freaked right now," she told Riley, "but I'm sure if we sit down and explain to them that I'm better at being myself, they'll realize they've been too harsh and—what are you doing?" Her gaze shifted in time to see Riley drop to her knees and reach for the bottom of Jaycee's Levis. Long, perfectly manicured fingers plucked at the denim hem.

"Rolling up your jeans."

"Why?"

"Because they're too long and the ends are frayed. Not that that's a bad thing. We can make it work for us. At least these things aren't two sizes too big for you like the last pair I saw you in."

"I like to be comfortable."

"That's the PC term for sloppy. There." Riley pushed to her feet and eyed her handiwork. "Instead of I-don't-give-a-shit, you look more I'm-a-daring-fashion-diva-and-I-can-pull-this-off." She reached for the hem of Jaycee's oversized Aerosmith T-shirt.

"Wait a second." Jaycee tried to pull away, but Riley's grip was too firm. "I like my shirts long." *And concealing*, a small voice added.

"Thankfully, otherwise, we wouldn't have anything to tie up. Would you stop wiggling and just turn?"

"But—"

"*Turn.*" Before Jaycee could respond, Riley blew out another exasperated breath and walked around her sister. She pulled the edges of the T-shirt and knotted them at the small of Jaycee's back. "Not great," she said, "but at least vintage rock tees haven't gone completely out the door yet." She plucked the shirt up an inch to reveal a sliver of Jaycee's stomach. "There. Now you look more your age." Her gaze dropped to Jaycee's black combat boots and her expression went from *maybe* to *why me?*

"They're comfortable," Jaycee told her. "Perfect for walking around a superspeedway."

"Maybe if you're leading troops, but these are young women." Riley glanced down at her own feet and seemed to think. She toed off her heels. "Here."

Jaycee took one look at the three-inch stilettos and shook her head. "I don't wear anything that requires a release form from a podiatrist."

"Since when are you so health conscious?"

"I'm an athlete. Finely tuned. Honed for speed."

"You're a garbage disposal who just happens to have a fast metabolism and good muscle tone. Now put on the shoes."

"I can't take your shoes. My boots won't exactly go with your outfit." Riley wore a tiny black skirt with a pink fitted jacket. She looked as perfect as ever with her shiny, straight hair and flawless makeup.

"I've got a spare pair in the car. I have so many shoes, there's always something extra lying around. Now come on. Hand over the boots."

For half a second, Jaycee actually considered telling Riley that she couldn't walk in the blasted things. But then, Riley hated her, so what would she care? "They're just shoes," Jaycee said. "I'm sure no one will even notice."

"Are you kidding? We're talking teenage girls. They live for texting and shoe shopping."

"And you know this because . . . ?"

"Been there, done that."

But Jaycee hadn't. Other than her one trip to the mall, that is. "I really think you're making a big deal out of nothing. Combat boots can be chic."

"In an alternate reality." Riley looked ready to throw up her hands and forget the whole thing. She seemed to think better of it and her gaze narrowed. "Put on these heels or I'll call Revved & Ready right now and tell them not to waste their time with us. You'll be out on your butt. The team will be out of a sponsor. I'll go back to the real world."

"And lose everything? You wouldn't do that."

"You know what? You're absolutely right. I *like* living out of a suitcase, arguing with you, inhaling exhaust fumes, arguing with you, wearing earplugs twenty-four/seven and did I mention, arguing with you? It's a charmed life."

For the first time, Jaycee noted the dark circles that marred her older sister's otherwise-flawless complexion. The tired light that gleamed in her bluer-than-blue eyes. She was out of her element, at her wits' end, and it was starting to get to her. She wanted out.

And the problem was . . . ?

It was too soon. As much as Jaycee hated to admit it, Riley was right. They needed each other right now.

She drew a deep breath and toed off her boots. Pulling off her socks, she stuffed them into her duffel and stepped into Riley's shoes. She wobbled and, before she could stop herself, she planted a steadying hand on her sister's shoulder.

"I'd like five seconds alone with the man who invented these things." She tried wiggling her toes. "It feels like I'm wearing a pair of Vise-Grips."

"Get used to it."

"What if I can't?" The words were out before she could stop them.

Riley looked ready to chew Jaycee a new one, but then she seemed to think better of it. "Walking in a pair of high heels is like riding a bike. Just keep moving and don't look down, and you'll be okay. Don't think so much about it," Riley added. Her voice was softer, as if she sensed Jaycee's insecurity.

As if she cared.

But she didn't. Not about Jaycee or the race team. It was all about money for Riley. Ditto for Jaycee. If she made it to the end of the season and accumulated enough points to push into the top three, she would make enough money to buy out Riley.

If.

The high-pitched sound of giggling pushed past the roar of the engines and the clang of tools and distracted Jaycee from a sudden rush of insecurity. She turned to see a group of girls standing at the security checkpoint several yards away. There were at least two dozen, a sea of plaid skirts and white button-down shirts. They all sported trendy haircuts, lots of lip gloss and cutesy purses. Some had iPods hooked on their belts, while others clutched cell phones.

Jaycee blinked, doing a visual search for grease smears and oil stains. "I thought you said this was an auto-shop group?"

"From an elite girls school," Riley reminded her. "Parents are all filthy rich. Some are celebrities, a few political officials, several high-powered CEOs. But make no mistake, these girls are race fans. They tune in every Sunday right along with everyone else." Riley pushed Jaycee forward. "I'll meet you back here in two hours. Now get on over there and don't forget to mention that Revved & Ready makes a teen energy drink that is low carb *and* low fat."

Chapter Eleven

"And this is the actual garage area where the cars undergo the majority of work in the days leading up to a race. Minor adjustments are made in the pits, but the gonzo stuff happens right here." Jaycee motioned around her before staring at the sea of blank faces.

Blank, as in tuned out.

Here she was torturing herself, and no one even gave a flip. It had been less than an hour, and already her feet throbbed and her back ached. If only she could ease her tootsies free for just a few minutes, maybe declare a quick cell-phone break and slide off the torturous shoes during the distraction.

But Jaycee knew the rules better than anyone. Shoes were mandatory behind the scenes, and Riley had confiscated her duffel bag. Which meant she was stuck in the pink high heels, and a break would just prolong the agony. She clapped her hands together. "Let's go. Let's move. We're headed to pit road to see the individual stalls."

"What about questions?"

Jaycee's gaze zeroed in on a petite redhead. She had earplugs stuffed into her ears and a silver MP3 player clutched in her hand. The name Dawn hung from a gold chain around her neck.

"You're going to let us ask questions, aren't you?"

"Of course." Jaycee ignored the screaming of her toes and forced a smile. "Ask away."

"Are you on, like, a first-name basis with the other drivers?"

"Sure." Jaycee nodded. "It's a small world and we see each other at the different tracks every weekend during the on season and at track tests when we're off. I know them all and they know me."

"But do you, like, *know* them? Do you hang out and stuff?"

"I usually do most of my hanging out—and stuff— with my crew. My crew chief is one of my best friends. But, yes, on occasion, I've actually kept company with some of the other drivers during various sponsor events." The comment stirred more enthusiasm than Jaycee's favorite high-powered hydraulic winch.

Shop girls?

Uh, yeah.

"A sponsor event? That's, like, sort of social, right?" one of the girls asked.

"A sponsor is more like your boss than your friend, but they do host promotional parties and banquets that drivers are required to attend. There's music and food. While it's work, it feels more social than the standard autographing or commercial shoot."

"Have you ever hung out with Rory Canyon?" Before Jaycee could respond, the girl rushed on, "He's, like, my favorite driver of all time. He's one of a kind."

"That's true. Not many drivers can boast eighteen first-place wins in one season."

"Who cares about his wins? I was talking about his eyes. They're so . . . *blue*. Not just a washed-out sky blue or anything like that. We're talking cornflower blue."

"Trey Calloway has blue eyes, too," one of the other girls piped in. "He's such a hottie."

"I like Linc Adams," said another girl.

"I think Trick Donovan is a total babe."

"Nobody but nobody tops Cowboy MacAllister," added another. "He's sooooo fly."

First off, Clint MacAllister, once a driver and now the owner of the MacAllister Magic Race Team, was in his late thirties. Married. With twin boys. He could be spotted any given Sunday with a burp rag over one shoulder and a pacifier clipped to his shirt pocket.

Second, Trick Donovan wasn't a driver anymore. He hosted the weekly race show *Life in the Fast Lane*, and the only two words that came to mind when Jaycee thought about him were *pushy* and *overbearing*.

Third, she'd raced against Linc Adams for years now and she'd yet to even notice his eye color. He ran tight most of the time. Incredibly so, which kept him slow in his turns. That was the sort of thing Jaycee noticed.

And Trey—sure, he was decent looking, but a hottie? She'd never really thought of him like that.

As for Rory . . . Was this girl kidding? He didn't have cornflower blue eyes. They were more of a flame blue. Hot. Bright. Intense.

Her heart kicked up a notch, and her breath caught as she realized that not only did she know the exact shade of Rory's eyes, but she could picture him in her mind, his gaze shining, his sensuous lips crooked in a grin. The vision was so clear, so real and straight out of her most erotic fantasy.

Her favorite was the one where Rory shoved her down on the mattress and stripped her bare without letting her get in a word edgewise. Then he leaned down and kissed and touched and—

"Time to go," she snapped, eager to distract her raging hormones and steer them back to a much safer subject—stock-car racing.

"Next"—she flashed an excited smile, despite her sore feet—"I'm going to go through each and every detail of what happens when I pit during a race, complete with job descriptions for all the members of my crew. From the jackman to the—"

"What about Rory? Can we find out what happens when he pits during a race?"

So much for safe.

Jaycee spent the next hour walking the length of pit road and doing her best to keep everyone engaged.

Fat chance.

By the time she finished the tour, she was more than ready to throw herself in front of Trey Calloway's Chevy. She'd had it with the shoes—her toes cried and the balls of her feet burned—and she'd *really* had it with the Sparkies. Forget an interest in race cars. They were teenage girls, which meant their attention centered on any and every male driver on the Sprint Cup circuit. They'd asked everything from Rory's favorite food—cold pizza, or at least it had been when they were kids—to Travis Calloway's shoe size. As if Jaycee knew.

She didn't, and so she'd had to head over to the Calloway stall and ask everyone from the jackman to the crew chief until she'd found the answer: size eleven. She might be fed up, but she was still conscientious.

She was also nailing the goddess thing, because no one at Calloway seemed to recognize her. Thankfully.

At the same time, the realization made her feel a teensy bit crappy. After all, she'd gone to a lot of trouble to fix herself up. The least someone could do was acknowledge her effort.

"That wraps up our time together," she declared once they'd gone full circle back to the security checkpoint where they'd started. Riley stood waiting with a large cardboard box overflowing with promo items.

"Thank you, Jaycee." Riley beamed as she drew everyone's attention. "Revved & Ready is donating free team shirts to each of you," she said as she started handing out the goodies. "I'm sure Jaycee would love to personalize—"

"Can we look around?" one of the girls cut in. "Or do we have to stay here?"

"Your bus isn't due for another fifteen minutes, so you're welcome to wander until—"

Her words were drowned as two dozen girls rushed forward, hands grabbing at the free shirts. The box emptied in less than a minute and everyone scattered toward the various pit stalls.

"Miss Anderson?"

Jaycee turned to see Dawn, who'd lingered behind. "Yes?"

"Cool shoes." The girl smiled before hurrying after her friends toward Xtreme Racing.

It wasn't an autograph request, or even a *Hey, you're a pretty decent driver*, but oddly enough it made Jaycee feel just as good. A warmth sparked in her chest and spread through the rest of her body, chasing away the aches and pains for a few blessed seconds as she glanced down at her feet.

Not that she liked the pink shoes. They pinched and cramped and hurt like hell. But they *were* sort of cool.

Rory rounded the corner of the Xtreme Racing transporter and came up short. The air stalled in his lungs as his gaze riveted on the bombshell who stood beyond the chain-link fence that separated the garage area from pit road.

She looked tall and leggy in pink high heels and faded jeans. The denim clung to her legs and hugged her round hips. A white Aerosmith T-shirt outlined her small shoulders and emphasized a perfect pair of voluptuous breasts. Long, blonde hair hung down around her shoulders and framed her heart-shaped face. She wore a tad too much makeup for his taste, but then, most women did. Even so, it didn't take away from her good looks. Her eyes sparkled and her full, pink lips curved into a smile.

A familiar smile.

While his brain tried to process the notion, his attention shifted to the woman standing next to her. Well dressed. Attractive. Irritated. Riley Vaughn. Which meant . . .

Jaycee?

His gaze swiveled back to the long-legged blonde and he blinked. She didn't disappear. Or morph into a cover-everything-up grease monkey. No, she actually had legs. And a hot body. And long, silky hair. And sparkling eyes.

And, holy shit. His heart slammed into his chest and started gunning for speed. Denial rushed fast and furious. No way. No friggin' way . . .

Rory's gaze swept her up and down again before colliding with her own. Sure enough, her eyes sparkled. Her smile grew wider. She lifted her hand and his shock eased up. This was it. The moment of truth. She would flip him off and the world would stop spinning backward.

She . . . waved at him.

His brain slammed to a stop and his heart paused as

he stared at Jaycee, who stared back at him. She smiled and her fingers wiggled and . . . Yep, sure enough. She was actually waving.

"Hey!"

A nudge followed the man's voice, and Rory half turned to see his older brother standing behind him. Cody wore a white polo shirt, XTREME RACING embroidered across the pocket in neon blue, and a headset hooked half on/half off his head.

"What's wrong with you?" Cody demanded.

"What do you mean?"

"I mean, you're just standing there, when you should be hauling your carcass behind the wheel of that car over there." Cody pointed toward pit road and the race car that sat in the Xtreme stall. "We have to work the bugs out of the new engine."

"I know."

"So why aren't you moving? What's wrong?"

"Nothing." He shook his head and turned back in time to see Jaycee pivot and head for the grandstand. The jeans tugged and pulled with each step. Her bottom swayed just enough to make him swallow.

Wait a second. Jaycee didn't sway. She stomped. And wore boots. And kicked ass.

". . . changed the shocks and the two rear tires to tighten you up," Cody's voice pushed into Rory's thoughts.

"Yeah." And she sure as hell didn't smile.

Sure, she'd done so at the *Vogue* shoot, but that had only been because the photographer had coerced her. It had been a PR thing, after all, and so she'd *had* to look pleasant. Even happy. But she didn't walk around doing it on her own.

And she sure as hell didn't strut.

He watched her take the last few steps before disappearing into the tunnel that ran beneath the stands, and his heart thundered. No doubt about it. She was definitely strutting.

"What the hell is wrong with you?"

"What?" Rory's gaze swiveled back to Cody.

"The car, remember? It was running loose in the turns, so we made a few adjustments and now you're supposed to get your ass over there and try it again. And again. And again, until we get it right. And then you're meeting with Martin to give him an update on how it handled." His eyebrows drew together and his forehead wrinkled. "Are you feeling okay? You're not sick again, are you? Because the doctor gave you a clean bill of health from one end to the other."

"Don't remind me." Rory started walking, eager to leave behind the sudden memory. "I'm fine."

"You don't act fine." Cody kept pace next to him. "You're acting weird."

Distracted.

But he wasn't. Why would he be? So what if Jaycee was prancing around, smiling and waving? There'd be a few hundred yards of concrete and a chain-link fence between them. As long as she kept her distance and he didn't have to see her up close and personal, he could deal with the situation.

He *could*, he told himself, as he walked over to the pit stall and found himself surrounded by a handful of teenage girls. He welcomed the diversion—anything to get his mind off Jaycee and her sudden change in behavior.

He spent the next several minutes smiling for pictures, signing autographs and revealing everything from his shoe size to his favorite food: cold pizza.

When the crowd dispersed, Rory slid inside the car and settled himself behind the wheel. He slipped the HANS device over his shoulder and plugged himself into the radio. Pulling on his helmet, he shoved his hands into his driving gloves and flicked on a switch. The starter caught and then the engine roared.

Waving, of all things. The notion pushed its way in, but he pushed it right back out.

"You're on, bro." Cody's voice came over the earpiece a few seconds later.

Rory shifted into gear and hit the gas. The engine screamed, the car launched into action and everything faded in a blur of concrete.

Chapter Twelve

"Trust me. Everything's taken care of," Riley told Aaron Jansen when he called for the fifth time and she finally answered her cell phone. "She just finished the tour with the Sparkies and they loved her." She rounded a corner and pushed through a doorway into one of the owner's boxes. The room was already crowded with team owners who had cars testing that day, as well as guests and sponsor representatives. "She fit right in."

"Really?"

"Yes." She snagged a bottled water from the bar and nodded a few greetings as she inched her way toward the row of seats that faced the floor-to-ceiling window overlooking the track. "It went flawlessly."

"That's hard to imagine, when I happen to know for a fact that she canceled the meeting with the personal shopper."

"There was a mix-up in her schedule. She's busy, Aaron. She drives for a living."

"Not for me, if she doesn't get her act together. If she isn't going to cooperate, then there's no reason to waste my company's time and money—"

"She did some shopping on her own," Riley cut in, sliding into a vacant seat. "She worked around the scheduling glitch and took the initiative. She's committed to this, Aaron. We both are."

"Jaycee went shopping?" he asked after a long pause. "By herself?"

"That's right. And trust me, she looks as trendy as possible." Riley stared toward pit road at the cluster of people near the Calloway pit stall and searched for a familiar blonde head. "You would be pleased."

"Really?"

Sort of. "Most definitely. Stop worrying. I'll see to it myself that she makes every appointment set up by Image Nation once we get back to Dallas. The hair-and-makeup sessions went off without a hitch," she added, trying to detour them toward a positive route. "She looks really fabulous."

"Danielle sent over some before-and-after shots. The difference *is* incredible."

"I'll admit I was a little skeptical in the beginning," Riley went on, "but after seeing the finished product, I'm feeling more and more confident that this is going to work. Jaycee is perfect for Revved & Ready."

If she continued to cooperate and give it her all. And if all the planets lined up.

Riley forced aside her doubt. "The Sparkies really took to her."

While they hadn't fallen all over themselves for autographs, no one had thrown a spitwad or walked off the tour. Yet. She studied the small group for any sign of rebellion, but from such a distance it was hard to tell.

"Make sure you take a few pictures of her with the girls and be sure to get the release forms signed," Aaron remarked. "I'll have marketing post the pics on our Web site."

"Of course. But remember, she didn't have her own

personal arsenal of experts to get her ready this morning. She had to do it herself, so naturally she's having an adjustment period."

"How much of an adjustment?"

"She's a NASCAR driver, not Max Factor."

"It's a little mascara and some lipstick. How hard can it be?"

So sayeth the typical man.

"Putting on makeup isn't as easy as it looks. Not that Jaycee can't do it," Riley went on. "She'll get it. But you have to give her a little time."

"She has less than five days."

"Excuse me?"

"We've volunteered her for the Dallas Regional Chamber's charity auction being held on Wednesday at the Doubletree Hotel. It's the perfect PR op. All the proceeds benefit Happy House, a local girls' shelter."

"Of course. Race Chicks can donate free race tickets and pit passes."

"It's not that kind of auction."

"Exactly what kind is it?"

"Attendees bid to win an evening with their favorite local celebrity."

"You want to auction off Jaycee?"

"She'll be in good company. There will be several news anchors up on the block, along with a few local cable-TV actors and actresses, and even the guy that does those commercials for that car dealership."

"The chicken guy?"

"He's a duck. 'Buy from the duck and save a buck,'" he repeated the familiar slogan. "He'll be auctioned off, in addition to three members of the Dallas Rockets, the women's pro-basketball team. Anyhow, we'll be sponsoring a table at the event and Jaycee will be our contribution. We were playing around with the idea that attendees could bid to have Jaycee whip up a healthy home-cooked dinner. What do you think?"

Riley mentally rifled through the past six months of memories for any clue that Jaycee might know her way around the kitchen. But other than seeing her at the race shop or on the track, they'd had little contact. No cooking marathons or sleepovers or all-night gabfests like most sisters.

Because Riley and Jaycee weren't most sisters. They were little more than strangers. Thanks to Ace. He'd undoubtedly feared Riley's influence on Jaycee, so he'd kept them apart. He'd protected Jaycee. Meanwhile, Riley had been on her own. Shut out. Forgotten.

Thankfully.

Ace had caused her enough heartache. The last thing she needed was a female version of him stirring even more grief.

"I'll find out if she can cook," Riley told the Revved & Ready CEO.

"Good. Let me know something by tomorrow. If we can't offer up dinner, we'll have to think of something else."

"What about a workout session or a personally guided tour of the race shop?"

"My marketing guys thought of both and vetoed them. We'd really rather have her cook. Putting on an apron and tinkering with a few pots and pans will soften her image."

Or kill it. Particularly if Jaycee set someone's house on fire.

"If she can't cook now, maybe she could learn," Aaron went on. "Once she gets back from Daytona on

Sunday, she'll have a good three days until Wednesday's event."

Aaron obviously didn't cook any more than he put on makeup.

"You could help," he added. "Surely you can teach her how to make something?"

"Of course." *Not.* "I'll see what I can do."

"Darlene's rescheduled the meeting with the personal shopper for Monday morning. Make sure she doesn't cancel this time."

"She'll be there," Riley assured him before punching the off button.

She'd just lifted the bottled water to her lips when she heard a familiar male voice directly behind her.

"The plot thickens."

Her grip on the water bottle faltered, and cool liquid dribbled down her chin. She blotted at the moisture as her heart stalled in her chest.

It couldn't be.

She half turned and dread washed through her. Trick Donovan smiled back at her. He looked even more handsome in person, with his sun-streaked brown hair and his twinkling green eyes. He was tanned and rugged and her heart flipped before it started thumping again at an incredibly fast pace. The way it did every time his face flashed on the TV screen.

Not that Riley watched him on a regular basis. Not out of choice. She turned in because keeping up with the latest when it came to NASCAR was her job.

For now.

She frowned. "How long have you been standing there?"

"Long enough to know that you're going to auction off Jaycee." His mouth crooked into a grin. "I'm assuming that's after you shoot her up with tranquilizers."

"I'm sure she'll be more than cooperative."

"Only if they're performing brain surgery along with the makeover."

"Very funny. Any chance you'll give up the Speed Channel and switch to Comedy Central?"

"Sorry, slick. Racing's my life." He eyed her. "So tell me about the auction. Are you going up on the block with her?"

"They need celebrities who'll rake in the big donations. No one knows me from Adam."

"I'd bid on you." He gave her a slow, lazy grin that made her breath catch.

It was a crazy reaction, because she knew his flirting meant nothing. He was a smooth-talking ladies' man with a reputation to uphold. Of course he was dishing out the lines and laying on the charm. That's what he did. It's what all players did, and she'd had more than her share of those.

She frowned. "Don't you have someone else to torture?"

His grin widened before he glanced at his watch. "Actually, I have a meeting with Trey Calloway. An update on today's test for my weekly episode. I thought I would mention Jaycee's tour. Sort of build up to the actual race week's interview, so no one passes out from shock when they get a good look at her."

Riley shrugged. "I suppose that would be all right."

"I'm not asking your permission, slick. I'm just keeping you informed."

"Are you always such a pain?"

"It depends on who you ask." He winked. "I'll have

my assistant call you and set up an actual time and date for the interview. Later, slick." And then he turned and walked away.

Riley drew a deep breath and turned back toward the track. She took a long gulp of water, but it did little to calm her pounding heart. Trick Donovan was more than just a pain in the ass. He was the ass itself. Granted, he looked good enough to eat when he smiled. But personality-wise, he was about as appealing as a horse's backside. Why anyone—let alone millions—tuned in to watch him each week, she would never know.

Not that she was going to waste her time trying to figure it out. She had more important things to contend with. Including whether or not Jaycee could actually cook. Since she lived in the race shop, Riley was willing to bet on the *not*.

She tamped down the sliver of panic that streaked through her and took another drink of water. She watched as the neon blue and black Xtreme car took the track and started gunning for the red, white and blue sixty-five car.

Behind Riley, a steady stream of conversation buzzed. She turned to see a dozen corporate execs from Bubba Beer, the major sponsor for Xtreme Racing, standing near the bar. Word Canyon himself stood in the center of the group and cited specs for his latest vehicle. He sounded extremely knowledgeable and excited, and for a split second, Riley actually envied him. He had passion for the sport. A passion she'd once felt herself a long, long time ago. Before things had soured between Ace and her mother. She'd loved watching him race back then. When the engine had revved, her heart had pounded. When the green flag had come down, her breath had caught. She'd spent each and every race completely caught up in the action, her adrenaline rushing, her emotions seesawing between excitement and fear.

She turned back and eyed the track in time to see Rory come up on the Chevy's bumper. Close . . . Too close.

She waited for the air to stall in her lungs, for her throat to tighten, for her stomach to flutter, but nothing happened. Her heart kept beating and her lungs kept drinking in oxygen and . . . Nothing. Sure, she felt the usual concern for the drivers who were moving at such high speeds, but no real excitement. Because Riley Vaughn had lost her passion when she'd lost her father.

Good riddance. She didn't need racing any more than she needed him. At least that's what she'd been telling herself since the moment Ace walked out of her life and turned it upside down.

Chapter Thirteen

"Twelfth," Cody told Rory later that afternoon. His older brother scratched his temple. "We're going to have to do a hell of a lot better than twelve out of fifteen if we want to win a championship."

Twelfth. An entire day of testing and he'd run a crappy twelfth?

Thanks to Jaycee.

While he'd managed to push her out of his head, she'd bounced right back in when he'd spotted her near the Race Chicks transporter. She'd been deep in conversation with Savannah, no doubt going over specifics for her track test tomorrow. She'd still been wearing her pink high heels, her T-shirt knotted at the waist, her hair long and flowing. She looked much too female for his peace of mind, and he'd found himself remembering more than once their first kiss.

Their last kiss.

He stared across the stretch of concrete toward the pink rig parked across from the garage. She was inside with her car and her crew, probably fine-tuning things for her session tomorrow.

That, or putting on more lipstick. Slathering the stuff onto her full, pouty lips. Licking them, pressing them together.

"Let's wrap this up, boys," Cody told the other team members clustered around him. "We need to get back to the shop and figure this baby out."

But it hadn't been the car that was off. While there'd been the usual adjustments, overall the car and its new engine had performed as anticipated. Fast. Smooth. Aggressive. Rory had been the part of the equation that had been off. He'd been preoccupied. Surprised and freaked and extremely wary. Because, distance or no distance, he knew what Jaycee could do to him if she put her mind to it.

She'd been the only one who had ever haunted his thoughts, and now here she was, putting it all out there, reminding him that she was every bit the woman from his fantasies. And that he wanted her. Bad.

"So, what do you think?" Cody asked him. "Any suggestions?"

"It's probably the tire pressure," he told his brother. "Or the track bar." He couldn't very well tell Cody the truth: he had the hots for Jaycee Anderson and it was wigging him out. Sure, Cody would understand, because he had Cheryl leading him around by the nose hairs. At the same time, he had a responsibility to his family. He needed this win as much as Rory did, so while he might understand, he wouldn't be the least bit sympathetic.

Forget explaining himself. Rory needed to get things together. To keep his focus. Now more than ever.

He rubbed a hand over his face. It was late in the afternoon, well past five o'clock, and his day wasn't nearly over. "We still have another test session before the race," he told Cody. "We'll get it right by then."

Cody nodded. "You look like hell. Why don't you

call it quits and catch a nap before your meeting with Martin?"

Rory thought of the soft, cushioned mattress waiting back in the motor coach and shook his head. The last thing, the very *last* thing he needed right now was to crawl into bed. Not with Jaycee still so vivid in his head.

His dick throbbed and he turned. "I'll be fine. Stop worrying."

"Make sure you give Martin as many details about the run as you possibly can," Cody called after him. "Maybe he can help."

If only. The only help Rory was going to get came in the form of a cold shower.

He spent the next half hour standing under the icy spray and rethinking the afternoon. Jaycee was up to something. That's what his gut told him. But his head wasn't nearly as suspicious.

By the time he shut off the water, he'd managed to put things back into perspective. Yes, he'd had three run-ins with her in less than a week, but they were all just flukes: those crazy coincidences that defied explanation and just sort of happened, with no rhyme or reason. Which meant he was jumping the gun, stressing over a conspiracy that didn't exist. Jaycee wasn't out to get him. Hell, she didn't have a clue that she *could* get to him. If she did, she would have played her trump card long before now.

No, it was better just to forget all about it, forget all about her, and get on with his job. Starting with his meeting with Schilling.

Just march right over there and plead your case.

The command echoed in Jaycee's head as she stood

in the doorway of the Fun & Sun Diner—a small dive located near the racetrack. The diner served up its signature monster burgers with a side of southern hospitality that was unmatched by the dozens of fast-food restaurants that populated Daytona.

The place was packed, as usual. The sound of hamburgers sizzling and popping rose above the steady chatter of voices and the slow twang of a Tim McGraw song that drifted from a beat-up jukebox. The delicious aroma of hot French fries and onion rings teased Jaycee's nostrils. Her stomach growled, reminding her that she hadn't eaten since the granola bar and bean-sprout sandwich she'd had at lunch.

Her gaze snagged on the chocolate meringue pie that sat on a pedestal beneath a glass lid, and for a long, breathless moment, she forgot all about the man who sat in the corner booth.

"Can I help you, hon?" The question came from a petite redhead wearing a white blouse and red-checkered apron. "You here for a take-out order?"

"No. I'm meeting someone."

The waitress smiled. "Well, have a look around then. I'll be over in a flash to take your drink order."

Do it, her courage whispered as the redhead disappeared through a set of swinging silver doors. *Walk over and tell him you can't sleep at night because you can't stop thinking about him and his brilliance. Tell him you need his help in the worst way. Then he says yes, and since you've been so faithful—you've done the bean-sprout lunch twice now, not to mention the black-bean burger for last night's dinner—you reward yourself with a piece of pie.*

And if he said no? Forget the pie.

Jaycee started walking.

"I need you," she blurted when she reached the table.

Martin Schilling glanced up from his half-eaten burger and eyed her. "I beg your pardon?"

"I need your help. With my engine."

He adjusted his black-rimmed glasses and let his gaze sweep from her head to her toes and back up again. "Do I know you?"

"Jaycee," she offered, wishing she'd had the good sense to wipe off the makeup and pull her hair into a ponytail. But she'd been so busy during the afternoon with the prep for tomorrow's track test that she hadn't really thought about it. "Jaycee Anderson. I drive for Race Chicks."

"I know who she drives for. But you're not her." Another visual sweep and realization seemed to strike. "Christ, it *is* you. You look—"

"Different? Don't remind me."

"Actually, I was going to say good." His gaze collided with hers and he smiled. "You look really, really good."

Warmth bubbled through her and temporarily distracted her from the engine and the pie. She smiled.

"So what can I do for you, Miss Anderson?"

"The name's Jaycee." She smiled. "I need your expertise."

He shook his head. "I wish I could help, but I don't have time for any new designs. I just filled up my schedule."

"I don't need you to build me an engine," she said as she slid onto the seat opposite him. "I already have one. It's my own design and it's fast. But it could be faster. That's where you come in. I want you to take a look at it and see if you can offer any suggestions."

He seemed to think. "I already agreed to consult on that. My secretary called to set up an appointment, but you weren't interested."

"My *sister* wasn't interested. She's tightened the team's belt, so to speak, and we're a little short on consultation fees right now. *But*," Jaycee rushed on before he could turn her down, "I know you're not 100 percent interested in money."

"I'm not?"

"You haven't gotten to be the best in the business by being blinded by a stack of green. You're in it because you like to see your engines win. And that's what I plan to do. I'm offering you a chance to share in the credit when I race into the top three and make history." She shrugged. "Or you could just stick with Xtreme and watch Rory Canyon eat my exhaust fumes."

"Rory is driving my latest and greatest. You won't beat him."

"Probably not, but what if I do? If I beat him with a Schilling engine—and I'm willing to give you full credit, if you help me out—then you'll bask in the glory no matter who wins."

"And glory is better than a consultation fee?"

"Much better."

He eyed her for a long moment. "I'll tell you what. I'll forfeit my consultation fee."

"That's great."

"But I won't work for free," he added. "And I won't do it for the glory alone."

"Which means?"

"That I'll take it out in trade." His gaze found hers. "I'll consult if you'll accompany me to an annual awards dinner sponsored by the National Association of Motosport Engineers. I've been nominated in a couple of categories. It's the weekend before Daytona, and it's being held in Charlotte at the Omni Hotel. It'll be dinner followed by two hours of industry awards and then a champagne reception."

"Are you asking me out on a date?"

"Not asking. Bartering."

A *date?* With Martin Schilling?

She'd anticipated a lot of things—including his telling her to get lost when she made the glory proposition. But she hadn't considered he might want more.

A *date?*

For the first time, Jaycee took a good, long look at the man responsible for the most winning engines in NASCAR. From the neck up, he was average looking with ho-hum brown hair and pale blue eyes that he kept hidden behind a pair of glasses.

And from the neck down?

He bypassed average and pushed the meter into semihot. Although he spent his days making calculations and working on a computer, it was obvious he found the time to work out. He wore a black polo shirt that revealed ripped biceps and heavily muscled forearms. She had no doubt that he had a six-pack hiding under the shirt and a hard, toned gluteus maximus parked on the cracked vinyl.

"Why do you need to barter for a date? You're a decent-looking guy. Why not just ask someone?"

"Because I work behind the scenes in a male-dominated sport and I don't have much time for a social life. I don't meet very many women. The few that I do are usually wives and girlfriends of different team members. You're single and, more importantly, you want something from me." He grinned. "Which means you'll more than likely say yes."

"Ah, the fear of rejection."

"Something like that. So what do you say?"

"What if I say I'm involved with someone? A mega-hot boyfriend that I'm keeping hush-hush from the press?"

"Are you?"

Only in her wildest fantasy. "No."

"Then do we have a date?"

The notion should have sent a rush of excitement through her. It would have, if Jaycee had been the average woman who enjoyed dinner and industry awards and champagne receptions. Or if the offer had come from a certain sexy, infuriating NASCAR driver who'd starred in the above-mentioned fantasy.

She nixed the last thought and concentrated on the matter at hand: securing Schilling's help and earning herself a piece of chocolate pie.

"It's a deal."

"Great." He pulled a BlackBerry from his pocket and started punching buttons. "I'll be flying to Dallas tonight to make some adjustments on the Xtreme car. I'll call you in the next few days and we can set up a meeting to look at your engine."

Jaycee gave him her cell number and signaled for the waitress. "Anything else I should know?" She watched the redhead pause to plop down two plates overflowing with chili cheeseburgers a few tables over before making a beeline for their booth. "About the ceremony?"

"It's formal and it's being televised on the Speed Channel."

Which meant she would have to squeeze herself into a floor-length dress à la *Vogue* and parade around on national television.

"Can I get you something, hon?"

Jaycee glanced longingly at the chocolate cake and

swallowed her disappointment. "You wouldn't happen to have a bean-sprout sandwich, would you?"

She was definitely up to something. Rory came to that conclusion the moment he walked into the diner for his meeting with Schilling, only to find Jaycee seated across from the engineer.

He watched as she smiled before taking a sizeable bite of the grilled-chicken salad that sat on a plate in front of her. First yoga and now salad?

Duh, buddy. She's this close to the top three and she's trying to give herself an advantage. She's gunning for you. One slipup on your part and you not only lose your standing, but you get your ass whipped by a woman.

The thought struck, and suddenly the past few days started to make sense. The way she'd smiled at the *Vogue* shoot. The way she'd shown up at his gym. The way she'd dolled herself up today and pranced around in her high-heeled pink shoes during his track test. The way she'd waved at him. The way she was now nibbling a slice of carrot while sitting across from Rory's ticket to the Sprint Cup.

His heart pounded and the air lodged in his chest. She was trying to distract him on purpose, to throw him off his game, because some way, somehow, she'd finally figured out that he wasn't half the jackass he pretended to be. No, she knew he was attracted to her and she meant to use the knowledge against him. She was trying to get under his skin, to make him want her that much more, to make him jealous.

It was working.

Rory watched her smile at Schilling and his gut tightened. Anger rushed through him along with a desperate longing as he watched her long, willowy fingers hold a fork that speared a piece of grilled chicken. Her full lips parted and hunger grumbled inside of him.

And not because he wanted a taste of her dinner. No, Rory wanted a taste of *her*. He wanted to press his mouth to Jaycee's and savor the sweet flavor of her pink lips. He wanted to drink in her intoxicating scent and bury his face in her long, silky hair. He wanted to strip off her clothes and slide between her legs and press himself deep, deep inside.

And she knew it. She was using that knowledge to push him beyond the point of control and screw up his focus. She wanted him to slip up on the track so that she could slide right into his spot.

Keep the faith, buddy.

Even as the encouragement rolled through his head, he knew it came too late. He wanted her too much to keep pretending otherwise.

He had to *do* something. Before he blew the season and lost his last shot at the cup.

She dabbed at her delectable mouth with the edge of a napkin and he swallowed. Forget hauling ass in the opposite direction; he was going to have to turn around and try going after her instead. Maybe if he stopped fighting it and just took her to bed, he could get her out of his system once and for all.

Rory grasped at the notion and refused to let go. He *could* work her out of his system. The key was to stop torturing himself by staying away. He needed to get close. To get intimate. To get Jaycee Anderson into his bed and out of his head. Then he would see that she was nothing special.

Even more, he would beat her at her own game because no way—no friggin' way—was he going to let her beat him on the track.

Chapter Fourteen

"Looks like the meeting started without me."

The deep, familiar voice stirred the hair on her neck. Jaycee's grip on her fork faltered and salad rained down on her plate. Her gaze swiveled to the man who towered over her.

Rory looked as handsome as ever in soft, worn jeans and a black T-shirt that read COWBOY UP! in silver letters. The sleeves had been cut off to reveal his heavily muscled arms. A thin line of flames encircled his left bicep like a slave-band tattoo. His blue eyes twinkled as he stared down at her, into her, and she swallowed.

"We're not having an official meeting," Martin offered. "Jaycee just showed up to ask me a favor and I invited her to join me for dinner. Isn't that right, Jaycee?"

"Yes." She held up a celery stalk. "That's exactly right."

"It looks delicious," Rory said.

You look delicious. That's what his gaze seemed to say, and the sliver of vegetable slipped from her hand and clattered to the plate.

Way to go, Jaycee.

"It's healthy," she blurted. She snatched up her fork, stabbed at a piece of lettuce and braced herself for the sarcastic dig that would surely follow. She had no doubt he would give her a hard time. He *always* gave her a hard time.

He smiled, a slow tilt to his sensuous lips, and her stomach hollowed out. "Can I have a bite?"

Wait a second. No *It looks like rabbit food* or *What? No fertilizer to go with that grass?* Just an easy grin and those twinkling eyes, and the deep, seductive question that held a world of hidden meaning.

"You want a bite?" He nodded. She held up a carrot stick minus her favorite ultrafat ranch dressing. "Of this?" He nodded again and she shrugged. "Um, sure. Be my guest."

Definitely the wrong thing to say. His gaze held hers, his eyes hot and bright and hungry as he leaned down. His lips parted. His mouth grazed the tips of her fingers as he snapped off a chunk of the raw vegetable. His strong jaw moved, working at the mouthful as he chewed. The muscles in his throat flexed and he swallowed. His Adam's apple bobbed.

"Not bad."

And how.

Her skin buzzed where his mouth had touched her. Her nerves tingled. Her nipples pebbled and her thighs gave an answering quiver.

She fixed her attention on what was left of the carrot stick. A bad move, because there was something extremely intimate about eating after him. As if his mouth were actually touching hers—

"Jaycee?"

Her name pushed into her thoughts and her head snapped up. Her eyes met Martin's and she realized he'd asked her a question.

"You don't mind, do you?" he went on.

"Excuse me?"

"Rory and I have a meeting scheduled and I have to catch a plane in a half hour, so we need to do it now."

"No problem." She started to climb from the booth. Before she could slide free, Rory folded himself in next to her and blocked her line of escape.

"We can talk in front of Jaycee," he told Martin as he wedged her back in the seat. "She's already seen me on the track. I don't think what I'm going to say will come as any surprise." His gaze zeroed in on her. "Isn't that right, Trixie?" He used the nickname he'd called her years ago. She'd been a die-hard Speed Racer fan and Trixie had been that character's female sidekick. "I saw you today." His deep voice slid into her ears and whispered over her nerve endings. Heat rushed from her head to the tips of her toes, and paused at every major erogenous zone in between. "You waved at me."

"I did?" Her mind rushed back and she remembered her afternoon with the Sparkies. She'd been riding her first goddess high, courtesy of her cool shoes. And then she'd spotted him. And then . . . "I did." Her mind raced for a plausible excuse that didn't involve shoes. It was one thing to prance around in the damned things and quite another to admit that she'd liked prancing around in the damned things. For about an eighth of a second, anyway.

"I, um, was fanning myself. The heat."

"Is that so?"

She nodded. "It was really hot at the track. Almost as hot as it is in here." She blew out a deep breath and took a long drink of her iced tea. The cool liquid did little to cool the sudden rise in her body temperature. Her chest heaved and she felt Rory's gaze zero in on her nipples, which pressed provocatively against the front of her T-shirt.

"So, how did it go today?" Martin asked, drawing Rory's attention. *Thank you.* "What do you think of the new design?"

"Jaycee?" Rory's gaze swiveled back to her.

"I, um, wasn't the one driving." She took another long draw of her tea. Icy condensation dripped onto the front of her T-shirt, soaking through the thin cotton to the hot skin beneath. "It's your call."

"Not necessarily. You were watching me. You were, weren't you?"

No. It was there on the tip of her tongue, but damn if she could spit it out. She ended up nodding.

"Based on the observation," he went on, "what did you think?"

"Well . . ." She cleared her throat and inched slowly, carefully toward the wall to escape the solid mass of hot, hunky male currently stealing her breathing space. There. Now she could drag some much needed oxygen into her lungs. "I'd say you were tight. You had trouble in the corners."

"Did you?" Martin cast an expectant gaze toward Rory, who nodded.

"The lady's right." Rory leaned back and settled his arm across the back of the booth, directly behind Jaycee. "I was definitely running tight."

Lady.

Oddly enough, the description didn't drip with the usual condescending tone. Realization hit as she sat there with Rory so close, his hard male thigh a scant inch from hers, his breaths echoing in her head, his warmth reaching out to her, surrounding her.

Somehow, someway, things had changed between them.

He'd changed.

Uh-oh.

"Cody made a few adjustments," Rory went on. "The usual. But it didn't make a difference in how the car handled. I don't think the fuel is pushing hard or fast enough through the engine, which is slowing her down and making it difficult to steer."

Martin nodded. "It's possible. I'll take a look at the pump. And the plugs. You might not be getting enough spark when you're giving it the gas."

"I also noticed the car fishtailed when I hit the straightaway. . ."

Rory's voice faded as he shifted in his seat and his blue jean–clad thigh brushed Jaycee's. Her heart bolted, slamming against her ribs. Heat rushed to her face. Her hands started to tremble. And just like that, his close proximity made her go all soft and warm inside.

It's not the car. It's you. You drive like an old lady inching through the grocery store. The comments rushed to her lips. She needed to fortify the wall between them that was fast crumbling.

At the same time, she'd committed herself 100 percent to the makeover. External and internal. Which meant keeping her smart-ass remarks to herself. She was no longer a rough-around-the-edges tomboy. She was a goddess.

Jaycee focused on her salad and did her best not to remember the way Rory had looked when he'd taken a bite of her carrot. And, more importantly, the way he'd looked at her as if he'd wanted to sink his teeth into her and nibble away.

As if.

Rory Canyon didn't like her like that. Not then. And not now.

It's a game, she told herself. *He knows you're gunning for his spot and he wants to distract you.*

But as much as she wanted to think he was a low-down, dirty, conniving snake in the grass, a man willing to use his sex appeal to weaken the competition, she couldn't quite believe it. Any more than she could forget the hunger that simmered in his eyes whenever he glanced at her.

Maybe he really and truly wanted her.

Maybe . . .

The notion played through her head and haunted her for the next fifteen minutes as she sat and did her best to concentrate on the conversation between the two men. Just when she'd managed to forget Rory and focus on what was being said, his thigh would brush hers. Or his arm would slide against her skin. His scent filled her breathing space. And more than once, Rory filled her line of vision when her gaze, the traitorous thing, slid his way.

By the time Martin Schilling stood up and said good-bye, Jaycee was this close to ripping off her clothes and throwing herself at Rory whether he wanted her or not. Because she wanted him.

Not that she was about to act on the feeling. Noway. Nohow. Not happening. She'd already put herself on the line once before and he'd run right over her, full speed ahead. She wasn't doing it again.

Not over a measly *maybe*.

"Can you give me a lift?" she blurted as Martin pocketed his BlackBerry and pushed to his feet.

"I'm headed back to the track," Rory told her. "You can ride with me."

"I'm not going to the track." She wasn't? "I—I'm headed to the airport."

Rory frowned. "But you're testing tomorrow morning."

"They, um, lost some of my luggage on the flight in, and they, um, just now found it. I have to go and pick it up." She smiled at Martin. "If you don't mind, I could tag along, retrieve my bag and then catch a cab back to the track."

Martin smiled. "Sounds like a plan to me."

"Great." She motioned to Rory. "Can you hurry up and move? I wouldn't want Martin to miss his flight."

Rory didn't budge for a long moment while Jaycee's heart pounded a frantic rhythm. "No, we wouldn't want that," he finally said. Still, he didn't budge. Instead, he trailed one fingertip across the back of her neck in an intimate caress that she felt between her legs.

Her breath caught and her gaze hooked on his lips. He was so close. All she had to do was lean forward just a fraction—

"We'd better get going then." Martin's voice shattered the thought and jerked her back to reality. To the all-important fact that she wasn't kissing Rory, or stripping naked for him or doing any of the very erotic things racing through her head at that moment.

Martin's voice seemed to galvanize Rory as well. He slid from the seat and turned, holding out a hand.

Don't do it, her hormones whispered. *Don't touch him.* But she couldn't very well refuse. Not without looking like a spoiled kid. Or worse, a stubborn woman with raging hormones and the burning desire to have wild and wicked sex.

"Thanks," she mumbled, sliding her hand into his. His palm burned into hers. Her nerves buzzed and her body hummed as she eased across the vinyl.

He pulled her to her feet beside him, but he didn't

let go of her hand. Instead, he kept his fingers wrapped around hers, his heat seeping into her for several heart-pounding moments.

His gaze dropped and he murmured, "Cute shoes."

For a split second, Jaycee forgot all about her sore toes and she actually smiled. "Thanks." Smiling? Because he liked her *shoes?* Who cared if he liked them?

Me, me, me!

She ignored her chanting hormones and pulled her hand from his. "Thanks for letting me sit in. It's been interesting."

"Yeah. A real eye-opener."

He seemed almost reluctant to let her go, but he did. His gaze glittered hot and potent as he stared down at her before shifting his attention to Martin. If Jaycee hadn't known better, she would have sworn he looked ready to lunge for the engineer's throat.

Jealous?

Maybe in her hottest, most erotic dream. But there was absolutely no reason for Rory to be jealous unless he actually liked her. Not in a let's-share-our-feelings-and-become-soul-mates way. Not the way Mac liked Savannah. No, this was more like a let's-get-naked-right-now thing.

Cute shoes. His voice echoed in her head and suddenly the past half hour made perfect sense. He was a man, after all, and now, albeit under duress, she was emphasizing her womanly attributes. Walking the walk. Talking the talk. Putting it out there. It only made sense that Rory would respond.

Martin Schilling had.

If she'd shown up covered in grease from head to toe, the engineer never would have asked her out on a date. She knew, because in all the years she'd been racing NASCAR, no man had ever bothered. Because she'd hidden behind her baggy clothes and ugly shoes and baseball caps.

But now . . .

She adjusted the T-shirt still knotted at her waist and combed her fingers through her long hair.

Martin had asked her out because he was attracted to the way she looked. Ditto for Rory. Not that it mattered. She wasn't sleeping with him. She couldn't, because she did feel more for him than just lust. It was a crazy feeling that spiraled deep inside of her.

Still, the tables had turned, and there was no denying that it felt good.

"See you later," she said.

"You can count on it." And Rory's sultry promise rang in her ears long after Jaycee strode from the diner and left him staring after her.

"The same thing happened to me last year when I was on my way to Dover," Martin said as he held open the car door for her. "They lost one of my suitcases," he added when she turned a puzzled stare on him as she climbed into the passenger seat. "Actually, it was a garment bag." He shut the door, rounded the front of the car and climbed into the driver's seat. "But they never found it. They ended up reimbursing me for the cost of the bag and its contents. You're lucky."

"You're not kidding." A few more seconds with Rory and she would surely have done something she would later regret. Like start with the smack talk again and totally blow the goddess image. Or worse, kiss him.

Her mouth watered and she licked her lips. Yes, she really wanted to kiss him right now.

"So which airline?" Martin gunned the engine.

"Excuse me?"

"Which one lost the suitcase?" He shifted the car into reverse, backed out of the parking space and turned onto the main road. "That way, I'll know what terminal to drop you off at."

"Actually, it's a really old bag and I've been meaning to get a new one. You can just drop me off at the next corner." She motioned up head. "I've got my cell. I'll call a cab to take me back to the track."

"Maybe we can catch Rory—"

"No," she cut in. "I would much rather take a cab." When he looked doubtful, she added, "Really. I like cabs. It's great having someone else do the driving. Someone who doesn't drive one-eighty."

"A cab it is." He gave her a knowing look and flipped on his turn signal to pull over. "Too much fraternizing with the enemy for one night?"

If only.

But Rory Canyon was much more than just her competition. That's what scared the daylights out of her.

Chapter Fifteen

"It's definitely you." Danielle Savoy stood in the dressing room of Dallas's most exclusive boutique and flashed a perfect, bleached-white smile. *"Tres chic."*

Jaycee rolled her shoulders. The seams of the jacket pulled. "It's really tight."

"It's fitted."

Jaycee glanced down at her legs, bare from midthigh down. "And short."

"Miniskirts are all the rage."

"And bright."

"Chartreuse is a great color for blondes."

Jaycee eyed her reflection in the floor-length mirror and tamped down the urge to peel off the linen suit and fast pitch it at Danielle.

I am a goddess. I am a goddess. I am a—

"An apple," Riley declared as she walked through the arched doorway, a glass of champagne in her hand. "You look like a Granny Smith."

"It's the latest color for this season," Danielle assured them. She glanced at the tall, thin, tastefully dressed woman who stood in the corner and studied Jaycee's reflection as if she were contemplating Einstein's theory of relativity. "Isn't it, Millie?"

Millie Handeland, personal shopper and fashion diva, wore a tailored orange dress—tangerine, Danielle had called it—tied with a wide black sash and matching open-toed sandals. She held a BlackBerry in one hand and a swatch book in the other. She rounded Jaycee, studying her from various angles before she finally nodded. "This color is all the rage in Milan," she finally announced.

But this is Texas, Jaycee wanted to say. Stifling heat. Raging humidity. Loads of hospitality. And a little something called pride.

As if Riley read her thoughts, she shook her head.

Jaycee clamped her lips shut and finished her mantra. She drew a deep breath and tried to ease the pounding in her temples. Her hands trembled and her stomach jumped. She was definitely having the stinkiest Monday of her life. Which only made sense, since she'd just come off of the worst weekend ever.

Careerwise, the past two days had actually been pretty sweet—she'd come in a reputable third out of sixteen cars during Saturday's track test.

Personally? We're talking bad with a capital *B*. She'd spent every free moment thinking about Rory and how much she wanted to kiss him, and touch him, and peel off his racing suit to see if he looked even half as good naked.

Okay, so she'd thought about more than kissing him. Much, much more. Enough said. Whew . . . Was it hot or was she hyperventilating just because of the suit?

She slid open the top button on the apple nightmare and drank in a deep draft of air.

Back to her reeking Monday . . .

It had started when Riley had shown up early that morning as Jaycee was on her way out the door to yoga.

Since Jaycee had been dreading running into Rory at Chucky's Muscle and Fitness, she'd let her sister wrangle her into the car. Thirty minutes later, they'd met Danielle and Millie in the plush reception area of Giovanni's. The elite boutique catered to the rich and famous and, in Jaycee's case, the most fashion challenged.

That had been eight hours ago. Yes, *eight.* Jaycee had spent the entire time trying on everything from dresses to blouses, shoes to belts. She now had a complete wardrobe that made her feel about as attractive as a fruit bowl. Which explained the headache.

And she hadn't had a decent burger or slice of pizza or even a lone French fry in six days, two hours and sixteen minutes. Which explained the bitchiness.

To top it all off, she'd yet to hear from Martin Schilling. Which explained everything else—anxiety, insecurity, sheer desperation. Maybe he'd changed his mind about consulting with her.

Or maybe, she hoped, he was just busy. He'd said a few days, and it had only been three. Two, if you discounted Sunday, which was really a good idea, since he more than likely took Sundays off right now—the race season had yet to start.

Which meant two days. And counting . . .

As if her thoughts had willed it, her cell phone chose that moment to ring. Jaycee almost ripped off a sleeve reaching for it. One glance at the display and her hopes plummeted.

"Where are you?" Savannah demanded when Jaycee said hello.

"Finding my external goddess."

"You're still shopping?"

"Don't rub it in. What's up?"

"I'm at the race shop going over the fuel system for

the car. I think maybe that's what was making you loose in the turns. I noticed that once the fuel burned up, you got a little tighter. I'm going to tweak and then we'll try her out again before the race."

"Sounds good. I have to go. Riley's giving me the evil eye."

"That's not why I called. You had a phone call. Someone named Betty. She said something about an awards ceremony for engines. Or maybe an engine for an awards ceremony. Something like that. The engine was gunning so I couldn't really here her clearly. But I got her digits."

Jaycee copied down the phone number, killed the cell phone and smiled. Maybe today wasn't so bad after all.

"I think she needs a hat." Millie stepped forward with a wide-brimmed creation—complete with green satin ribbon and a fuzzy-looking feather—clasped in her perfectly manicured fingers.

On second thought . . .

"I'm not wearing the hat," Jaycee said for the hundredth time since they'd left Giovanni's.

"Fine." Riley flipped on her turn signal and braked to a stop. "Don't wear it." She turned down the main road leading to Race Chicks headquarters.

"I mean it." Jaycee snatched up a stray bean sprout that had fallen from the sandwich they'd picked up right after leaving the boutique. She popped this last morsel into her mouth and braced herself against the hunger that still gnawed at her gut. "I'll wear all the clothes, even if they make me feel like a stuffed sausage, but I am *not* wearing a hat. Not the green one or that red one, or even the pink one they picked out to go with that sundress." That's right, a *sundress*. Since when did NASCAR drivers need a sundress?

Jaycee fought down the rebellious thought and held tight to her newfound goddess.

"You don't have to wear the hats," Riley said as she bypassed Race Chicks and headed for Jaycee's place just a few blocks over. "I've never been a huge hat fan myself."

"Really?"

Riley shook her head. "They can look good with the occasional outfit, but I never liked having anything on my head." She hung a left at the first corner. "They make me feel closed in."

"You're claustrophobic?"

She shook her head again. "I can deal with small places. I just don't like anything over my head."

"I like hats. Not the frilly kind, but baseball caps and race helmets. I'm good with both."

"You would be."

"What's that supposed to mean?"

Riley shrugged. "Just that you're a driver, so it would stand to reason that you wouldn't have a problem shoving something over your head. Especially since you're the daughter of a race-car driver. You were probably putting on Ace's helmet and gloves while most girls were playing pretty princess dress-up."

A memory stirred, and Jaycee saw herself standing in front of the mirror with her dad's suit dwarfing her, his helmet weighing her head down. She'd actually been scared to death at that moment. While the suit had looked like fun, when she'd put it on she'd felt as if someone had locked her in a closet. One that she couldn't escape.

She'd been right.

"I put on Ace's helmet one time." Riley shook her head. "I didn't like it." That's what she said, but Jaycee couldn't help but wonder if she really and truly meant it. Or if she was just saying the words more to convince herself.

Yeah, right. Riley Vaughn had made no secret that she disliked the sport. She was here now not because she liked racing, but because she stood to gain from it. When the season ended, she would gladly leave. The sport. The team. Jaycee.

Especially Jaycee.

Jaycee swallowed against the sudden lump in her throat. What did she care what Riley did or didn't do? So long as she sold her share of the team when the season ended, everything would be fine.

Silence stretched between them as the sisters covered the last few blocks to the two-story Colonial Jaycee had bought several years ago before she'd really started to climb. It was modest, the only luxury a custom-designed garage she'd had added onto the rear of the house after she'd won her first race. Most people would have gone for a pool, but Jaycee was a NASCAR driver and she liked to get her hands dirty.

"Are you going back to the shop?" she asked Riley after they'd wended their way up the front drive and come to a stop in the driveway.

Her older sister shook her head as she put the car in park. "I've got a meeting with a few members of the Dallas Area Chamber of Commerce." Reaching for her purse, she retrieved a silver lamé bag. "They're having a charity auction on Wednesday night to benefit Happy House. They want us to help them out with a donation."

"I volunteered at Happy House last year. I helped paint their new recreation room. I'd be glad to donate some signed T-shirts and caps." Jaycee watched her sister pull a tube of Luscious Pink from the bag and swipe her mouth a few times before rubbing her lips together.

Uh-oh. While Jaycee was clueless for the most part when it came to her sister, the one thing she'd picked up on over the past six months was that Riley liked to put on makeup when she was stressed. Nervous. During Ace's funeral, she'd held a rose in one hand and a compact in her other. She'd spent the entire reading of the will trying out different shades of blush. The first race following Ace's death, she'd glossed and reglossed her lips to the point that Jaycee hadn't been worried about the glare from the setting sun. No, she'd been more concerned about the reflection off her older sister's bee-stung lips.

"I don't think shirts and caps are exactly what they need." Riley swiped at the corners of her mouth before shoving the lipstick back into her bag. "It's not your typical auction." She retrieved her mascara and added another layer to her already-caked eyelashes.

"I can help out with some posters," Jaycee suggested.

"I'm afraid that's not what they're really interested in, either."

"An autographed five-by-seven?"

Riley swiped her cheeks with blush. "No."

"One of my old driving suits?"

Riley added bronzer over the blush. "That wouldn't work either."

"Free pit passes?"

"Nope." She applied more bronzer and then a sprinkling of dusting powder.

"A driving lesson?"

"Uh-uh."

Jaycee's hand shot out and she caught her sister's powder puff. "Then what do they want?"

Riley's gaze met Jaycee's and *Oh, shit* glittered there as she spoke the unspeakable: "A meat loaf."

Dinner with NASCAR driver Jaycee Anderson.

The words echoed in Rory's head for the umpteenth time since he'd read them in the lifestyle section of the newspaper early that morning. After he'd gone to Chucky's to work out.

He'd gone to the gym fully expecting to run into her. She was purposely trying to throw him off his game, so Rory had had no doubt that she would take every opportunity to rattle him. Then again, the fact that she hadn't shown up had rattled him even more. He'd left Chucky's with every intention of driving by Race Chicks for a little confrontation of his own. But then he'd seen the newspaper and a prime opportunity to get up close and personal, so he'd decided to back off.

Until Wednesday and the auction, that is.

He'd also decided to call her publicist and wangle a PR schedule. He wanted to know what Jaycee was up to before reading about it in the newspaper.

"Is that the last bolt?" A boy's voice pushed its way into Rory's head and drew his attention.

He glanced at the group of twelve teenage boys who hovered around him. "This is it," he told them. "Then we're done with the gas tank."

"Can I hold the impact wrench?" one of the teens asked.

"No way. It's my turn, dude," said another.

"Yeah, right. I'm up next."

Rory's gaze swept the dozen familiar faces before landing on one boy in particular. He was tall and lanky, with deep brown eyes and a crooked nose. The eyes had come from his mother, who'd given him up to a foster family five years ago because of her drug addiction. The nose was courtesy of her dealer/ex-boyfriend.

The boy stood back from the others as if he weren't the least bit interested in what was going on, but Rory knew better. He'd seen the spark in those brown eyes the first day the group had walked into Rory's shop over six months ago. It was an excitement he had felt himself when he'd found the courage to finish restoring his mom's Harley.

"What about you, Mike?" he asked the boy. "You want to do the honors?"

Mike shrugged. "That's okay. You can let someone else take my turn."

Rory wanted to argue, but the teenager looked so hesitant and guarded that he decided to let it go. For now.

"Okay . . ." He motioned to one of the others. "Bennie. You're up next." He watched as the boy checked his safety goggles to make sure they were firmly in place before reaching for the state-of-the-art air impact wrench. With a look of pure awe, he stepped toward the chopper tank. The loud *whirrrrrr* of the wrench soon bounced off the walls of the massive garage.

Several minutes later, Rory patted the newly installed tank and clapped the boy on the shoulder. "Good job."

"Thanks." Bennie grinned and turned to high-five his buddy.

Rory ran his hand over the smooth metal surface. "She's coming along nicely, guys."

"She sure is."

Rory turned to see a fiftyish man framed in the doorway. Eddie Dougal was the youth coordinator for the local YMCA. He was the one who'd initially contacted Rory about doing the class for the foster kids. The teenagers had all been placed in good homes, but due to their ages, they still had self-esteem issues that made them susceptible to bad choices. The sessions, Eddie had hoped, would not only teach the boys some valuable shop skills, but give them something productive to do with their time.

Rory had been more than happy to help. He'd opened up his home shop to the boys and had been hosting them every Monday afternoon since, with the exception of a few holidays or race conflicts. They'd started the first lesson with nothing more than a sheet of metal and an arc welder.

"Come on, guys." Eddie clapped his hands. "Everyone on the bus. I've got to get everyone home in time for dinner."

Rory pulled off his safety goggles. "You guys be sure to rest up, because next week we're going to cut out the rear fender. I need everybody to bring their A game."

The steady chatter of voices echoed through the room as the boys headed for the doorway. Eddie shook Rory's hand before motioning everyone outside.

Rory had just turned to pack away the dozen pairs of safety goggles when he heard the footsteps behind him.

"Rory?"

He turned to see Mike lingering a few feet away. "What's up, guy?"

Mike shrugged. "I just wanted to say thanks. I really appreciate you letting me come here and everything."

"You're very welcome. The chopper's really taking shape. You've got a really good eye for fabrication. That gas tank wouldn't have come out half as good without you behind the welder. I can't wait to see what you do with the rear fender."

Mike grinned a split second before the expression faltered. "About that . . ." He stared at his feet. "You'll have to let someone else do the welding. Today was my last class."

"But I thought you liked coming here?"

"I do."

"Then what's the problem? Is one of the other boys giving you some trouble? I could talk to Eddie—"

"No," Mike cut in. "The other guys are all cool. Really. It's not them." He shook his head. "It's just . . . my foster mom, Carol, wants me to take violin lessons. She plays and she's been teaching me chords. I'm pretty good, so she thinks I should take formal lessons."

"And what do you think?"

"I think she's right. I should take lessons. But the only opening the instructor had is for Monday afternoons. There isn't enough time for me to do both. Since I'm really good with the violin, this has got to go."

"But you're good at this, too. In fact, you're the best I've ever seen. You've got a natural eye for detail."

"It's really interesting." Mike shrugged. "But it's not like this will actually lead to anything. That's what Carol says. She says if I start taking lessons now, I might actually be able to get a music scholarship. Carol went to Baylor and studied classical music. She says that I have a really good shot of going there if I buckle down and focus." His gaze met Rory's. "She's really excited about this. She loves to play."

"What about you?" He leveled a gaze at the boy. "Do you love it?"

Mike shrugged again. "I like it okay."

"There's a big difference between liking something and loving it," Rory pointed out.

"It doesn't matter. Carol really wants this and she's been good to me. I owe her, you know?"

Boy, did he ever. Rory thought of all the hours he'd put into restoring that Harley. And he thought of how busted up he'd been when Word had made him pack it away. The man had brought home an old Chevy Impala right after that to give Rory something to do. Something that didn't remind him of his mother. Something that didn't remind Word of his wife. Rory had watched silently as his father had rolled the Harley into the shed and padlocked the door. Then he'd climbed behind the wheel of the Impala, because that's what Canyon men did. They were drivers. And because his dad was all he had left and he'd wanted to please him just as much as Mike wanted to please Carol.

As soon as the thought struck, Rory pushed it right back out. Sure, he'd learned the ins and outs of the Chevy because of his dad, but he'd hauled ass to the nearest track for himself. Because he'd wanted to race. The need for speed—he'd had it in the worst way. He could still remember his first win. The rush of excitement. The jolt of pure pleasure. Nothing could touch the feeling—not even tinkering with a bunch of chopper parts.

No, the motorcycles were just a hobby. A way to distract himself and deal with the stress of competitive racing. Some drivers turned into gamers, and others raced go-carts. Hell, a few even played golf. A distraction. That's what Rory had always told himself. But as he watched Mike turn and walk out of the garage, he wasn't so sure he actually believed it anymore.

Chapter Sixteen

While Jaycee liked doing community service and volunteering for the various organizations that requested her time—particularly when she could help a deserving group of underprivileged girls, like the residents at Happy Home—she drew the line at making a fool of herself in public. A girl had her pride, after all.

Just as she'd told Riley, she would gladly autograph a stack of publicity photos. Or do a marathon meet and greet. She would give driving lessons or rotate someone's tires or offer up a free oil change. She would even donate her autographed poster of the legendary Cecilia Marbury—*the* first woman ever to drive in a NASCAR race. But she was not making a meat loaf.

She was making spaghetti.

Not that she'd ever whipped up a batch of sauce any more than she'd cooked an actual hunk of meat. But when she'd gone through the endless stack of recipes she'd pulled off the Internet, spaghetti had been the simplest one with the fewest ingredients. Short and sweet meant less room for error. At least that's what Jaycee was hoping.

She stared at the recipe she'd downloaded one more time before tucking the paper into her white goddess diary. She packed the book into the large wicker picnic basket filled with all the ingredients for tonight's meal and closed the lid. She tugged up the bodice of her strapless evening gown for the fifth time in as many minutes before hefting the basket off the kitchen table and heading for the den, where Riley paced back and forth across the gleaming hardwood floor.

"I'm fully capable of driving myself," Jaycee told her sister as she set the picnic basket near the couch. "In case you've forgotten, driving is my thing."

"Race-car driving." Riley gave her a knowing look. "I wouldn't want you to miss your exit and bypass downtown."

"You don't trust me," Jaycee stated.

"I promised Aaron that tonight would go off without a hitch, and I intend to deliver. He'll be there along with a few corporate bigwigs from Revved & Ready, and I want everything to go smoothly." She eyed the strapless, floor-length creation Jaycee wore. "Nice."

"It's pink."

"Actually, it's called salmon."

"Same thing." Jaycee tugged at the bodice again. "I think it's too loose."

"Or maybe you're just nervous."

"I'm not nervous. I'm hanging out." Jaycee tugged yet again.

"You're going to rip the material if you keep yanking on it like that."

"I feel naked."

"You look fine."

"You're not the one with your boobs hanging out for the world to see."

"It's just a little cleavage."

"It's a Hooters calendar just waiting to happen."

Riley shook her head and Jaycee waited for another

Give it a rest, you look fine. Instead, her sister gave her a long, assessing glance before reaching for the salmon-colored silk wrap that lay over the back of the couch. She stepped toward Jaycee.

"Let's try this." She hooked the wispy material around Jaycee's neck and evened out the dangling ends. Then she rounded Jaycee and pulled either side under each arm.

"What are you doing?" Jaycee tried to turn.

"Just face forward and relax." Riley pulled and tugged at the material. "There," she finally announced. She circled Jaycee for another look. "Much better."

Jaycee walked toward the large mirror that hung near the fireplace and surveyed her reflection. "It looks like I have a collar. And sleeves." Albeit small ones, but still, the top portion of her arms was now covered.

"It gives a halter effect and kills the feeling of being half dressed." Riley left Jaycee staring at her reflection as she went to retrieve a couple of safety pins. "Lift," she said when she returned. She motioned to Jaycee's right arm and then went to work pinning the wrap material to the edge of the dress.

"Where did you learn that?"

"A little trick I picked up at my senior prom. I never really liked strapless dresses myself. My chest is too big. The dress has to be either really tight, which means I can't breathe, or loose enough to accommodate the twins here, which means it tends to inch south. Plus, I've got narrow shoulders. The illusion of a collar helps balance out everything." She wiggled the pin in place before moving around to the other arm.

"You wore a dress like this to your senior prom?" Jaycee broke the silence that stretched around them as Riley worked at the second pin.

"Actually, mine was even worse. It wasn't straight across the chest. It dipped for cleavage and gave new meaning to the word *skimpy*. I had to use a half dozen safety pins to keep the wrap attached." She shook her head. "One even came loose and poked my date during a slow dance."

"Seriously?"

"Cross my heart." She smiled to herself. "It was just the first of many pokes that night, I can tell you. Later, when we were making out, he kept trying to untie the wrap. By the time we said good night, I swear his hands looked like pin cushions."

"I bet he never wanted to take you out again."

"I wouldn't have gone if he had. I liked him so much—I'd had a mega-crush on him since freshman year—and I thought he liked me."

"I sense a 'but' coming on."

"*But* he didn't like me. It seems while I was picturing the two of us falling madly in love and tying the knot, he was picturing the two of us naked in his backseat." She shrugged. "He just wanted to get into my pants. So what about you? Who did you go to the prom with?"

Jaycee shook her head. "It was in April. Dad had a race that weekend."

Riley gave her an incredulous look. "You missed your prom for a race?" When Jaycee nodded, Riley asked, "What about homecoming? Surely you went to homecoming."

"Race weekend."

"Christmas dance?"

"I didn't really like that sort of thing."

Riley eyed her. "You didn't, or Ace didn't?"

Jaycee shrugged. "It doesn't matter."

But it did. All the regrets that Jaycee had buried

deep, all the schoolgirl fantasies she'd locked away and tried to ignore, came rushing back as she turned and surveyed her reflection in the mirror. "You're so lucky," she blurted before she could stop herself.

Riley arched an eyebrow. "How's that?"

"You *know* this stuff: the makeup, the clothes. You got to go on real dates and have a real life." Jaycee swallowed against the sudden lump in her throat. "Not that I regret anything. I mean, I love driving. It's just..." She shrugged. "I don't know. I sometimes wonder what it would have been like to be someone else's daughter." Her gaze met Riley's in the mirror. "But you don't have to wonder. You escaped all of this. You got away from him."

Riley's gaze met hers. "Yeah, but you're the one he kept." And before Jaycee could reply, her sister turned away and busied herself finishing with the last safety pin.

The one he kept? Yeah, right. He hadn't *kept* Jaycee. He'd pushed and molded and done his damnedest to turn her into the exact opposite of his oldest daughter. Because he'd loved Riley and he'd missed her, and he'd wanted no reminders of what he'd lost.

That's what Jaycee had been thinking ever since her sister had walked into her life. Because she couldn't imagine that Ace had been the kind of man who could have abandoned his child. Yes, he'd been hard. Tough. Even an asshole at times. But he'd still *been there*. For every important moment—when Jaycee had climbed behind the wheel for the first time, when she'd changed her first fan belt, when she'd learned how to use a torque wrench, when she'd driven her first NASCAR race— Ace had been there for all of it.

No, Riley and her mother had been the ones to walk away. They'd left him. Abandoned him. That explained why Jaycee had grown up not knowing she even had a sister.

But it didn't explain the hurt she'd seen in Riley's eyes.

Maybe Ace really had turned his back on Riley and her mother. Maybe not.

And it matters because . . . ?

It didn't. Either way, Riley still hated racing, while Jaycee loved it. Riley was walking away when the season ended, and Jaycee was staying. They were polar opposites who didn't see eye to eye on anything.

Jaycee adjusted the edges of the wrap sleeves. Okay, so maybe they both had an aversion to strapless dresses. But that wasn't enough to base any kind of relationship on. Riley still didn't like Jaycee and Jaycee still didn't like Riley.

"Thanks," she said, despite the truth.

Because of it.

"You didn't have to help me out," she went on. "You could have made me walk out of here with my dress hanging to my ankles, but you didn't. I just want you to know that I appreciate that."

"Maybe I didn't do it for you, so much as I did it for myself. The more you cooperate, the easier things will be for me."

"Maybe." But Jaycee knew better. She could tell by the sudden glimmer in Riley's blue eyes and the way her expression softened. "But I still appreciate it."

"It's all in a day's work." Even as her sister said the words, her voice wasn't as harsh as usual. "We'd better get going. The auction starts in a half hour."

Thanks.

Jaycee's voice echoed in Riley's head as she steered her car onto a busy street in downtown Dallas. She would never have thought her spoiled kid sister capable of genuine gratitude, but she'd been wrong. In more ways that one.

Riley turned and caught a quick glimpse of the woman who sat in the passenger's seat. Jaycee looked so unlike the tomboy who'd stormed into the lawyer's office for the reading of Ace's will. She'd done a complete one-eighty. Under duress, of course. Still, Jaycee had stepped up to the plate. She was making a genuine effort to please Revved & Ready, and she wasn't bitching about it.

That was why Riley had taken pity on her back at the house. She knew what it was like to feel uncomfortable and she'd wanted to ease Jaycee's misery.

Because?

Because she wanted to help herself, of course. It was all about securing the means—a solid sponsorship—to see them through the race season, so that Riley could get her share of the pie when it ended. It certainly wasn't because she liked Jaycee.

There was nothing whatsoever to like. The younger woman was stubborn and bossy and a know-it-all when it came to racing. Nope. Jaycee scored a big, fat *nada* when it came to amicable qualities.

But there was something kind of sweet about the insecurity she'd noticed in her sister's eyes. Jaycee wasn't a full-fledged badass, as she'd first appeared. No, she was as insecure as the next person.

And even more alone.

She'd never had a mom to help her out with clothes and makeup. While Riley's own mother had been far from a prize, she'd still taught her daughter the ropes, when it came to all things feminine.

Jaycee had looked so vulnerable when she'd tugged

up the bodice of her dress that Riley hadn't been able to resist. She'd offered her help. But it hadn't been because she liked Jaycee. Or respected her. Or admired her. She was just a means to an end.

"Wow." Jaycee's voice slid into Riley's thoughts and drew her attention to the half-moon drive that bustled with traffic in front of the Doubletree Hotel. "I didn't realize there would be this many people here." Local news crews clustered here and there. Cameras flashed and pictures snapped as familiar faces exited the endless stream of cars that poured through the drive.

Riley veered toward the left and eased the BMW up behind the last car in line. "More people mean higher bids."

"So you really think someone will bid on me?" Jaycee asked after a long, silent moment while they inched closer to the entrance.

"You don't?"

"If I were doing something really cool like showing them how to drive, yes. They'd be paying for my expertise. But for me to make them dinner?" She suddenly looked ready to throw up. "I just don't want to get up there and make a fool of myself."

"Someone will bid on you. Hell, I'll bid on you, if no one else does."

And just how are you going to manage that, genius? Riley was already up to her neck in debt and the salary she drew from Race Chicks was barely enough to pay the rent on her miniscule apartment.

She opened her mouth to take the statement back, but Jaycee looked so hopeful that she couldn't make herself say the words. Besides, she was already so far behind, what was one more month?

"I have to eat just as much as the next person," Riley added. "Besides, I love spaghetti."

"You do?"

Not. Riley gave Jaycee her most reassuring smile. "It's my absolute favorite."

"Sold!"

The announcement thundered through Jaycee's head and she blinked against the blazing spotlight, hoping to get a peek at the person who'd just made the winning bid. But the ballroom was too large, and she was *this* close to being blinded for life after standing on the chopping block for over twenty minutes while the auctioneer wrangled her asking price from a measly fifty dollars to ten thousand.

She still couldn't believe it.

Riley hadn't had to make good on her promise, because the bids had started the minute Jaycee had hit the stage. Then again, she'd had an autographed door panel off last year's Daytona car go for twenty thousand dollars at another charity auction, so she shouldn't have been surprised. She drove for the fastest-growing sport ever, so it only made sense that *someone* would bid on her.

"You can collect your prize at the auction table located at the entrance to the ballroom," the auctioneer said, smacking down his gavel again. "Next!"

Jaycee turned to walk toward the edge of the stage as a local weatherwoman went up for bid.

Relax, she told herself. *You're home free now. The hard part is over.*

But as much as she'd studied the recipe, she hadn't actually had the chance to try it out. After the shopping spree on Monday, she'd had a full day of sponsor commitments on Tuesday. She'd been at the race shop all day Wednesday checking and rechecking the progress on the Daytona car. She'd barely made it to the grocery store and then home in time to shower and pack up the picnic basket. Which meant she would be trying out her culinary skills for the first time tonight.

Then again, maybe whoever had bought her might not even expect her to cook. Maybe they just wanted to get to know her, to talk shop.

Jaycee latched onto that possibility as she made her way around the edge of the ballroom toward the entrance. By the time she reached the table that had been set up to handle the transactions, her nerves had calmed.

"Thank you again, Miss Anderson," the coordinator, a fifty-something woman named Rose, told her. "Your contribution means so much to the girls."

"My pleasure."

As in the opposite of pain. Meaning, she shouldn't be dreading the next few hours. No, she should be looking forward to them. It was a prime opportunity to go one-on-one with a loyal fan, and she loved her fans. Race fans in general were the greatest people on earth. Excited. Gracious. Understanding. Tonight wouldn't be so bad. In fact, she might actually enjoy . . .

The thought faded as a familiar solid mass of warmth stepped up next to her.

"I hope you brought plenty of food." Rory Canyon reached for the picnic basket she held in her arms. He looked smoking hot in a black tuxedo and a sexy-as-hell grin. Jaycee's tummy tingled and her hands trembled.

No. It couldn't be.

"I really don't have time for this." She held tight to the basket, doing a little tug-of-war with him. "I'm waiting for a fan," she blurted, despite the truth that blared in her head. "You're not a fan."

"No, but I'm hungry." He pulled a check from his pocket and set it down on the table before giving the basket another pull. "Starved."

"Yeah, but that doesn't mean what I think it means," she said, as if uttering the words out loud could make them true. Rory would disappear and some crazed groupie would appear, and all would be right with the world. "You didn't just do what I think you did." She swallowed. "Did you?"

His grin turned to a full-blown smile. One that promised heart-stopping kisses and bone-melting sex. He winked.

"Guess who's coming to dinner, sugar."

Chapter Seventeen

Jaycee was stuck in the middle of her worst nightmare. She stood at the island stove, smack-dab in the middle of a large kitchen, surrounded by pots and pans and black granite countertops cluttered with ingredients. Rory was behind her.

She glanced down at her bare feet—she'd chucked the high heels the minute she'd walked into the tiled kitchen—which peeked from beneath the hem of her fancy dress. Give her a baby on the way, and she would have been the picture of domestic bliss.

Okay, so it would have been her worst nightmare, except that at one point in time, it had actually been one of her hottest fantasies.

About a zillion years ago.

But times had changed, and Jaycee had outgrown her adolescent thoughts about Rory Canyon. At least that's what she told herself as she moved about his kitchen while he leaned against one of the countertops and watched. He'd shed his jacket and unfastened the top buttons of his shirt. The vee afforded her a glimpse of silky chest hair and tanned skin and—

Uh-oh. Her stomach tingled and her nipples tightened. She fought to keep the tremble from her hands.

You're a grown woman. You're a successful driver. You've

got it going on and he totally missed the boat. And while you're as horny as hell, you're not some naïve virgin. You know he's bad for you. You can resist him.

Um, yeah.

She rolled the last of several meatballs and scooped them up. She could feel his eyes following her as she dropped them on a cookie sheet and popped them into the oven. She turned back to the sauce, her skin prickling with awareness, and added more garlic. Then a can of crushed tomatoes. Her nipples tingled. Some basil. Her tummy quivered. Then thyme—

"Why don't you set the table?" she blurted, eager to put some much-needed distance between them and calm her traitorous body.

"I'm the one who forked over a ten-thousand-dollar check for dinner. I pay, you do the work."

She bit back a sarcastic reply and gave him her sweetest smile. "It would really mean a lot to me if you could help out."

He gave her a disbelieving look, as if he expected her head to start spinning around. When it didn't, he finally shrugged. "I guess I could do that."

She turned back to the sauce and heard the clink of plates, the clatter of silverware. A few moments later, the kitchen door rocked shut as Rory headed for the adjoining dining room, and she breathed a sigh of relief.

Temporary, of course. He would be back, and the sultry glances and sexy grins would start all over again, and her body would wave the white flag.

He really *was* attracted to her. Duh. The guy was out of his mind with lust. She'd come to that conclusion the minute she'd crawled into the passenger's seat of his Hummer for the long ride to his house in suburban Dallas. She'd seen the truth in the sparkling intensity of his eyes when he'd looked her way. She'd felt it whenever his arm happened to brush hers. And she'd heard it in the deep, husky timbre of his voice as he talked about everything from the weather to the upcoming race at Daytona. The air had practically sizzled between them.

Things had gotten even worse once they'd arrived at his house. He lived in a two-story Colonial several blocks over from hers. Like her place, the house itself wasn't monstrous, but it had all the amenities. Pool. Weight room. Sauna. Professional garage.

He'd given her a quick, heart-pounding tour that had led to the kitchen, where she'd spent the past thirty minutes trying to calm her frantic heart while he stood nearby and observed her every move. Attracted. All thanks to the makeover.

She braced herself against the sudden rush of regret that washed through her. Yes, it was the makeover rather than the real Jaycee that had finally snagged his full attention. The hair. The makeup. The clothes. The image. That's what had Rory panting like a dog in heat. He hadn't so much as spared her a glance before. No, he'd spent the past fifteen years keeping his distance when he could, and aggravating her when he couldn't. There'd been no heated glances or sexy flirting or outright ogling. And no panting. Definitely no panting. Because he'd never really and truly liked her. Not the way she'd liked him.

She ignored the thought and reached for the brown sugar. Tonight was all about dinner. He'd paid for her spaghetti and she intended to give it to him. Dinner and nothing but dinner. No sprinkling herself with whipped cream and doubling as dessert.

While she might have been foolish enough to hand

him her heart on a silver platter once, she wasn't making the same mistake twice.

Not that he wanted her heart. No, he wanted something a good twelve to fifteen inches lower.

The body part in question throbbed, and a tiny thrill of excitement zipped up her spine. Jaycee stiffened. Forcing her attention to the recipe card, she concentrated on adding a pinch of brown sugar to the bubbling sauce.

A pinch? What the hell was a pinch?

"It's like a smidgeon," Riley told her a few seconds later, after Jaycee had pulled out her cell phone and punched in her sister's number.

"I know I'm no expert, but I'm pretty sure there's no standard measurement called a smidgeon." Jaycee stared at the cooking utensils strewn across the granite countertop. "I need something recognizable." She stared at the measuring utensils. "A teaspoon. A tablespoon. A quarter cup."

"It's less than a teaspoon."

"A half teaspoon?"

"Give or take."

"You don't know, do you?"

"I usually do takeout. Listen, it's no big deal. Just toss in a half teaspoon or so and don't worry about it. The real reason you're there isn't to cook. The person who bought dinner with you doesn't give a flip what you're serving. It's all about having a brush with greatness."

"You don't know who bought me, do you?"

"I was talking to Aaron backstage about next week's PR schedule. Listen, I'm sure that whoever the lucky fan is, he or she is even more nervous than you. This isn't about cooking. It's about interacting. You're fulfilling someone's fantasy."

If only.

Jaycee ignored her panting hormones, said good-bye to Riley and hit the off button on her phone. She tossed in half of a teaspoon of sugar. Watching the pale brown granules disappear into the thick, spicy sauce, she wondered how such a minute amount could make any difference in the gigantic pot.

Then again, Riley had said a half teaspoon *or so*.

Translation? Less or more. She couldn't imagine it being less, since she was cooking enough to feed a small army. Which left more.

She opened the box and held it over the open pot. She flexed her wrist and the brown granules sprinkled into the sauce.

"It looks good."

The deep voice stirred the hair on the back of her neck and sent a jolt of awareness through her. Her hands trembled and her grip on the box faltered. Cardboard dove into the pot and sauce splashed.

Rory's deep chuckle sent tingles through her body. "I usually make mine with mushrooms." He eyed the sinking box. "Trying something new?"

"Maybe." She scooted a few feet away toward the utensil drawer. "Do you always sneak up on people?" She tossed him a sideways glance as she rummaged for a pair of tongs.

His eyes twinkled and his sensuous mouth crooked. "Are you always so touchy when you cook?"

"I don't cook very much." The words were out before she could stop them. Ugh. *Way to blow your new image, Jaycee.* "I mean, I usually don't have time to cook," she rushed on. "My PR schedule has been so busy that I barely sleep, much less whip up gourmet meals."

She retrieved the tongs. Before she could rescue the

box with them, Rory leaned over the sauce and gripped the edge of the cardboard that hadn't gone under yet. He pulled out the dripping mess and tossed it into a nearby stainless-steel trash container.

Jaycee set the tongs on the counter and reached for her spoon. "Mushrooms, huh?" She eyed the list of ingredients.

"And lots of garlic."

"I've got the garlic, but my recipe didn't say anything about mushrooms."

"It's a matter of taste. You can add cherry tomatoes, Vidalia onions, bell peppers, grated cheese, zucchini—all sorts of things to vary it up. On top of that, you've got sausage, ground meat, chicken, venison—"

"Venison spaghetti?"

He nodded. "You can use most any type of meat. Wieners, too."

"You're kidding, right?"

His grin faltered. "It was all Cody knew how to cook, so we ate it a lot after my mom died. He thought we needed something besides fast food—my mom was never much of a cook because of her career, but she always made sure we had something nutritious—and so he made dinner for us every night."

Jaycee's mind rushed back and she remembered the first time she'd ever met Rory. He'd been a lanky kid with faded jeans and a *Dukes of Hazzard* T-shirt. She'd only been five at the time and she hadn't really noticed anything except that he hadn't been like the other boys. He'd been nice. Even more, he hadn't seemed the least bit annoyed when she'd followed him around the racetrack, the garage, the pits. Rather, he'd slowed his pace and let her keep up with him. He'd even talked to her back then.

"He sounds like a good brother."

"The best. He helped us with homework and made sure we had clean clothes and nagged the hell out of us whenever we did something wrong. He was a good guy. He still is. Best crew chief in the business."

"Says you."

"I'll give you props. Savannah's not bad, but Cody works for the winning team. This is my year. My cup."

Say something cordial. Something nice. Something that would go with her new image.

She meant to, but when she opened her mouth, all that came out was "I hate to break it to you, buddy, but you'll be eating my dust."

He arched an eyebrow and his blue eyes twinkled. "Before or after your next hair appointment?"

She frowned. A crazy reaction, because her remark had obviously hit a bull's-eye and jarred him back into his teasing, obnoxious ways. But instead of sarcasm, there was a flirtatious edge to his words that made her tummy tingle and her heart flutter that much more.

Bad heart.

"You'd do well just to cut your losses and get out while the getting is good," she said, turning back to her cooking. "Better yet, you could save face and switch places with Cody. That way I can humiliate him on the track while you wait in the pit stall like a good little crew chief." She retrieved a baggie full of tomatoes from her picnic basket. "After my next hair appointment, that is."

His laughter slid into her ears and rumbled over her nerve endings. Her hands trembled as she reached for a nearby cutting board.

"How are things going with Riley?" he asked.

"Aside from the fact that she hates me and I hate her?

Okay, I guess." She retrieved a knife and started to slice one of the tomatoes. "We're not killing each other. Not yet, anyway."

"I figured you would have taken her out when she had your car painted pink."

"I came close."

"But you didn't," he pointed out.

"What can I say? I'm allergic to prison food."

Silence settled for a few seconds as she diced and chopped and he watched.

"Maybe you don't hate her as much as you think," he finally said. "She *is* your sister."

"She's a royal pain."

"It's part of her job description. I should know. I've got brothers and they're each a pain in the ass. There isn't a day growing up that I didn't suffer at least one wedgie."

"At least you had the chance to grow up with them." *What?* "Not that I wish Riley and I had grown up together," she rushed on, desperate to ignore the strange regret that suddenly niggled at her. "But it would have been nice to have at least known about her. Instead, I walked into that lawyer's office thinking I was an only child and walked out joined at the hip with a sister I never knew existed. And now I'm stuck with her for a full race season."

"Why do you think Ace did that?"

She tried to swallow past the sudden lump in her throat and reached for the next tomato. "Your guess is as good as mine."

"You must have a theory."

She did, but the last person she wanted to tell was Rory Canyon. She shook her head and concentrated on dumping several diced tomatoes into the sauce. She wasn't going to say anything. She *wasn't*.

That's what she told herself, but her memory stirred. She remembered all those nights in Rory's garage when she'd helped him with his mom's old Harley. The years slipped away. The kitchen seemed just as quiet, as cozy, as the garage, and suddenly they were friends again. Talking. Sharing.

"I always knew my father was a cold man," she said, her words soft. "But I thought that beneath the hard exterior and the criticism, he really and truly loved me. That's why he pushed me so hard. But when I met Riley, I knew that wasn't true. He pushed me because he loved her. So much that he didn't want anyone to take her place. He discouraged the dresses, the makeup, the fancy hair products—all because he didn't want any reminders of the little girl he'd lost. That's why he left her the race team. Because he loved her the most and he wanted to prove it."

She remembered her sister's words. "Riley says he's the one who left, but I don't believe her." She shook her head. "What kind of man would do that?"

"The kind who wants to win."

Rory's voice brought her around and her gaze collided with his.

"What's that supposed to mean?"

He shrugged. "Maybe he walked out on Riley and her mother because they were holding him back from his dream of racing. Maybe he pushed you into the driver's seat to further that dream."

"I didn't know you were the expert on Ace."

"I'm not, but my dad raced with him for years. Ace was tough. Hard. Competitive. If you were on his team, he would do anything for you. If you weren't, you were the enemy and he would run you over."

Jaycee turned back to the tomatoes as the memories rolled through her head. She thought of the time she'd rushed home to tell Ace she'd been picked to play Cinderella in the school play. He'd told her she would look silly in the dress and had handed her a socket wrench so she could follow him around the shop. Then there'd been the time she'd begged to go to her sophomore homecoming because Michael Martin Miller had asked her. Ace had shook his head and told her it was just a joke. No way would the captain of the football team really be interested in her. He'd gone on to ease her wounded pride by letting her drive one of his cars. He'd pushed her onto the track instead of letting her take a wrong turn.

Or a right one.

"You're saying he never loved either of us."

"I'm saying it wasn't about love. It was about business. About winning."

It was. That's why he'd committed suicide when he'd discovered he was sick. Because he'd hadn't been able to stand the thought of losing to an invisible enemy like cancer. He'd taken matters into his own hands. He'd crossed the finish line into the afterlife before the illness could catch up to him and force him to crash and burn.

It explained his death, all right.

But not the will. Only one thing explained that.

"He didn't abandon them."

"He might have. People do crazy things. I never thought my father would turn his back on Cody, but he did."

"Your dad is a caveman. He thinks women should be barefoot and pregnant."

"Yeah, but he still loves his sons. He's always loved us. Cody, too." He shook his head. "But the day Cody married Cheryl, my father disowned him. He barely speaks to him now and he won't even acknowledge the girls."

"Because he hates women."

"Maybe." The admission brought a sadness to Rory's eyes that reached down inside Jaycee and made her chest tighten.

"He loved your mother," Jaycee heard herself say. She wasn't sure why she said it, except she couldn't forget the one and only time she'd seen Word with his wife. He'd been in the winner's circle and she'd been in his arms and there'd been a softness in his eyes that was no longer there.

"I always thought he did, but when she died, he just turned his back and acted as if she never existed. He forgot her so easily."

"Maybe it hurt too much to remember."

"Maybe." When he said the word this time, it wasn't laced with the same pain she'd heard before, and the tightening in her chest eased.

Silence settled between them for several long moments. "You're not like him, Jaycee," he finally said. "You're not like him any more than I'm like my dad."

But she was. Rory had had Cody to pattern himself after. He'd seen an alternative to Word and his prejudiced views against women. Even more, he had his mother's memory to hold on to. Jaycee had only had Ace. She'd grown up in Ace's shadow, following in his footsteps, determined to earn his love by being just like him. Just as smart. Just as skilled. Just as cold.

But not at this moment. Not with Rory so close, his body heat curling toward her, sympathy gleaming so hot and bright in his eyes. Instead, she felt warm.

Too warm.

"Can we change the subject?" she blurted, eager to douse the strange heat coursing through her.

"That's a really great dress."

The comment slid into her ears and upped her body temperature a few more degrees. She became even more conscious of his gaze that followed her every move. Thanks to her new image, of course.

She stiffened as her traitorous hormones sped into Victory Lane and started doing donuts. "Why don't you set the table?"

"I already did that, remember? I'm just waiting on you." He gave her a long, sweeping stare. "I like the color."

"What about wine?" She unearthed a bottle from the picnic basket, along with a corkscrew. "Why don't you go out to the dining room and pour yourself a glass while I cook?" She thrust the Cabernet into his hands and turned back to the recipe, determined to tune him out.

A *dash* of oregano . . . And she'd thought engineering specs were hard to translate?

She grabbed the spice, popped the cap and shook once, twice, a third time.

"That's not enough." Rory's deep voice whispered into her ears as he came up behind her. The wine bottle settled on the cabinet just to her left and then his arms came around her. One hand closed over hers while the other slid around her waist.

"But it said a dash."

"Recipes aren't written in stone, Trixie. Trust me, it'll be much better with more."

The fingertips that held her frantic grip on the oregano bottle slid down until his thumb massaged the inside of her wrist. The heat from the bubbling sauce drifted up, bathing her face and making her cheeks burn. Air lodged in her chest and she couldn't seem to catch her breath.

"Give it another shake," Rory murmured, the words little more than a breathless whisper against the sensitive shell of her ear.

She wanted to say something, to argue the point, but she couldn't seem to find the words.

"That's it." His thumb slid from the inside of her wrist, up her palm, leaving a fiery trail. "Now you're cooking."

Boy, was she ever.

She became instantly aware of his hard male body flush against hers, her bottom nestled in the cradle of his thighs. His erection pressed into her, leaving no doubt that he was turned on.

Extremely so.

Her mouth tingled and she had the insane urge to turn into the warm lips nuzzling her ear.

Jaycee wasn't sure what happened next—if he took the initiative or if she led the way—but one minute she was thinking about kissing him and the next she was actually pressing her lips to his.

Chapter Eighteen

She was kissing *him*.

Rory felt a split second of victory as her lips parted. Her tongue touched, swirled and teased. She didn't hold anything back.

At the same time, there was something tentative about her touch. While she put the pedal to the metal on the track, she didn't seem nearly as up to speed as he did when it came to sex.

The thought intoxicated him even more than the sweet taste of her cherry-flavored lips. He planted one hand on the back of her head, tilted her face to the side and kissed her with everything he had.

He nibbled her bottom lip and plunged his tongue deep, exploring, searching. When he couldn't breathe, he slid his lips across her cheek and along her jaw. His mouth slipped to the side of her neck and he pushed her hair down her back. She smelled of peaches and warm, feminine skin. He breathed her in for a long, heart-pounding moment and closed his eyes. He thought of all the things he wanted to do with her.

Everything.

He ached to see her soapy and wet in his shower. Naked and panting against his sheets. Laughing and smiling across the breakfast table—

He killed the last thought and concentrated on the lust that rolled through him like a ball of fire that dive-bombed south. He edged her sideways until they were clear of the stove, then bent her back over the counter-top and captured her lips again.

He fed off her mouth for several long moments, tasting and savoring, before nibbling his way down the sexy column of her throat.

His dick throbbed, and it was all he could do to keep from shoving his zipper down, parting her legs and plunging fast and sure and deep inside her hot, tight body.

Easy.

He forced himself to slow down, to concentrate on the small cry that bubbled from her lips when he licked her pulse beat. He liked pleasing her, so he held tight to his control and paced himself. With each touch of his lips, she sighed or gasped. The sounds fed the desire swirling inside of him.

When he reached the neckline of her dress, he traced the edge where her skin met the material with his tongue and relished the breathy moan that slipped past her full lips. His hands came up and he touched her, a feather-light caress of his fingertips over the soft fabric of her dress. He traced the contours of her waist, her rib cage, the undersides of her luscious breasts.

He slid his hands up and over until he felt the bare skin plumping over her neckline. Heat zapped him like a live wire and his pulse jumped. He tugged at the bodice. Safety pins popped and her luscious breasts spilled over the top.

Grabbing her sweet round ass, he lifted her, hoisting her onto the countertop. He stepped between her legs and caught one ripe nipple between his lips. He suckled her and she arched against him.

He pushed her back down, still sucking as he caught the hem of her dress. He shoved the material up until he felt the quivering flesh of her bare thighs.

She felt even softer than he'd imagined. Wetter.

He slid a finger deep inside her slick folds and her body bucked. He drew away from her swollen nipple and caught her delicious moan with his mouth. He plunged another finger inside, wiggling and teasing.

He wanted to feel every steamy secret. Even more, he wanted to taste her.

Tearing his mouth from hers, he worked his way down, kissing and teasing and tasting until he reached the dress bunched around her waist. He glanced up and his gaze caught hers for a brief moment before he dipped his head.

He licked the very tip of her clit with his tongue and she shuddered. She opened wider, an invitation that he couldn't resist. He trailed his tongue over her clit and down the slit before dipping it inside.

She was warm and sweet and addictive, and suddenly he couldn't help himself. Hunger gripped him hard and fast. He sucked on the swollen nub and plunged his tongue inside until her entire body went stiff.

"Come on, baby," he murmured. He gripped her thighs and held her tight. "Let go."

A few more licks and she did. A cry rumbled from her throat and tremors racked her body. He drank her in, savoring her essence until her body stilled.

Then he pulled away and stared down at her.

Her eyes were closed, her face flushed, her lips parted. Her chest rose and fell to a frantic rhythm that made his groin throb and his entire body ache. She was so beautiful. So damned dangerous. He wanted her more than he'd ever wanted any woman. He had the gut feeling that getting Jaycee out of his head wasn't going to be nearly as easy as taking her to bed.

Nope. And this was because she wasn't just in his head. She was under his skin. In his heart.

Like hell.

He was *this* close to busting his pants, and being as hard as a rock made a man think crazy things. He wasn't in love with Jaycee, that was for damned sure.

As for falling in love . . . He wasn't nearly as sure about that.

"I need some fresh air."

Her eyelids fluttered open. "What?"

Yeah, *what?*

He took a huge drink of oxygen and forced his hands away from her. "It's stuffy in here."

"Stuffy?" Her gaze swiveled toward the oven. A stream of smoke slivered through the vents. "Oh, no." Her cheeks fired a brighter red as she shoved at the hem of her skirt and tugged up her bodice.

Jaycee Anderson blushing, of all things. It was definitely a first. He liked it. He liked it a hell of a lot.

What he didn't like was the fact that she'd scrambled away from him faster than he could blink. As if she'd just realized she'd made a big, big mistake. One that had nothing to do with the smoke that slowly filled the room.

"I think my meatballs are burning," she murmured as she reached for pot holders and threw open the door. But he had the distinct feeling she was talking about him rather than dinner. "I knew this would happen. I just *knew* it."

She gripped the edge of the pan and pulled out the charred lumps of meat. Her eyes brightened as she set the baking sheet on the counter and waved her hand at the smoke.

"I'm not much of a meatball man," he heard himself say. "I'm sure the spaghetti will be just fine without it." Wait a second. What happened to *stuffy?* But suddenly he wasn't half as anxious to get away from her as he was to ease the anxiety pinching her expression.

"Spaghetti?" Her gaze swiveled toward his, and he knew then that dinner was the farthest thing from her mind. Realization seemed to strike, and she blinked frantically. She glanced at the pot. "I—I'm sure the sauce will mask the taste." She grabbed the balls and started chucking them into the pot. "There's so much garlic in here you won't be able to taste anything else." She tossed in the last ball and reached for a spoon. After making as if to shove it into the pot, she seemed to think better and handed it to him. "Just stir a little more, season to taste and serve." She turned and started to gather up her picnic basket. "Have a great dinner."

"Hold up. You're supposed to eat with me."

"I can't." Her brain seemed to scramble. "I—I'm allergic." She nodded. "My throat closes up and I start coughing up all this phlegm and I break out in this horrible rash. It's really disgusting." She smiled. "Enjoy." And then she snatched up the basket and beat a hasty retreat toward the door.

"I'll drive you home—"

"I can walk. It's only a few blocks to my place. You just eat before it gets cold." She motioned him toward the stove.

"It's after dark. You're not walking."

"I'm a grown woman."

"And therein lies the problem." He swept a gaze from her head to the tips of her toes and back up again. "You look too good to go prancing around after dark."

"I do?" Insecurity gleamed in her gaze, and Rory mentally kicked his own ass for turning away from her in the first place. This wasn't about her. It was about him and his damned feelings. Feelings that were going to get him into a world of trouble if he didn't control himself.

But she didn't know that. She thought it was her, and he meant to keep it that way.

"Let's go. I'll take you home." He turned off the stove and set the lid on the spaghetti sauce.

"Forget it." She started toward the door. "I can make it just fine on my own."

"I'll toss you over my shoulder if I have to."

She stopped in the doorway and turned on him. "You wouldn't."

"Oh, wouldn't I?"

She looked as if she wanted to argue, but then she caught her bottom lip and he knew she'd decided against it. Her hands tightened on the picnic basket. "Okay. But for the record, I would much rather enjoy the fresh air. It *is* pretty stuffy in here." *Thanks to present company*, her gaze seemed to add.

"We'll take my Mustang." He snatched up his car keys and started for the garage. "It's a convertible."

Third note to goddess: never, ever climb into a convertible while wearing a strapless dress.

The wind rushed at Jaycee, sneaking underneath the material of her bodice and tugging it away from her chest, as she and Rory sped the few blocks to her house. Another rule leapt to mind.

Fourth note to goddess: never, ever climb into a convertible while wearing hair.

The long blonde strands on her head whipped her, slapping across her face with enough force to make her eyes water. Where was a good buzz cut when she needed one? She clutched at the gaping material with one hand and tried to hold her hair down with the other.

The only saving grace was that, with the top down and the V-8 running wide open, the car was too noisy for conversation. Forget talking. Now was the time to think. To try to figure out what had happened and why—dear Lord, *why*—she'd gotten herself into this mess.

She'd kissed him. She still couldn't believe it. One minute she'd been cooking up a storm and the next she'd been trying to swallow him whole. It was as if the past fifteen years had ceased to exist and she was the same naïve thirteen-year-old who'd shown up on his doorstep and thrown herself at him. She'd not only worn a dress that first time, but she'd planted one on him. A quick peck on the lips that had ended in disaster. Just like tonight.

Her nipples tingled and she felt wetness between her thighs.

No . . . tonight had been far worse. She hadn't just kissed him. She'd followed it up with a full-blown orgasm. And he'd pulled away from her. Just like before.

That truth haunted her as they rounded a corner and zoomed a few more blocks before the car finally slowed in front of her house.

He'd barely turned into the long drive when she whipped off her seat belt and reached for the door.

"Thanks for the ride." She jumped from the front seat the moment he started to brake, and almost toppled onto the pavement. She managed to catch herself as he slammed to a stop.

"Are you nuts? We were still moving."

"Just practicing for Daytona." *Lame, Jaycee. Really lame.*

"The point is to stay in the car. Not climb out."

"Yeah, but you never know when you'll need to bail. There's always a chance of fire."

He stared at her before shaking his head. "Friggin' nuts," he muttered.

"Just because I'm prepared for an on-track emergency and you're not is no reason to start name-calling."

"I'm completely prepared."

"Sure you are." She turned on her heel. "See you around."

Not. Never, *ever* again.

Rory watched Jaycee disappear in a flash of pink. He could still taste her on his lips. Her scent clung to him and made his pulse race. Sexual frustration clawed at his gut and he came dangerously close to following her inside.

Love?

He wasn't in love. He already knew that. As for the falling part . . . All right, so he might be on his way down, but he hadn't hit the ground yet. And he wouldn't. If there was one thing he'd learned from his father, it was to control his feelings.

Jaycee was right. Word had locked away the Harley not because he hadn't cared, but because he'd cared too much. He hadn't been trying to forget. He'd been trying not to remember. Not to hurt. He'd turned his back on the grief and refused to feel it. He'd controlled it, and Rory could do the same.

But not tonight. No, right now he was too worked up, his control too shaky. He backed out of the driveway and shifted the car into first. He hit the gas and welcomed the wind that rushed at his face.

A few minutes later, he hit the highway and watched the speedometer climb. But he couldn't go fast enough to ease the anxiety that ate away inside of him—not without breaking several laws and landing himself in a world of trouble—so he took the next exit and turned around. He reminded himself that she was just playing a game with him. She was gunning for his spot and trying to distract him. That's why she'd morphed into a bombshell. Why she'd come on to him tonight. Why she'd hooked up with Schilling.

A surge of jealousy went through him, so fierce that it confirmed the strange feelings swimming inside of him. He'd never been the possessive type. Then again, he'd never seen Jaycee with another guy before.

He's isn't just some guy. He's her ticket to the top three.

Rory knew that. He also knew that it wasn't the thought of her with another man that had him tied up in knots. He was rock hard and desperate. Crazy with desire.

Not for long, he promised himself. He might have put on the brakes tonight because he'd been momentarily freaked, but he wasn't going to make that mistake a second time. He was going full speed toward the finish line next time. He was going to have sex with Jaycee Anderson. That would get her out of his head once and for all and solve all of his problems.

Personally.

But . . . professionally?

He didn't have any professional problems. Schilling was tweaking the engine and making the necessary adjustments at that moment. Cody was working on the handling issues they'd had. Everything was good to go for a winning season.

At least, that's what he thought until he pulled up to his house to see a familiar black Escalade sitting in the driveway. Worry prickled as he walked up the front steps and went inside.

"What's wrong?" he asked as he walked into the kitchen to find his brother scarfing down a plate of spaghetti.

Cody's head bobbed up and his gaze collided with Rory's. "I . . ." His brother swallowed a mouthful. "I brought the data from the track test." He motioned to the stack of computer printouts that sat on the countertop. "The new engine ran like a dream. The specs are all what we expected."

"She was running loose."

"That's what you say, but from everything I've seen, it doesn't seem like the car. It looks more like your timing was off. Kip said he had to repeat himself twice because you couldn't hear him." Kip was Rory's spotter. "The earpiece was working. I checked it myself. Which means you weren't listening. You—"

"Do Cheryl and the girls know that you aren't really a vegetarian?" Rory cut in, determined to steer them onto a safer subject.

Cody looked like a deer caught in the headlights. "You mean there's meat in this?" He feigned a look of surprise as he glanced down at the plate.

"That's what those big round things are. They're called meatballs. As in balls of *meat*."

"Meat?" He tried to look outraged. "I—I thought they were tofu. That's what Cheryl always makes them with. Talk about some good stuff."

"You're full of it, you know?"

"And you're distracted." Cody set down the plate. "We've got a lot riding on this race. It sets the pace for the entire season. A winning season, or a losing season. We need a first-place win."

"We'll have one."

"That's what you keep telling me, but I'm not seeing it yet."

"What does Dad think?"

"That you can do no wrong." Cody shrugged. "At least that's what Jared said."

"Why don't you ask him yourself?"

"And have him ignore me? I had enough of that when I tried to explain my marriage to Cheryl to him."

"Maybe he's mellowed over the years."

"And maybe you're living in a fantasy land. Dad's not going to change his mind about Cheryl. He doesn't like her and he'll never accept her as long as she's flying a 747."

"Maybe she could downgrade to a Cessna."

"And maybe she'll make me a pot roast for dinner tomorrow night." Cody shook his head. "She's not going to change. I wouldn't want her to. As for Dad . . ." He shook his head. "He'll never forgive me, but it's okay. I know I made the right choice. I've got beautiful daughters to prove it."

Daughters that Word had yet to even acknowledge. Because he was a chauvinistic caveman who didn't give a shit for anyone's feelings but his own? Probably. That's what Rory told himself. But he couldn't forget what Jaycee had said, or the slim possibility that she was right.

"Can you just get back on the ball?"

Cody's voice snapped Rory back to reality. He caught his brother's stare. "Have I ever let you down? I haven't," he said before Cody could reply. "And I won't. The race isn't for another three weeks. That gives you plenty of time to find out what's up with the car and get her ready." When Cody didn't look the least bit convinced, Rory added, "And it gives me plenty of time to watch the track test and listen to the audio feed and see what I'm doing wrong. *If* I'm doing something wrong."

The lines around Cody's eyes eased. "That's all I'm asking. Just take a look for yourself and listen in and let's get the kinks ironed out."

Rory nodded and watched his brother set the plate aside. "You, um, won't mention this to Cheryl, will you?" Cody nodded toward the half-empty plate. "I wouldn't want to upset her or anything like that."

"Especially since upsetting her means that you sleep on the sofa, right?"

"Mom's old futon. Cheryl set it up in the guest room and it's the only place I'm allowed to crash whenever we have a fight."

"You are seriously whipped, brother."

"Maybe, but there are enough perks to make it worth it."

"Such as?"

"Cheryl gives the best backrub after I've had a long day. And last weekend when my old Chevy cruised into first in San Antonio . . ." He smiled for a long moment. "Let's just say she was very proud of my driving and she sure as hell didn't mind showing it."

"Congratulations by the way. You drove a helluva race."

"It's not even close to the big leagues, but I can hold my own."

"You ought to try moving up."

"Dad would never let that happen."

"You never let Dad stop you before."

"This is different. No team worth their weight is going to hire me, and Dad sure as hell would never give me a shot." He shrugged. "It doesn't matter. I'm happy on the short tracks. I get to haul ass and satisfy the need for speed, and you get the best crew chief in the business. It's a win-win."

That's what Cody said, but Rory didn't miss the flash of longing in his brother's gaze. Rory opened his mouth to pursue the subject, but Cody flashed him a warning. "So, being married isn't all that bad, huh?" he asked instead.

"Being married, bro, is really bad. And really good. And everything in between. That's the beauty of it. There's never a dull moment." Cody grinned and motioned to the dishes. "Wish I could help you tidy up, but it's past my curfew. Gotta go." And then he left.

Rory spent the next thirty minutes cleaning dirty dishes and storing the leftovers in his refrigerator. It was a job that would have taken ten, if he had known where everything went. But since he rarely cooked for himself—he had a service that prepared meals whenever he was home—it took longer than expected. That, and he couldn't seem to get his mind off a certain blonde.

When he picked up the dirty spoons, he thought of the way she'd looked standing in his kitchen in her fancy dress and bare feet. And when he put away the spices, he thought about the way she'd trembled in his arms when he'd helped her with the oregano. And when he wiped down the cabinet, he thought of the way she'd tasted when she'd climaxed.

By the time he cleaned up the last trace of spaghetti sauce, he was even more worked up than he'd been when he'd first arrived home. Too worked up to sit in the media room and watch the tapes from the track test. He didn't want to think about Jaycee. Or seeing her again. Or kissing her again.

No, he wanted to *do* something.

He headed out to his shop. Flicking on the light, he walked over to the sheet metal that sat on a large workbench. He usually let the boys do everything, but he figured it wouldn't hurt to get a head start and at least have the thing shaped before Monday's lesson. Besides, none of the boys liked the metal work. Except for Mike.

But, he reminded himself, the boy wasn't coming back. He wasn't coming back any more than Rory was going to hand over his helmet and retire from NASCAR. They'd both made their choices to please the people in their lives and it was all a matter of seeing things through. That meant violin lessons for Mike and a Sprint Cup for Rory.

If Jaycee Anderson didn't beat him to it.

Rory flipped on the arc welder, fired up the torch and tried to force aside the sudden vision that filled his head. He wasn't going to think about her right now. No, he was going to relax, work on the fender and make it through the next few hours without thinking about her. Or how pretty she'd looked in her pink dress. Or how sweet her mouth had looked so wet and puffy from his kisses. Or how red and swollen her pussy had been when she'd come against his mouth.

Cut. Cool. Smooth.

The instructions ticked off in his head, killing her image as he shaped and molded the metal.

Yep, he was on the last lap, *this* close to the victory lane. It was just a matter of maintaining his control and holding steady until then.

That, and getting Jaycee Anderson into his bed once and for all.

Chapter Nineteen

"It's about ever-lovin' time you showed up. I was just about to cart the blasted thing back to the store and get my eighty dollars back."

"I'm here now, Momma. Just calm down." Riley handed over the plastic bag she carried and closed the door behind her. She found herself standing in the kitchen of the small mobile home where she'd grown up. The place was a single-wide with a kitchen, living room, two bedrooms and one bath. In that order. Riley eyed the square kitchen table that still overflowed with that morning's breakfast dishes. "Where is it?"

"In the living room." Arnette Vaughn held a cup of coffee in one hand and a cigarette in the other. She had her dyed red hair teased and puffed to perfection and a face full of makeup.

But no amount of cosmetics could doctor the truth. Thanks to too many years of being a single mother desperate to make ends meet and a decade-long battle with emphysema, she was far from the beautiful woman she'd once been. Her voluptuous figure had shrunk and deep lines marred her once-flawless complexion.

She took a long drag of her cigarette, then let loose a hacking cough.

"I thought you were giving up the Marlboros?"

"They're Lights, and I've cut down to one pack a day."

Riley eyed the overflowing ashtray that sat on the counter next to a box of Cap'n Crunch. *Those aren't all from today.* She opened her mouth but then clamped it back shut. Arnette wouldn't listen to her any more than she listened to the long line of specialists at Dallas General. Each one had advised her to stop smoking, or else.

Arnette was obviously opting for the *or else*.

"I'm gonna stop," the woman said, as if reading Riley's mind. "Just you wait and see." She settled into a kitchen chair and started rummaging in the bag Riley had handed her. "You brought a strawberry face mask. But I wanted oatmeal and honey."

"They were out." Riley walked the few feet into the living room and eyed the vacuum cleaner pieces strewn across the worn living-room floor. She picked up several magazines that lay scattered across the back of the couch and straightened the sofa cushions before kicking off her shoes and settling Indian-style on the floor. "Where are the directions?" she called out.

Arnette appeared in the doorway separating the two rooms. "Somewhere in there." The cigarette wagged between her lips with each word. She had the plastic bag hooked in the crook of her arm as she searched inside. "What about my Racing Red nail polish?"

"They didn't have it. I got Candy Apple."

Riley studied the directions as her mother settled on the sofa, the nail polish in one hand and the cigarette in the other. "I don't know why I need a new vacuum in the first place. I still have the old one."

"Because the old one doesn't work. It hasn't worked for about six months."

Arnette shrugged. "That long?"

"Yes." Riley eyed the fuzz balls on the worn shag

carpeting. "The doctor says you should vacuum daily. It'll help your breathing."

"Doctor, schmoctor. That man just wants to collect a paycheck."

Tell me about it. Riley had been feeding that paycheck with the income from Sunny Side Up until she'd stepped in to head the racing team. Debts had been piling up since. "Dr. Merriweather is a good man. A patient one."

"Patient? I waited forty-five minutes for my last appointment. I always have to wait on him."

"I'm sure the feeling is mutual, but he sees you anyway, despite the fact that we haven't paid him in over six months. And he's a hundred times better than the doctor at the county hospital." Riley turned back to the plastic parts. "This thing has one of those HEPA filters on it. He said those really help."

"I didn't see any filter when I opened it." Arnette settled the cigarette between her lips and rolled the bottle of polish between her hands before opening it.

"This is the filter." Riley held up a small cardboard box.

Arnette spared her a glance. "Hmpfff," she muttered as Riley grabbed a screwdriver and went to work.

In less than ten minutes, Riley had pieced the vacuum cleaner together, complete with the extra hose and attachments. "There you go." She pushed to her feet and bent to retrieve the screwdriver. "All done."

"So soon?" Arnette paused midtoenail to stare at the finished contraption. "How come I couldn't do that?"

"Because you didn't really try?"

"Bullshit. I read those directions at least a dozen times. I'm just not good at mechanical stuff."

Nor was she good at cooking. Or dusting. Or doing

laundry. No, the only thing Arnette Vaughn was good at was primping. She could give a mean perm and a rockin' manicure.

Riley's mother coughed, the nail-polish brush shaking in her hands. Hands that had once been so long and elegant, the skin like porcelain.

That's the one thing Riley remembered the most about her childhood: those soft, flawless hands tucking her into bed at night, touching her forehead whenever she was sick, brushing her hair every morning before school. Riley had wanted hands just like that, until she'd realized that they weren't a sign of beauty.

No, they were proof that Ace Anderson was right. Arnette *was* lazy. She wasn't driven or motivated or dedicated. She couldn't hold down a decent job. Her brief stint waiting tables had ruined her manicure, so she'd quit. Then she'd tried answering telephones for an insurance company, but the constant pressure of the receiver had smashed her hairdo, so she'd quit that as well. Her longest job had lasted for eight months. She'd been the head shampoo tech for a fancy salon in downtown Dallas when Riley was in kindergarten. She'd actually enjoyed that job until she'd accidentally doused a customer's hair with nail-polish remover rather than conditioner, and had been fired.

An honest mistake, Arnette had claimed, that anyone could have made. Anyone who didn't know how to read. Arnette was dyslexic. Not that she would ever admit as much. She'd grown up in a time when they had yet to diagnose the learning disability, so she'd gotten by on her good looks and charm. Until she'd gotten sick.

Riley had been thirteen at the time. With only Ace's monthly child support between them—a modest amount, since Arnette had agreed to the first measly figure he'd tossed at her—Riley had been forced to get a job after school to make ends meet. She'd bagged groceries for tips and, when she'd turned sixteen, she'd gone to work as a cashier. She'd been supporting her mother ever since.

"So, tell me." Arnette finished her toes and recapped the polish. "Are you meeting any nice men? Those drivers are so handsome. And well-to-do. I bet you've been out dozens of times since I saw you last month."

"The only driver I spend any time with is my own." Not that Riley was bemoaning the fact. After her last relationship—a banker by the name of Tom, who'd pawed her as a cat did his favorite toy—she'd had her fill of the opposite sex. She was on hiatus where men were concerned. At least until the season ended and she managed to get her life back on track. Then maybe she would think about dating again. Maybe not. As it was, she was too busy to sleep, let alone have a social life.

Arnette made a face. "I was hoping you'd found someone and could give up all this ownership nonsense. You think that sorry SOB could have left you something decent, what with all the money that man had."

"Actually, he didn't have that much money." Wait a second. Did she actually sound defensive? On Ace's behalf?

No, she was just being truthful. She'd seen the financial records herself.

"He put everything he had into the racing team to make it thrive and he took out several loans to expand. He was running teams in both Busch and Sprint." Teams that had sucked up more money than they'd brought in. While Ace had been a great driver, he'd sucked as an owner. "He overextended himself."

"Stupid." Arnette shook her head. "You'd think he

would have put some of that money up and left you enough to at least buy a house. Or even a car."

But Riley would be able to buy both if she could keep Revved & Ready on board through the season.

If.

Despite her obvious commitment, Jaycee wasn't progressing quite as well as expected. She still didn't look like a hot, hip, trendy, ultrafeminine woman. Rather, she looked too much like she was trying too hard to look like a hot, hip, trendy, ultrafeminine woman. She didn't seem genuine.

Yet.

Then again, she still had to face the lifestyle coordinator, whom she'd meet first thing the next morning. The woman would follow her, rearrange her lifestyle and then babysit Jaycee to make sure she followed through. Then, if everything still didn't fall into place, Jaycee would face The Reinforcers to help her embrace her new look and behavior.

They still had four weeks until Daytona and the live interview with Trick. Plenty of time for things to jell.

Or not.

The doubt stuck in her brain, and Riley did the only thing she could to distract herself. She motioned for the red nail polish. "Hand it over. It's my turn."

"You look different in person."

Jaycee sat behind a six-foot table near the front entrance of Forever Fit, a new health food store in Fort Worth, and smiled expectantly at the twenty-something girl who stepped up for an autograph. "Is that so?" She signed her name across the back of a Revved & Ready T-shirt and waited for the girl to elaborate. To give the usual *You look taller* or *You look shorter* or *You look thinner* or *You look fatter.* Jaycee had heard it all before during the gazillion meet and greets she'd done for various sponsors over the years.

"You look stiff," the girl finally said.

"You *do*," offered the woman who flanked Jaycee.

Jaycee glanced over her shoulder. "I thought your job was to observe?"

The woman, a tall brunette wearing a sleeveless pearl-colored turtleneck and a pair of matching slacks, shrugged. "Just voicing an opinion." She went back to her PDA and keyed in a few notes.

Tina Windsor was the lifestyle coordinator from Image Nation. She'd shown up on Jaycee's doorstep at five A.M. and had been following her around ever since. Her job? To document Jaycee's routine.

She'd started with Jaycee stumbling into the kitchen, desperate for coffee—Jaycee had bypassed the coffee, albeit slowly, for a glass of orange juice—and had stuck to her like Super Glue ever since.

"Are you nervous?" the girl asked, her voice turning Jaycee back around. "Maybe that's why you look stiff."

"Yes." Tina's voice drifted from behind. "That could be the problem."

"I'm not nervous. Hungry, yes. Tired, yes." Annoyed, hell yes. She caught her lip in her teeth against the last comment.

I am a goddess . . .

"You know what they say." She did her best to look cheerful. "The camera makes everybody look stiff." While she had in the past signed more than her share of T-shirts and scribbled her name on everything from a ball cap to a leg cast to a man's bare stomach, she'd never done so wearing a tailored suit, her feet stuffed into ridiculously high heels.

"I thought the camera added ten pounds."

"That, too." Jaycee wiggled for some breathing room. Her lime green skirt bulged at the seams. The jacket—a synthetic blend of something that made her itch—scraped across her skin as she flexed her shoulders.

"It's fitted," Riley had told her again. Which, Jaycee had come to realize, was goddess lingo for *friggin' tight*.

"You're prettier than you look on TV," the girl added as she took the autographed T-shirt. "A lot prettier."

Okay, so the suit wasn't *that* bad.

"Did you get that?" Jaycee cast over her shoulder as the fan walked away. "She said I was pretty."

"First she said you were stiff." Tina kept clicking away on her PDA. "And first impressions are of monumental importance."

Jaycee ignored the urge to snatch the small machine from Tina and make a lasting impression. One that would surely make the front page of every sports section, along with the caption NASCAR DRIVER KICKS BUTT AND GETS KICKED OUT. Bye-bye, Race Chicks.

She drew a deep breath, took a sip from the R & R can next to her and beamed at the next person who stepped up to the table.

Over the next two hours, Jaycee signed more than two hundred shirts and greeted over three hundred and fifty fans, half of whom were women. It was a huge coup, especially with Tina tapping away behind her, except that most were there to get autographs for their husbands/brothers/sons/fathers. But a few, a precious few, were there because they actually liked Jaycee.

"See there? That woman is going to name her first-born after me," Jaycee told Tina, pointing at the star-struck fan who'd just asked for a signature on her maternity smock. "I do have a few adoring female fans."

"She's pregnant."

"And?"

"One minute she likes you. The next minute, she could be totally in love with Linc Adams or Trey Calloway. You can't rely on a woman who eats pickle-and-sardine sandwiches. It's the hormones talking."

"Thanks for the vote of confidence."

"I'm not here to pump your ego. I'm here to observe." She motioned Jaycee to turn back around. "Continue, please."

Jaycee smiled at the next person in line, a woman in her midthirties who herded two teenage boys with her. "What's your name?" she asked as she took the T-shirts the woman handed over.

"Oh, they're not for me. They're for my boys here. They just love you. I'm a Trey Calloway fan myself. His car is unstoppable."

Why me?

"Aw, Mom," one of the boys chimed in. "Everybody knows it takes more than just a fast car. You gotta have a good crew. Your pit crew's the bomb," the boy told her.

But what about the hair, kid?

"Yeah," the other boy added. "Your guys did 12.5-second pit stops for the whole race at Talledega last year. We watched the whole thing on our Uncle Ned's big screen."

"We were definitely on the ball during that race," Jaycee said, raising her voice just enough to make sure that Tina heard loud and clear. *Tap that into your PDA.*

"And in Vegas. And at Napa," the first boy added, ticking off two more of Jaycee's best races last year.

Before Ace had passed away.

He'd had the best of the best, half of whom had

walked when Riley had taken charge. Not because they didn't want to work for a woman, but because they didn't want to work for an inexperienced woman.

But the new crew—made up mostly of women, and a few token men—were slowly but surely getting with the program. Savannah had been drilling them over the past few months and they'd gotten better. Faster. More efficient.

But Daytona would be the real test.

"Wait until you see us this year," Jaycee promised, despite her own doubts. It didn't matter if the new crew was as fast as the old one. *She* was fast. And so was her car. Or it would be, after she met with Martin Schilling next Sunday.

She'd called his assistant back and the woman had arranged everything. He was flying into town next Friday. He'd agreed to stay over until Sunday night and meet her after hours at Race Chicks to go over her engine. Then he would head back to North Carolina to work with a few of the Carolina teams. After a breakfast with a local women's group the following Friday—just a week before race weeks officially launched in Daytona with the preliminary races—Jaycee would fly up and accompany him to his awards ceremony, to be held that night at the Omni Hotel in Charlotte.

She still couldn't believe he was going to help her in return for a date. Then again, she—Jaycee "the Tomboy" Anderson—had morphed into NASCAR Barbie, and it wasn't Halloween. There wasn't much that could shock her anymore.

Except maybe several dozen walking pink roses. Jaycee stared at the cluster of flowers and the long, muscular, jeans-clad legs that stepped up to the table.

"Delivery for Jaycee Anderson," a familiar male voice drawled.

Jaycee's heart started to pound even before she saw Rory's head peek from behind the wall of pink.

Chapter Twenty

Jaycee stared at the cluster of flowers. The rich, fragrant aroma tickled her nostrils as her gaze shifted to Rory. "What is this?"

"A token of my appreciation. For last night. The spaghetti was great."

"It was?" She stiffened. "I mean, of course it was. I always make a mean spaghetti." She fingered one of the fragrant petals and something softened in her chest.

Wait a second. Rory Canyon was bringing her flowers?

It's the image, honey. It's all because of the image.

That, or maybe they were the trick kind that would spray her with ink and ruin two hours of makeup and an hour and a half with the blow-dryer.

She gave him a suspicious glance. "You really brought these because of the spaghetti?"

"Why else?"

"I don't know. Maybe they're wired with explosives and you're going to knock me off before Daytona." Or maybe he actually regretted putting on the brakes last night.

Not that it mattered. She still wasn't setting herself up for possibly more hurt and humiliation by getting close to him again.

She'd picked her pride up off the floor twice now, she wasn't going for number three. It was now obvious to Rory and the world that she lusted after him.

But everything stopped there.

He didn't know that she actually *liked* him. Not yet anyway.

Not ever.

She frowned. "They're booby-trapped, aren't they?"

"I'm a driver, sugar. Not a terrorist." He grinned.

"Sorry. I just didn't expect this."

Not that Jaycee hadn't received her fair share of gifts in the past. She'd gotten everything from Mylar balloons to fruit baskets to an NFL jersey collection from her fans when she'd dislocated her shoulder during a race a few years back. She'd even gotten a few plants, including a cactus she'd named Rosie and a couple of palms she'd managed to kill because she'd been on the road too much to water them properly. But soft, velvety, delicate roses? She'd never been the type.

At least that's what everyone thought. Including Rory. Especially Rory. Until now.

The notion sent a tingle of disappointment through her, but then he smiled and she forgot everything except the pounding of her heart and the sudden rush of heat through her body. The sweet, intoxicating smell of the roses teased her nostrils and made her blood rush that much faster.

"I thought I'd give you a lift to Lean Machine," he went on. Lean Machine was a fast food chain that specialized in low-carb, low-calorie fare—a healthy alternative to greasy burger-joint eating. Since Revved & Ready was their primary beverage, Jaycee had been lassoed into appearing at the grand opening of their newest restaurant north of Dallas.

"How did you know—"

"Morgan Bakeries is one of my sponsors."

Jaycee ran through a mental list of the numerous patches and logos that decorated Rory's famous car.

"Since when?"

"A few years now. They're not a major player, but they're still part of the team. They just came out with a new pita chip that Lean Machine just started selling." He shrugged. "Looks like we'll be keeping each other company for the next few hours."

After yesterday, the last thing she needed was to spend time with Rory. In fact, she'd made up her mind to stay as far, far away from him as possible.

Oh, no. That's what her heart said.

Her hormones, on the other hand, had their own opinion on the matter: *Oh, yeahhhhh.*

She wasn't going to listen, obviously. She had her own sanity to think of. Her career. Her team. Her pride.

"I already have a ride." She motioned to Tina. "She's my . . ." She started to say *shadow*, but then she remembered that the entire makeover was supposed to be hush-hush. Gradual. Believable. "She's my, um, cousin who's visiting from, um, Idaho. Aunt Sophie and Uncle Nick's daughter. Isn't that right, Cousin Tina?"

"Idaho?" Tina paused her PDA tapping to look startled.

"Yeah. Famous Potatoes. Home sweet home."

"Idaho?" Tina's mind seemed to race before everything started to sink in. "Um, yes." She smiled and shook her fist in the air. "Give me carbs or give me death."

Tina might be a kick-ass lifestyle consultant, but when it came to improv, she needed some major help.

"She's still trying to come to terms with the whole

home and hearth versus healthy living thing." She lowered her voice and mouthed, "She has issues."

"I do not." *Tap, tap, tap.* Jaycee could only guess what she was typing.

Jaycee shrugged. "Thanks for the offer, but Tina and I are sharing a cab. Parking downtown is murder, so we figured we would make it easy on ourselves."

"I could give you both a ride." Rory winked. "I'll even drop you at the door."

"I don't think so."

He arched one dark brow at her and his blue eyes sparkled. "Afraid you won't be able to control yourself?"

Again.

"Look." She licked her lips and tried not to notice the way his eyes followed the motion. "I know you probably have a few misconstrued notions because of last night—"

"Yeah," he cut in. "You want to have sex with me."

Jaycee swallowed and silently begged the Race Official Upstairs to forgive her. "I *do not* want to have sex with you."

Tap, tap, tap.

"Last night . . . It was all just a mistake," she went on. "I'm following this new healthy eating thing and it's really messing with my head. I'm not thinking clearly."

"And here I thought it was my irresistible charm."

She ignored the smile that tugged at her lips. "I've been really nervous and anxious, so I think it's best if we just forget all about last night. I really didn't mean to, um, *kiss* you." *Or do an imitation of Old Faithful*, a voice added silently. "And I certainly won't do it again."

"So you're done with the healthy eating?" He eyed the empty cans of Revved & Ready that sat near her

Sharpie, along with a half-eaten multigrain bagel, minus her beloved cream cheese.

"Well, no."

"Then there's still a chance you might go bonkers again and try to compromise my virtue."

"Yes. I mean, no." She shook her head, finally giving in to the smile that tugged at her lips. "Yes, there's the chance I might go bonkers again, but no, I won't compromise your virtue. I'm not interested in you sexually. Not at all."

Liar. She tamped down the sudden burst of guilt and gave him her most convincing look. "You're not my type," she added. "I like my guys, um, shorter. Without so much"—she motioned to his broad shoulders and massive biceps—"muscle."

"So you like short, skinny guys?"

"No. I mean, yes." He gave her an amused grin and she shook her head. "It's not about appearance. Not completely," she added when he arched an eyebrow. "Sure, it's great if a man's attractive. But the real deal breaker is this." She tapped her temple. "I like men who are thinkers."

"Guys like Schilling?"

Okay, so she hadn't thought of Martin when she'd started down this road, but no reason to detour now.

What better way to sound credible than to describe the actual man—the smart, attractive man—who'd asked her out on a date? "Martin is totally my type. He's nice-looking *and* brilliant." When he didn't look convinced, she added, "And he wears glasses. I love a man in glasses."

"Glasses?"

"The black-rimmed kind. They just scream hot,

hunky genius." She nodded vigorously while he seemed to digest her words. Ditto for Tina.

Tap, tap, tap, tap, tap.

Rory's bright blue gaze was unreadable. "And here I thought a cool pair of Ray-Bans was enough to cinch the deal."

"Hardly." She finally killed the nodding for fear of whiplash. "Well, then. I'm glad we're on the same page."

"We're there, all right. Tina, you don't mind riding with me, do you?" His gaze moved past Jaycee.

"Uh, not at all."

"Good. Tina doesn't mind. I don't mind." He held out a hand. "I think we're good to go."

Warning bells sounded in Jaycee's head as she stared up into Rory's blue eyes. She should say no. Catch a cab. Sit as far away from him as possible at Lean Machine.

She would have, but suddenly she knew it wouldn't make any difference. He wanted her and she knew it, and so the awareness would continue. No matter if she sat right next to him or if an entire racetrack separated them.

Even more important, she wanted to sit next to him. To enjoy the feeling of being wanted by a man she'd dreamt of night after night. A feeling that would be all too brief. Once Rory realized that she was still the same old Jaycee inside, he would lose interest and turn away. Again. She would beat him at Daytona and they would go back to being enemies again.

But until then she could simply enjoy the attention. And the conversation. She'd never realized how much she'd missed talking to him until last night. Besides, it wasn't as if anything could actually happen. Not with

Tina documenting her every move. Which meant
Jaycee was safe from her raging hormones.

For now.

She slid her hand into Rory's.

If he didn't touch her soon, he was going to lose his
fucking mind. That knowledge weighed on Rory as he
signed his last autograph at Lean Machine and took a
bite of the chocolate mousse someone had set in front
of him. Taste exploded on his tongue, but it did little
to sate the hunger that churned inside of him.

They'd been at it for four hours: Signing autographs. Sitting next to each other. Flirting every once
in a while. Talking even, particularly during the small
breaks. He'd actually been surprised at how easy the
conversation flowed, as if the past fifteen years had
never existed and they were friends again. He'd gotten
an update on things at the newly restructured Race
Chicks, and he'd filled her in on Xtreme. On how his
dad was satisfied with his performance, but he wasn't.
He'd been sitting number three far too long and he
was getting antsy.

Telling her that was the worst thing he could have
done. At the same time, it also felt like the best.

She hadn't goaded or patronized him. Nor had she
offered any words of encouragement. No, she'd simply
stared at him, her eyes full of understanding and compassion, and just like that, he'd felt a little less anxious.
Jaycee knew what it was like to want something other
than what she had. She'd wanted a life and she'd been
stuck living Ace's. Just as he was stuck.

As soon as the thought hit, he pushed it back out. He
liked driving. He liked it a hell of a lot, and no way was
he so frustrated that he wanted out.

No, he wanted to win.

And so did she.

"If I don't make enough money to buy Riley out, she'll sell to someone else. If we even make it through the season, that is."

"You'll make it," he heard himself say, and he believed it. Jaycee had drive. Determination. Courage. He couldn't help but admire her.

Admire, not love. Not yet.

He reminded himself of that over the next hour as they finished the meet and greet, said the necessary good-byes to sponsor reps and lingering fans, and climbed into his Hummer. He'd left the convertible at home on purpose, because he'd had to transport the flowers. That, and he'd wanted some privacy with Jaycee.

"That went well," she was saying to Tina, who sat in the backseat.

"If you say so." The woman kept tapping on her PDA. Rory turned on the radio, found an old ZZ Top song and fired up the volume just enough to drown out the irritating sound.

"This is a nice vehicle," Jaycee told him.

She trailed her hand over the maroon leather seat and Rory felt the stroke down his spine. His hands tightened on the steering wheel. *Easy, boy. Now's not the time or the place.*

"I bought it last year. . ." They spent the next few minutes talking about his Hummer while "La Grange" pounded away in the background. Metallica came on next, along with a heated discussion regarding the mandated car specs NASCAR had implemented.

"Overall, I like the new car," she told him.

"It handles for shit."

"If you don't know how to control it. It's all about skill."

"All the skill in the world can't make up for a difficult car."

"No, but it can compensate to a certain degree. If the car is hard to handle in the turns, then you work on your upper body strength and build more muscle to put behind the wheel. It might not solve every problem, but it'll make any easier to deal with."

She had a point.

That was the thing about her: she never opened her mouth unless she had the insight and knowledge to back up what came out. That's the way it had been with her when she'd been a kid. She'd never been chatty like all the other girls who'd pursued him, but quiet. Shy even. But when she'd opened her mouth, she'd always said something meaningful. Whether offering advice on his mom's Harley or making a comment about his favorite television show, she'd made him think. And rethink. He'd never met a woman like her who knew more about NASCAR. Then again, he'd never met a woman like her, period.

The sex, he reminded himself. He was infatuated with her because she was the one thing he couldn't have. The one thing he'd never been able to have. He had no doubt that one night would kill his curiosity and he could get back to the business of winning.

At least he hoped like hell.

"Thanks for the ride," she told him when he followed her to her front door later that evening, vase of flowers in hand. Cousin Tina had already taken her PDA and her incessant tapping inside the house. They stood on the front porch alone.

Moths flitted around the porch light, casting dancing

shadows across Jaycee's pale blonde hair. Her eyes were rich and warm, and his heart kicked up a beat.

"Thanks again for the spaghetti."

"Thank you for the donation."

Do something, a voice whispered. But Rory couldn't very well push her into the house and get naked in the hallway with Tina right there.

"I guess I'll see you later." He handed her the flowers.

His fingers brushed hers. Skin met skin. Electricity rushed from the point of contact, zapping every nerve and making him stiffen.

Her gaze snapped to his, and he noticed that the color darkened. Other than that, she gave no indication that she'd even noticed the contact.

"Take care." She stepped inside and started to close the door.

He turned.

"Rory?"

He whirled back around, his lips parted and ready—

"I really like the flowers." She smiled, her luscious mouth parting to reveal a row of straight white teeth.

Pure satisfaction somersaulted through him and he found himself grinning before he could stop himself. "My pleasure."

And it was.

Seeing her smile, her expression so sincere and unguarded, and knowing he was the cause, made him feel better than any orgasm.

Before he could dwell on that startling thought, her soft voice drew his attention. "No one's ever given me roses before," she added, almost as an afterthought. As if she didn't want to admit the truth to him but couldn't help herself. "You're the first."

And I'll be the last.

The notion struck as he gave her a quick peck on the lips, but he turned on his heel and walked toward his car before he said to hell with Tina and tossed Jaycee on the nearest horizontal surface. Climbing behind the wheel, he gunned the engine, backed out of her driveway and headed home—straight into an ice-cold shower.

Chapter Twenty-one

"On the right side of the screen is an actual day in the life of NASCAR superstar Jaycee Anderson." Tina's voice bounced off the walls of the conference room as she motioned to the huge flat-screen monitor mounted before them. "On the left side is an ideal day in the life of Jaycee Anderson the woman."

"How about Jaycee Anderson the sorry excuse for a BFF?" Savannah whispered in Jaycee's ear. "I can't believe you didn't tell me that Rory bought you at the auction!"

"I didn't have time. Tina showed up on my doorstep and started writing down my every move."

"You couldn't ditch her to go to the bathroom and call me on your cell?" Savannah reached for her water bottle and took a sip. "This is a big deal. *He's* a big deal."

Because Jaycee liked him. She always had, and Savannah knew it. Which was why Jaycee had been dodging her phone calls since the auction news broke.

"I'm sorry. Really sorry." They sat at a U-shaped table in the main conference room at Image Nation. Riley sat to Jaycee's left, and Savannah sat to her right. Danielle was positioned on the other side of Riley, along with a few other people from the makeover team. Aaron Jansen sat nearby next to two other men: his vice president and the head of marketing at R & R. "It's no big deal. He just bought me because of the image."

"And?"

"And he put the moves on me, but nothing happened. We didn't have sex." *Oral sex*, maybe, she added silently. "His clothes never came off. Swear."

Savannah wasn't going to be satisfied that easily. "What about yours?"

"I was just cooking for the man." *And how.* "That's it." Jaycee cast her a glance that said, *Please, please, please give it a rest.*

Savannah eyeballed her a few more seconds before she shrugged. "I'm sorry I'm being such a nagging bitch." She took a sip from her water bottle. "I'm cranky because I'm ovulating and Mac is track testing in Daytona."

"Sorry," Jaycee mouthed before turning back to Tina.

"Notice the overlapping categories," the lifestyle consultant was saying. "Such as the time required at the race shop and various sponsor commitments, but otherwise, I've tried to tailor the activities to fit with the new and improved lifestyle."

Jaycee scanned the second column and panic rushed through her. "You want me to meditate?"

Tina nodded. "First thing every morning. That should kill your insatiable need for caffeine."

"But I didn't drink any coffee."

"No, but you spent at least thirty seconds sniffing the coffee can."

"It helps curb the craving."

"It's a waste of time that could be better spent doing something constructive."

"Like meditation?"

"Exactly. I meditate every morning."

"So do I," Danielle chimed in, wiggling her manicured fingers. "Right before my shower. It keeps me centered."

"I'm already centered."

"You're stiff," Tina reminded her. "Which says you're nervous. Which says you're far from centered."

"That's true," Aaron chimed in. Clad in his usual jogging suit, he presented the picture of good health as he sipped a Revved & Ready energy drink and munched on a piece of whole-wheat toast from the breakfast cart. "You do look somewhat stiff, Jaycee."

She wanted to tell Aaron that he, too, would look stiff if he were wearing thigh-shaping underwear that cut off the circulation in his—big surprise—thighs, but she managed to swallow the comment before it rushed past her lips.

She was a goddess. And goddesses—at least the ones who drove for NASCAR—didn't talk back to their main and only sponsor.

She smoothed the silk material of her skirt—flimsy, which explained the thigh shapers, but softer than yesterday's suit—and drew a deep, controlling breath. "I can do meditation."

"Good." Aaron smiled, popped a piece of dry toast into his mouth and turned his attention back to the screen.

"You'll also note," Tina said when he motioned for her to continue, "that I've included time for at least one major soap opera. Statistics hold that women—whether on the fast track with career, family or both—make time for their soaps. The new schedule also eliminates the hour wasted on David Letterman and dedicates it to a brand-new activity—MySpace chitchat."

"No Letterman?" Jaycee blurted. "But—"

"MySpace is more important."

"But I already have a MySpace profile."

"One that you don't personally monitor. Your publicist takes care of that, and while she's more than adequate when it comes to the usual Net-keeping chores, she isn't taking an aggressive role. She isn't combing profiles and friending possible fans. And she certainly isn't staying in contact with your preexisting ones." Her gaze shifted to Aaron. "Compared to the profiles of male drivers on MySpace, Jaycee has only a tiny number of friends. Her profile page doesn't even reflect her image. Her wallpaper looks too much like something you would find lining the walls of a young boy's room. There are too many cars, too many images of her number. Too much clutter. We need something that's simpler. Something feminine." Tina smiled. "Something cute." She turned back toward the screen. "Something like this."

Jaycee found herself staring at a hot-pink background that bubbled with hearts and flowers and—

"You have to be kidding me," she blurted, pushing to her feet. Her heart pounded and her throat tightened and she had the sudden urge to hit something.

Or pass out.

She eased back down into her chair and the room stopped its sudden spinning. She was definitely light-headed.

The thigh shapers, a voice whispered as her gaze riveted on the screen.

Stay calm.

Breathe.

Focus on the positive.

"The pink," she finally managed, "is bright, but I can deal with it." *Atta girl*. "And the hearts aren't so terrible." *You tell 'em.* "And the flowers . . ." She swallowed, and the tightness in her chest eased. "Well, I actually like flowers." *Thanks to Rory.* "But Kenny G?" Her heart stalled as the music echoed in her head. "This is NASCAR. What happened to my Fuel song?"

"I like Kenny G," Aaron declared, tapping his fingers along with the smooth tempo pouring from the overhead speakers. "And my wife loves him. She does three miles on the treadmill every day to his greatest hits."

"My wife loves him, too," the head of R & R marketing added.

"Mine, too," said the R & R vice president.

"I have a few of his CDs myself," Riley offered, though she didn't look half as excited as the men. No, she looked almost sick. Worried.

"Kenny is an icon among women ages eighteen to forty-six," Danielle piped in. "Our target market in this situation." The Image Nation execs nodded in agreement.

"That's right," Tina said. "That's why we chose him. No one comes close to matching his fan base, except maybe Michael Bolton." Her gaze shifted to Jaycee. "We could do Michael if you'd like."

Jaycee weighed the two options for an eighth of a second. "Kenny is fine."

"It's a go, then." Tina reached for a stack of copies that sat next to her briefcase. "I've printed out Jaycee's new schedule, which includes all of the behavior modifications." She walked from one end of the table to the other and handed out the information. "I want everyone here to have a copy; that way we can help monitor Jaycee and keep her on the right track should we see her veering off course."

"What happens if she commits one of the seven

deadlies: pride, sloth, envy . . . stuffing her face with an entire bucket of fried chicken?" Savannah asked.

"There's a phone number at the bottom of the schedule. Call me and I'll deal with the situation."

"I hate you," Jaycee mouthed to her crew chief, who grinned.

"To ensure that she complies with the changes," Tina went on, "I'll need everyone to really keep their eyes open. I'll monitor the MySpace activity myself." Her gaze found Jaycee's. "I know the changes seem overwhelming, but with your drive and determination, you'll make it. And if you're the least bit tempted to cheat, just remember . . ." She smiled and gestured around her. "We'll all be watching."

"Are you headed back to the shop?" Savannah asked when they reached the ground floor of Image Nation after the presentation. Riley lingered several feet away with Aaron and the R & R execs.

"Let's see." Jaycee eyed the schedule before stuffing it into her pocket. "I'm supposed to be meditating right now. I suppose I could do that at the shop."

"Sure you could. With all the gas fumes around that place, meditation is a piece of cake."

Jaycee's stomach grumbled, reminding her of the miniscule breakfast she'd eaten before leaving the house. "You're trying to torture me, aren't you?"

"Follow me back to the shop and I'll pick up lunch on the way." Savannah waggled her eyebrows. "There's a new deli just a few blocks over. I've been craving their fudge cake for days now."

"You are trying to kill me."

"I'm not going to eat it in front of you. I wouldn't do

something so cruel when you're giving your all to this makeover."

"I knew I could count on you."

"I'm going to buy you your own piece."

"You're trying to get me into trouble so you can take over the car and drive it yourself."

"Actually, I'm trying to make up for the fried chicken comment." She blew out an exasperated breath. "I'm so sexually frustrated right now I feel like my head's about to pop off."

Jaycee remembered Rory and the chaste kiss that had kept her tossing and turning for most of the night. "I know the feeling."

"The thigh shapers getting to you?"

"They stopped bothering me about fifteen minutes ago when I stopped feeling my legs."

Savannah grinned. "You definitely deserve some chocolate. Come on. You can eat your piece in the storage closet so no one sees you. I'll guard the door."

"In that case"—Jaycee followed her crew chief out into the bright morning sunshine—"you're on."

Jaycee didn't eat the piece of cake.

No, she ate two pieces.

She'd had to. When she walked into the shop, she'd found Rory waiting for her. He'd shown up on the pretense that he'd missed her at the gym and wanted to make sure she was okay. Then he'd proceeded to make a lame excuse about being intrigued by the changes Savannah was making to Jaycee's Daytona car. And so he'd hung around.

Jaycee had wanted to boot him out on his butt. He was the competition, after all—but that excuse didn't really wash, because NASCAR policed so many aspects of the car that there really was little secrecy in the sport. It all came down to the skill and innovation of the team members in finding the right balance between all the factors involved, rather than any major structural modifications.

In other words, having Rory look around was no big deal to anyone, so she'd kept her mouth shut.

That had been three hours ago. She now stole a glance over the hood of the bright pink race car and saw him eyeballing the fuel system that sat on a nearby counter. His gaze lifted and collided with hers.

Awareness rippled up and down her spine. Her heart drummed. Heat rolled through her body. Hunger stirred, fierce and demanding in the pit of her stomach. Her nipples sprang to full, throbbing awareness.

"You don't have any more of that cake left, do you?" she asked Savannah once she managed to corner her crew chief a few minutes later.

"Sorry."

"A cupcake?"

"No."

"A candy bar?"

"Nada."

"Gum?"

"I knew it." The crew chief's gaze followed Jaycee's to where Rory now stood near the undercarriage of the car. "You got naked with him, didn't you?"

"I most certainly did not." She swallowed. "He had his clothes on the entire time."

"But you didn't," Savannah pressed.

"Technically I did." The dress had been up around her waist the entire time.

Savannah grinned. "He likes you."

"He likes this." Jaycee motioned toward the silk skirt and blouse she wore. "He doesn't like *me*."

"So what?"

"So he doesn't want anything more than to get into my pants."

"And?"

"And he's all wrong for me."

"Actually, he's pretty perfect when you think about it. It's not like you want to fall in love at this point in your life. You're busy with your career. He's busy with his. You don't want any strings attached. He doesn't want any strings attached. You think he's hot and he obviously thinks you're hot. So stop worrying about all that *like* crap and have a little fun. What?" Savannah added when Jaycee gave her a pointed stare.

"I would have expected more from a die-hard romantic."

"So I'm hopelessly in love with my husband and I now firmly believe there's someone out there for everyone. That doesn't mean I think you should strap on a chastity belt until Mr. Right shows up." Savannah's eyes twinkled with excitement. "Go talk to him."

"I have work to do."

"Actually, *I* have work to do." Savannah adjusted the strap on her overalls, and Jaycee stifled a pang of longing. "I've got a few more things to do to the fuel system, and none of them require assistance from you. You're after the fact. I don't need your input until the track test at the end of next week."

"But—"

"*Go.* Before I call Tina and tell her about the cake."

"You're evil."

"And don't you forget it."

Jaycee turned, drew a deep breath and started for

Rory. When she reached him she said, "Since you're determined to spend time with me, let's go."

He grinned. "Where do you have in mind?"

"My place." Before the smile could settle on his face, she added, "It's time for *General Hospital.*"

Over the next few days, every time Jaycee turned around, Rory was there. He showed up at her house on Friday morning and gave her a lift to the gym. He showed up to take her to lunch. He showed up at her speech to a local Girl Scout troop. He showed up at her guest appearance at a local meeting of Avon representatives.

He was everywhere. And he was driving her crazy. Not in the would-you-go-crawl-back-under-your-rock sense. No, he was driving her hormones crazy.

He didn't do anything overly forward. He pretty much played the perfect gentleman. But when he looked at her and whenever he happened to touch her, however innocently, she felt the bone-deep reaction clear from her head to her toes.

And when they talked . . . That was the real killer. Rory actually seemed interested in what she had to say. She told herself that he couldn't care less. That it was just an act to get her into bed.

She tried to remember that, to keep her defenses up.

Instead, she found herself relaxing around him. Because as intense as the chemistry that burned between them, there was an even stronger sense of camaraderie. They were friends.

Were—as in past tense, she reminded herself time and time again. They weren't friends now.

But it felt that way. The more time she spent with him, the more she felt connected to him, and the louder common sense demanded that she turn and walk away. Now. Before she got to know him even more. Before the situation became more complicated.

Before she got her heart broken all over again.

Jaycee forced aside the thought and held tight to her resolve early Saturday morning. They were at Chucky's Muscle and Fitness. She'd done yoga while Rory had done cardiovascular training, and now they'd paired up for some weight lifting before calling it quits.

She stood at the head of the weight bench and spotted him as he pumped a two hundred–pound barbell. Up and down. Over and over.

His face was set, his lips drawn into a thin line. Sweat beaded on his forehead and the muscles in his neck bulged. He was so handsome. So strong. So determined.

"Done," he grunted, letting the bar collapse onto the metal stand. "Your turn." He eyed her and suddenly the thought of him looming over her, staring into her, seemed too much for her to handle at the moment.

"I don't have much time before I have to meet Riley." They were meeting with Tina to fine-tune the schedule. Not that she could tell Rory that. She couldn't tell anyone. "I really want to get in a few minutes on the treadmill." She grabbed her water bottle and hightailed it across the room, an escape that didn't go nearly as quickly as she'd hoped, thanks to several race fans who wanted autographs.

She smiled and signed whatever they pushed into her hand, including a Chucky's towel that reeked of perspiration. Hey, it was part of the job, and Jaycee had learned to go with the flow a long time ago. She kept her game face on, all the while conscious of the man who followed her.

She made it to the treadmill and was just about to

plug in her iPod when Rory climbed onto the machine next to her.

Come on, she told herself. *Just plug it in and start walking. Before he says some—*

"So what are you and Riley doing today?"

"We've got a lunch." *There.* She plugged the headset in and was just about to slide the earpiece into her right ear, when—

"It's good that you guys are spending more time together."

"We're not really spending time together. It's just a lunch with Revved & Ready. They want to brief us on a new commercial idea." She tried for the left earpiece, but Rory seemed determined to keep her engaged.

Turn it on and forget him.

That's what she wanted to do. But she was a goddess, remember? A nice goddess. And nice goddesses didn't act like cold, distant bitches for no good reason. Not when they were out in public.

She draped the headset over the bars of the treadmill and concentrated on picking up her steps. "What about you?" She forced herself to make small talk. "Any big plans today?"

"Just paperwork at Xtreme. I've got a charity banquet tonight. I was thinking that we could do dinner tomorrow night."

Her heart skidded to a halt. "A date?"

His gaze collided with hers. "Yeah."

"An *official* date?"

He grinned. "Yeah."

As the truth sank in—Rory Canyon, *the* Rory Canyon, was actually asking her out on an official date—she remembered one all-important fact.

"Tomorrow night is Sunday, isn't it?"

"Let's see . . . Today is Saturday which means that, yes, the day after would be Sunday."

Her meeting with Schilling.

"I . . ." *Yes, yes, yes.* That's what she wanted to say. She'd waited so long, and while she knew that he wasn't interested in her sparkling personality, she wanted to say yes anyway. To burn off some of the sexual energy driving her bonkers.

Because that's what he wanted. He didn't really like her. He never had.

"I—I can't. Tomorrow just isn't good for me."

"Why not?"

"Because I've got another date," she blurted. And then she snatched up her headset and left him staring after her.

Chapter Twenty-two

Rory picked up his speed as he hit Turn Two. It was three days later, and he'd yet to push Jaycee's words out of his head. A blaze of multicolored bullets whizzed past him and he urged the car harder.

A *date*.

And why was this such a big shocker? It shouldn't be. Jaycee looked 1000 percent better with her new clothes and makeup. At the same time, she was still far from a knockout. She was pretty, all right, but in a subtle way. With Jaycee the appeal was all about the little things. The two dimples that cut into her cheeks when she smiled. The twinkle in her eyes whenever she talked about her driving. The two crinkles that furrowed between her eyebrows when she got really pissed.

No, he shouldn't be the least bit surprised. But he was.

He'd convinced himself that her effort to play up her assets had all been for him. To get under *his* skin and shatter *his* concentration and zoom into the top three.

He'd been dead wrong. She was doing it all for some other guy.

He had a sudden vision of her, her lashes at half-mast, her lips parted, an expectant expression on her sweet face as she waited for some other man to kiss her—

The thought shattered as he hit Turn Three and swerved a little too sharp. *Easy, man.* But it was too late. His back end flew one way while the front end went the opposite. His gut tightened as the car went into a spin. Rory fought for control. The engine screamed. The crowd roared. The wall seemed to come from out of nowhere and, just like that, *bam!*

Rory tossed his video game controller to the side and stared at the smoking front end on the giant plasma TV that sat center stage in his media room.

Shit.

He cursed his loss of control and his wandering thoughts. But most of all, he swore because he wanted Jaycee and she obviously didn't want him, and that realization bothered him a hell of a lot more than the fact that, for the first time ever, he'd crashed and burned during his favorite video game.

Maybe she really was putting on a good show to nail his ass come race day. Maybe not. He didn't know.

There was one way to find out.

"I think your crew chief is right in her assessment of the fuel system," Martin announced Sunday evening after a full two hours spent examining the engines of both of the cars going to Daytona. "I think with her adjustments that you'll be running at top speed. Then it's just a matter of tweaking the handling, and you should be in top form."

"You really think I could win?"

He grinned. "I wouldn't be here otherwise."

"I thought you were here because you wanted a date."

"That's just icing on the cake. What I really want is

recognition." He grinned. "Money goes hand in hand with recognition. The more my name is associated with the winning cars, the more money I make. Throw in an escort to the most boring awards ceremony in the history of the world, it's definitely a win-win situation for me. It's strictly platonic, by the way." He shifted, looking suddenly nervous. "I mean, I am attracted to you, but I don't expect you to *do* anything in return for my help." His words sent a rush of relief through her because as good as his sudden interest had made her feel—because it had been proof that she was on target with the makeover—she wasn't interested in him like that.

Despite what she'd told a certain competitor.

"I don't want to go the torture chamber alone," Martin added.

She smiled. "Come on. It can't be that bad."

"The ceremony honors a measly four recipients. In a perfect world, the whole thing would be relatively short and painless. The usual overpriced rubber chicken, the association president says a few words, calls the four names, and it's over, right?"

"Wrong?"

"Exactly. The president's wife is bored and she sees the banquet as an opportunity to try out whatever hobby she's into at that particular moment. Year before last, she was into photography. She put together a three-hour slide show of her family's last vacation."

"But that doesn't have anything to do with the recipients," Jaycee pointed out.

"There were a few token pictures thrown in from various association functions. Very few. Last year, she was into cinematography. She made a documentary of the life of an engine. I know, I know. It sounds fascinating," he said in all seriousness. "But the woman knows zip about engineering. It was the most boring thing, complete with play-by-play commentary, that I've ever sat through. This year it's going to be even worse."

"That's hard to believe."

"She's into crochet. Rumor has it that she's going to teach everyone how to do a cross-stitch. Instead of place cards, we're going to have crochet frames."

"On second thought, maybe I don't need your expertise after all."

Schilling laughed. "Too late. I've already given you my expert opinion. Speaking of which"—he glanced at his watch—"I need to get going. I've got a plane to catch. I'll see you on Friday?"

"Unfortunately," she muttered.

He grinned. "Paybacks, as they say, are hell."

But well worth it, Jaycee told herself as she eyed the list of notes he'd made. She'd had a hunch that the car would do well, but now she felt even more certain. She'd covered all of her bases. Her pit crew was training full force. There was plenty of power under her hood. The handling had been good. It all came down to Jaycee now. Her skill behind the wheel. Her communication with the crew. And luck.

Since Jaycee couldn't influence the last one, she pulled out her phone and punched in Savannah's personal cell number.

I can't answer right now. Leave a message and I'll call you. Unless Mac is home and we're making babies. Then you're on your own. Beep.

"Meet me at the shop first thing in the morning before everyone else arrives. I want to go over a few things with you." Jaycee punched the off button, killed the lights in the shop and walked back through the building toward the front door. Locking up behind herself, she headed for her SUV, which sat on the far end of the parking lot.

Fifteen minutes later she pulled up in front of her house to find Rory's Mustang blocking her driveway. Her gaze swiveled to the man who sat on her front steps. Her heart jumped into her throat as she drank in the sight of him. He wore a sleeveless black T-shirt with XTREME emblazoned in liquid blue. Faded jeans hugged his thighs and calves. Biker boots completed the outfit. His arms bulged with muscle, his elbows resting on his knees. He looked hot and incredibly sexy and . . . worried?

Jaycee's pulse quickened and heat uncurled low in her belly as she slid from the driver's seat. Rory pushed to his feet as she started up the front walk toward him.

"What are you—?" she started to say when she reached him, but she didn't get a chance to finish. He pulled her into his arms and hauled her up against his chest. His mouth covered hers. Strong hands pressed the small of her back, holding her close as he kissed her long and slow and deep. He smelled of soap and fresh air and a touch of wildness that teased her nostrils and made her breathe heavier, desperate to draw more of his essence into her lungs.

"I can't stop thinking about you," he murmured when he finally tore his lips from hers. "I want you so bad."

Want. It didn't go beyond sex as far as he was concerned. It never would.

It doesn't have to, Jaycee reminded herself, her lips tingling from his kiss and her body buzzing with desire. Savannah was right. She was a grown woman now, not some young girl with fantasies of happily ever after. She could guard her heart and focus on the physical and just have a little fun. She would, because she wanted Rory and he wanted her, and holding back was no longer a possibility. This had been building far too long, and while tomorrow would only bring heartbreak, she wasn't going to worry about it. This was about now.

This moment. This man.

She slid her arms around his neck, leaned up on her tiptoes and touched her mouth to his.

The kiss that followed was hot and wild and consuming. Her head started to spin and her heart pounded faster. He tasted of impulse and danger and her adrenaline started to pump even more furiously than it did when she climbed behind the wheel. Her hands snaked around his neck and she leaned into him, relishing the feel of his body pressed flush against hers.

He pulled free long enough to sweep her up into his arms and carry her inside. A few minutes later, they were upstairs in her bedroom. He let her feel every inch of his hot, aroused body as he eased her to her feet.

They faced each other then, and she knew he was waiting for her to make the next move, to put her feelings out there.

Her physical feelings, she reminded herself. This was sex, pure and simple. One night. *Fun*.

She lifted her tank top over her head. Trembling fingers worked at the catch of her bra and freed her straining breasts. She unbuttoned her shorts and worked them down her legs. Her panties followed, until she was completely naked.

He didn't reach out. He simply looked at her, yet it felt as if his hot hand traveled the length of her body along with his gaze. His bluer-than-blue eyes tweaked her nipples and circled the vee between her legs and stroked the hot slick flesh between her legs. Desire rushed through her, sharp and demanding, and she reached for him.

She gripped his T-shirt and urged it up and over his head. Her fingers went to the waistband of his jeans. She slid the button free and her knuckles grazed his bare stomach. He drew in a sharp breath, and then another, when she slid the zipper down and her thumb trailed over his hard length.

She hooked her fingers in the waistband of his briefs and tugged his jeans and briefs down. His massive erection sprang hot and greedy toward her.

She touched him, tracing the bulge of his veins and cupping his testicles. He throbbed at her touch and a surge of feminine power went through her—a crazy feeling, because she knew it wasn't really *her* making him this hot and hard. It was the image. But at the moment she wasn't going to worry about the details.

She relished the feel of him for a few fast, furious heartbeats before he seemed to reach his limit. He reached for her, pulling her close. Capturing her mouth with his own, he sucked the breath from her body with his hungry kiss. She met him thrust for thrust, lick for lick, losing herself in the feel of him so close. A moment later, he pressed her back against the bed.

"Don't close your eyes," he murmured. "I want to know that you like it when I touch you. That you want me to touch you. *Me.*" He settled beside her and trailed his hand down her collarbone, the slope of one breast. "Do you like it when I touch you here?" With his fingertip, he traced the outline of her nipple and watched it pucker.

"Yes," she breathed, the word catching on a gasp.

Her nerves came alive as he moved his hand down her abdomen to the triangle of hair covering her sex. One rasping touch of his callused fingertip against her swollen flesh and she arched off the bed. She caught her bottom lip and stifled a cry.

With a growl, he spread her wide with his thumb and forefinger and touched and rubbed as he dipped his head to draw on her nipple. Sensation speared her, and she had to fight to keep her eyes open. But she managed. She fixed her gaze on the dark head at her breast and trailed her hands over his shoulders while he drove her crazy.

When he slid a finger deep, deep inside, she moaned. Her fingertips tightened on his shoulders, digging into the hard, muscular flesh.

"You're wet," he said, leaning back to stare down at her, into her eyes.

"So are you." She reached between them and touched the pearl of liquid that beaded on the head of his erection nestled against her thigh. She spread the liquid around the rock-hard shaft and watched his gaze darken.

"If you don't stop touching me, this is going to go a hell of a lot faster than I anticipated."

"Haven't you heard?" She continued circling, stroking. "I like it fast."

He shifted and reached for his jeans. His fingers dove into one of the pockets and he pulled out a condom.

Driven by her need for him, she took the latex and tore open the package. She eased the contents over the head of his smooth, pulsing shaft. He pulsed in her hands and hunger gripped her.

She spread her legs and waited as he settled between them. The head of his penis pushed a delicious fraction into her. Pleasure pierced her brain. She lifted her legs and hooked them around his waist, opening her body even more. He answered her unspoken invitation with a deep, probing thrust.

Her muscles convulsed around him, clutching him as he gripped her bare bottom and tilted her so that he could slide a fraction deeper, until he filled her completely. He thrummed inside her for a long moment as he seemed to fight for his control.

But Jaycee had already lost her own control and she wasn't going to crash and burn all by herself. Not this time. She lifted her hips, moving her pelvis, riding him until he growled and gave in to the fierce heat that raged between them. He pumped into her, the pressure and the friction so sweet that it took her breath away.

She met his thrusts in a wild rhythm that urged him faster and deeper and . . . *yes!*

Her lips parted and she screamed at the blinding force of the climax that crashed over her. Rory buried himself deep one last time and a shudder went through him as he followed her over the edge.

Rory collapsed on top of Jaycee, his face buried in the crook of her neck, her muscles still clenched tightly around him. He felt every quiver of her body, every erratic breath. Her heart pounded against the palm of his hand and a wave of possessiveness swept through him. He had the sudden, desperate urge to tighten his hold on her and never let go. Because she was his.

Now and forever.

Always.

He forced the thought aside, determined to ignore

the damned emotion pushing and pulling inside of him. Rather, he focused on the steady beat of Jaycee's heart and the sweet scent of her skin and the fact that they weren't finished yet.

Chapter Twenty-three

Jaycee opened her eyes very early the next morning and crawled over Rory's sleeping form. A rush of tenderness overwhelmed her as she remembered the past night and the sex. Breath-stealing, bone-melting sex that had gotten better and better as the night progressed.

Her gaze traveled from the splatter of freckles on one shoulder down the massive bicep encircled by the flaming slave band tattoo, the bend of his elbow, his thick forearm sprinkled with dark hair, to the purposeful hand resting on the pale yellow sheet that rode his waist. The early morning light pushed through the blinds and bathed his heavily muscled torso. He looked so dark and yummy stretched out on her bed, and she had the sudden urge to hop back in and snuggle up next to him.

To celebrate.

After years of wondering, of fantasizing about being in his arms, she'd experienced it firsthand. She knew what it was like to be kissed, touched, cherished by the one man, the only man, who'd ever made her knees quiver and her tummy tingle.

Yes, she knew, so she should have felt satisfied. She had her memory to tuck away and pull out when the nights grew lonely and the constant traveling finally got to her.

The thing was, she didn't want just a memory. She wanted the real thing. In her bed. In her life. In her future.

Fun, remember? Last night had been all about having a little fun. No strings attached. She knew that. At the same time, she found herself having the craziest thoughts. About climbing into bed and having more sex. And then climbing back out and sharing pancakes together. And getting married. And building a home. And having kids.

Crazy.

Jaycee was in the prime of her career. She couldn't have a kid. Sure, she liked them, but she didn't know the first thing about how to raise one. She thought of her own bedroom while growing up, filled with car models and NASCAR paraphernalia. She'd had a race flag hanging from the ceiling. A boy might think that was cool. But what if she had a girl? She didn't know the first thing about little girls. It didn't matter that she'd once been one; she'd been Ace Anderson's kid first and foremost. A chip off the old block.

The past swirled inside her: the kids laughing at her because she'd worn a pair of Speed Racer underwear when she should have been wearing My Little Pony panties, the isolation she'd felt when she'd watched the other girls wear their homecoming mums the Monday after a game, the silent tears she'd cried when her friends went off to the prom as she headed for the track. She wouldn't do that to her own daughter. She couldn't. And at the same time, Jaycee had been following in Ace's footsteps for so long, she wasn't so sure she could do anything else.

Not that it mattered. She didn't want kids right now. She wanted a winning season. A satisfied sponsor. Her very own racing team. All were within her reach. All she had to do was forget Rory Canyon.

It was her turn to walk away this time.

She picked up her clothes and headed for the bathroom. She took the world's fastest shower, pulled on one of the stretchy bodysuits her personal shopper had picked out—a lemon yellow number with orange trim—and headed downstairs.

She steeled herself as she passed through the kitchen—mere inches from the coffee cannister—and headed into the media room. She popped in a few race tapes from last year, put the volume on a moderate level, and settled herself in the center of the floor on a braided rug.

Then she closed her eyes.

"Ohhhhhhhhmmmmmmmmmm . . ."

Rory stood in the doorway separating Jaycee's kitchen from her media room and wiped a hand over his eyes. It was too early and he'd had a late night. Exhaustion had to be playing tricks on him.

His hand fell away, but she didn't disappear. She sat in the middle of the room, her eyes closed. Her arms rested on her legs, her palms upturned.

He blinked just to be sure. "Are you meditating?" he finally asked.

Her eyes popped open and her gaze zigzagged over to him. Hunger flashed in her expression, followed by a rush of regret.

Over last night?

His question lingered as she seemed to recover her composure. Her face went passive as she directed her attention in front of her and closed her eyes again.

"Yes," she murmured. "Meditation keeps me centered."

"But the TV is on."

"I'm not watching it."

"But you're listening to it."

Her eyes snapped open. "Look, this is my centering time. Either be quiet or go away."

What the hell? "Did you just tell me to *go away*?"

"Or be quiet. Your choice. I've only got fifteen minutes and then I'm meeting Savannah at the shop."

Her words slid into his ears and realization hit. She was giving him the brush-off.

So?

So, it didn't matter. That's what he told himself. He'd wanted to take her to bed, to work her out of his system once and for all, and he'd done it. No more lusting after her. No more thinking about touching her or tasting her or talking to her. He'd done all three. The race was now officially over.

And he'd won.

If only he felt the expected burst of happiness. Instead, he felt a dozen other emotions, and not a one of them put a smile on his face.

"I've got a busy day, too," he told her, determined to hide the whirlwind of emotion twisting inside of him. "Jam-packed."

"Ohhhhhhhhmmmmmmmmmmm . . ."

"I guess I'll just get dressed and head out." He started to turn, to get the hell away from her so that he could make some sense out of the nearly uncontrollable urge to say to hell with everything—his team, his racing, his father, his future—and stay here with her, in this place, this moment, for the rest of his life. He wanted to kiss it all good-bye, to snatch Jaycee into his arms and spend the rest of his life with her.

Like hell. He'd worked too hard to make it to number three. He had too many people depending on him. What's more, he *liked* racing. Sure, he'd been feeling restless lately. Unfulfilled. But that had nothing to do with his personal life and everything to do with his professional life. Because he'd been idling far too long and he wanted to gun it and zoom into first place. He wanted to win.

Winning was everything.

Start walking, buddy. Now, before you do something really stupid.

That's what his head said, but his his feet didn't seem to want to cooperate.

"Maybe we could whip up some eggs or something," he heard himself say. Hey, breakfast *was* the most important meal of the day.

"I already ate. Ohhhhhhhhmmmmmmmmmm . . ."

"I guess I should go then." He glanced at his watch, yet he didn't feel the usual sense of urgency. His gut churned. His body felt tight. His chest hurt. "I've got two meetings this morning."

"Good for you. Ohhhhhhhhmmmmmmmmmm . . ."

"This afternoon I'm doing one of those public service announcements." His heart hammered, echoing in his ears.

"Great. Ohhhhhhhhmmmmmmmmmm . . ."

"It's one of those antidrug things."

"That's nice. Ohhhhhhhhmmmmmmmmmm . . ."

If you're not too busy, maybe we can have dinner tonight. It was there on his lips, but he caught the words before they could slip past. She obviously wasn't interested in more than a one-night stand, no matter how great the sex had been.

Thankfully, he tried to tell himself. The last thing he wanted to do was hurt Jaycee. And that's what would happen if she got hung up on him again. No way could they have a real relationship now, with the season just starting and so much on the line for the both of them.

Still. Last night had been pretty great. Fan-fucking-tastic as far as he was concerned.

He glanced at the picture she made sitting in the middle of the floor, her face so calm and composed. There were no tears. No pain. No anger. She was completely oblivious to him.

And that's a problem?

It wasn't. It was the best thing that could have happened to him. Numero uno on his "morning after" list. Relief. That's all he should feel at the moment. Pure, blissful relief because she wasn't kicking and screaming and embarrassing herself because she wanted to spend every moment with him from this day forward.

That was the last thing he wanted.

Her reaction was a complete and total blessing. Like winning pole position *and* the friggin' race.

But damn if he didn't feel like he'd just smashed into the wall straight into the first turn.

The next few days should have been the best of Jaycee's life. Martin's suggestions turned out to be right on the money and the car was roaring like a lion ready for the hunt. Her new profile had attracted an extra three thousand MySpace friends. Riley was busy trying to iron out the details for the upcoming Daytona race, which meant she didn't have time to dog Jaycee's every step. And Rory didn't call.

They weren't great, though. They were the worst days of her life. Savannah was mad because Jaycee hadn't given her a heads-up about Martin's visit. The Image Nation lifestyle rep had killed the Kenny G My-Space music and replaced it with—big swallow—Michael Bolton. Riley was too busy to stalk in person, but she'd substituted with e-mail and voice messages. And Rory didn't call.

Not that she wanted him to call. She was glad he'd taken the hint and a hike. The last thing, the very last thing she wanted was to see him right now. Their night together was still too fresh in her mind. No, she needed to get her head on straight and forget all about him before she saw him at Daytona. She didn't want to see him.

Not that she had to worry about that now. She would deal with it when the time came. In the meantime . . .

She stood in front of the mirror on Friday evening and eyed her reflection. She'd hopped a plane from Texas and arrived in Charlotte just three hours ago for her date with Martin. She'd been primping ever since.

A fat lot of good it had done her. Her mascara was clumpy. She'd accidentally colored outside the lines when she'd done her lips. She'd fried her forehead trying to curl her bangs. To make matters worse, the silver lamé dress made her look washed out. And the cut—floor-length and skintight with a tulle bow that made her butt look huge—did absolutely nothing positive for her figure.

"It'll look fabulous." That's what the personal shopper had said before she'd left. Of course, she'd said that about everything else, including the mint green biker shorts and lavender tank top that made Jaycee look like an Easter egg.

Jaycee grabbed a brush and her blush and added more color. She looked like a walking corpse wearing a space suit—an overly long space suit, she decided, when she tripped over her hem on her way to open the door to Martin.

"Are you okay?" He reached out a hand to steady her.

"I'm fine."

"You want to throw on a different pair of shoes?"

"Yes." She glanced down at the sky-high silver sandals and shook her head. "But I won't. They match the dress."

"So?"

"I can't walk around in black shoes and a silver dress. It wouldn't look right."

"Why not?"

Yeah, why not? "I guess I could." She contemplated a few blissful hours in which she could actually feel her toes, before accepting the inevitable. "But I won't." *You go, girl. Just tough it out. That's what goddesses do.* Besides, there would be tons of press in attendance for the awards ceremony and they would surely be taking pictures. Not to mention there would be news crews, as well. Add in several NASCAR execs and members of some of the competing teams, and it was a PR opportunity she couldn't pass up. Time to drive her new image all the way home. She forced a smile. "I like these shoes."

He glanced down. "They are nice shoes." His gaze swept upward, but Jaycee didn't feel the same awareness she felt when Rory looked at her. "Nice outfit, too."

"Thanks. Listen," she rushed on, "I know you said this was platonic, but I just want to make sure that no one gets hurt here. You're a really nice guy and I like you. I really do."

"But?"

"But I think we'd make better friends. I don't do relationships very well."

"Neither do I. I've got three ex-wives to prove it."

"You've been married?" Jaycee arched an eyebrow. "I didn't know that."

"It's not something I list on my resume." He shrugged. "I have a bad habit of falling for the wrong women."

"Tell me about it."

He grinned. "You fall for the wrong women, too?"

"Men," she said. "Well, actually, just one man." Rory's image pushed into her head and she did her best to push it back out. "If I had an ounce of common sense, I would just forget him."

"But you can't," he said, as if reading her thoughts.

"I'm trying."

"It's not easy when you're really hooked on someone. I still think about Trudy—she was the third Mrs. Schilling. She's an investment banker. Brilliant woman. Beautiful. I couldn't have asked for a more perfect woman."

"What happened?"

"She wanted more time than I was willing to give. I haven't gotten where I am professionally by slacking. It's all about dedication. She liked that about me at first, until we tied the knot. Then she accused me of being married to my career. She was right, too. The thing was, I couldn't change it. I didn't want to. My career was too important to me. It still is. So don't worry. I won't get the wrong idea. The last thing I need in my life is another romantic entanglement." He grinned. "But a friend . . . That I could definitely use."

Relief washed through her. "Then let's get this show on the road." She hooked her arm through his and they headed downstairs to the ballroom where the ceremony was being held.

An hour later, Jaycee came to the conclusion that Martin Schilling had been dead wrong when he'd warned her about the ceremony. It wasn't nearly as bad as he'd described it.

It was worse. Much, much worse.

Her gaze swiveled to the man who sat across the room at one of the round tables. There were a half-dozen men seated with him—all decked out in tuxedos—but she found him instantly.

Rory Canyon turned from the man next to him and his blue gaze collided with hers.

Panic bolted through her, followed by a rush of *duh*. Of course he was here.

Now. *Here.*

There were several drivers in attendance. Owners. Sponsors. She should have anticipated it, but she'd been so determined *not* to think about him that she hadn't let herself entertain the possibility.

Big mistake.

She drew a deep, steadying breath and forced her attention back to Martin. He was talking to her about some new heat-conducting material he was researching for an aerospace company.

". . . use it to insulate the engine, then we can cut down on the temperature inside the engine space by at least thirty degrees."

"Really?" She stole another glance at Rory to find him still watching her, his mouth drawn into a tight line. As if he wasn't any more thrilled with seeing her than she was with seeing him.

". . . once the kinks are all worked out, it could actually be used under the hood of a stock car, as well. Which would cut down on the nearly unbearable heat inside the car."

"That's great." Jaycee busied herself sipping a glass of water. She was not going to look at Rory again. She was going to focus on Martin and the award adorning his place setting. He was her friend and this was his night. She wasn't going to ruin it by faking a headache and hightailing it up to her hotel room.

"Wine?"

Jaycee turned toward the waiter, who held up a bottle of Chardonnay. "Yes, please."

"A full glass?"

"That, or you could just leave the bottle."

He smiled and topped off her glass before moving to the next person.

"A good year," Martin said as he held up his own glass and took a sip. "Yes, a very good year."

"Hear, hear." Jaycee took a huge gulp and nearly spewed the stuff back out. She'd never been a big drinker, and when she did indulge she stuck to the occasional ice-cold beer with a slice of pizza. "It's good." *Not.* Her gaze swiveled to Rory in time to see a tall, scantily clad redhead lean over his shoulder. She whispered something and he smiled.

"Really good," Jaycee added, taking another huge gulp.

The funny thing about wine, she decided a half hour later, was that the more she drank, the better it seemed to taste. And the less she worried about Rory.

So what if the redhead had practically planted herself in his lap for the past fifteen minutes? Jaycee didn't care. She had no designs on him. No hope for the future, which was why *she'd* walked away from *him* this time. No, the only thing she wanted as far as Rory was concerned was to beat the pants off him come race day.

The thought stirred a memory of their night together, and she took another huge gulp before holding up her glass for a refill. The waiter topped her off again and she tried to focus on Martin. Her date. The most boring man in the universe, or so it seemed as he blathered on about engine specs.

She sipped more wine, but even the halfway-decent Chardonnay did little to ease her boredom. And so she didn't resist when Rory seemed to appear out of nowhere and reach for her hand.

"Hey there, Schilling. You don't mind if I borrow your date, do you?" Before Martin could reply, Rory pulled Jaycee from her seat. He grinned, but the expression didn't touch his bright blue gaze. "By the way, congratulations," he told Schilling before turning to lead Jaycee away from the table.

"How much did you have to drink?" he asked as they wound their way through the maze of tables.

"Two and a half glasses." She stifled a hiccup. "I think."

He shook his head and tightened his grip on her hand.

"Where are we going?"

"To dance."

"I don't think that's such a good idea." She dug in her heels as he tried to tug her onto the small wooden floor that had been set up at the center of the room.

"Too drunk?"

"Hardly."

"Then what's the problem?"

"I don't know how to waltz."

"Neither do I."

Before she could protest, the classic "Tennessee Waltz" came to an end. A steel guitar and a whining fiddle poured from the speakers, launching a fast, modern-day country tune.

"I don't two-step, either," she said, tugging against his hand. He stopped pulling and stared down at her, into her, and the words were out before she could stop them. "I don't dance, period."

"Ever?"

She shook her head. "Not in public. And not with a partner. And not with shoes like this." She indicated the three-inch strappy silver sandals. "I'll fall on my face."

"I'll catch you first," he promised, and as much as she wanted to turn and walk the other way, she found herself following him out onto the dance floor.

"Now what?" she asked as he turned to face her.

"Now you relax." He slid an arm around her waist and took her hand. "And follow my lead."

He started slow at first, his foot sliding forward, pushing against her leg and urging her backward. And then the move started all over with the other foot. Slide, move, switch. They moved around the dance floor, slowly, tentatively at first.

"See? It's not so hard."

It wasn't. The music slid into her ears and thrummed through her body as they picked up momentum, until they were moving as briskly as the other couples. "It's kind of fun."

"Yeah?" His eyes twinkled. "You haven't seen anything yet."

"What do you—? Whoa!"

Before Jaycee knew what had happened, he'd twirled her and sent her whirling in the opposite direction. She was dead certain she was about to eat some hardwood, but his fingers tightened around hers, and just as she teetered to the side, he pulled her back to him, turned her under his arm and the roller-coaster ride started all over again.

By the time the song faded to a close, Jaycee could hardly breathe. Her heart hammered and her pulse raced, and she felt as psyched as if she were on the last lap, gunning for Victory Lane. And she felt happy.

"Not bad for a rookie." He grinned and pulled her closer as the Righteous Brothers' "Unchained Melody" drifted from the speakers.

"I don't think—"

He pressed a fingertip to her lips. "Don't think. Just feel."

He drew her even closer. He was strong and warm and he smelled so delicious that she couldn't help herself. She leaned into him, molding herself to his hard frame, despite the warning bells that sounded in her head. The music faded until she heard only the pounding of her own heart and his deep voice. They swayed to and fro for the next few minutes, and Jaycee actually forgot how miserable she'd been the past few days.

It's another memory, she told herself, making up her mind to enjoy the moment and brand it into her brain. Reality would intrude all too soon, and she would be reminded that no matter how tenderly he held her, or how his frenzied heartbeat matched her own, he still didn't care for her. What's more, she didn't have the time or energy to care for him. She was busy, and this was all about lust.

"I've missed you." His deep voice slid into her ears and a rush of hope went through her. Followed by a great big dose of *No way*.

She went stock-still and stared up at him. He looked as surprised as she felt.

"What did you just say?"

"I said that I, um, kissed you," he blurted. He nodded. "Yeah, that's it. I kissed you. Last week. I was just thinking about that because you look pretty incredible with that lipstick."

What?

"That's a nice color. What do you call that?"

"Pink Glimmer. I—I really think I should get back to Martin. He *is* my date."

Rory's gaze darkened, and his mouth drew into a tight line. "Do you really like this guy, Jaycee?"

"Actually, I do." *As a friend*, she added silently. "What's not to like? He's the total package. Brilliant. Good-looking. Everything a woman could want in a man."

Rory's gaze narrowed and she knew he didn't believe her. Smart guy.

"Well, um, thanks for the dance lesson," she said as she turned to walk away.

"Anytime." His voice followed her as she wobbled toward the edge of the dance floor and worked her way through the maze of tables.

Forget him, she told herself. Forget the disbelief on his face. And the disappointment. No way was he disappointed. She was the only one headed down that road if she kept imagining things that weren't there.

Before she realized where she was going, she'd headed out the front doors toward the elevator. She paused to grab a nearby waiter and ask him to deliver a message to Martin.

"You want me to tell him what?" the waiter asked.

"Just tell him Mr. Wrong is here and—" She waved a

hand. "Never mind." She couldn't do this. She couldn't run away. Rory would never buy that Schilling was the man of her dreams if she bailed.

She turned to go back in. Her heel caught in the hem of her dress and a loud *rrrrrrippppppp* stopped her cold. She glanced down to see a gaping tear two inches above her knee.

Fifth note to goddess: never, ever flee the man of your dreams wearing a skintight, silver, floor-length dress without a change of clothes handy.

She closed her eyes and contemplated her choices. She could salvage her image, call it a night and head for her room. Now. Before someone saw her sporting a fashion disaster. But if she ran, Rory would realize she'd walked out on Martin—the supposed man of her dreams—and he might guess the truth: *he* was the man of her dreams.

She should deal with the situation and get her butt back to the table. If she did that, Rory, she hoped, would never know that she'd fallen head over heels for him.

Again.

She grabbed the ripped material and pulled. She kept pulling until she'd yanked off the bottom half of the dress and turned her floor-length formal into a mini. Seeing the tiny razor cut near her knee, she thanked the heavens above that she was getting better at the whole shaving thing. And then she turned on her heel and headed back to the ballroom.

Chapter Twenty-four

Stupid, stupid, *stupid!*

Rory stood near the bar and reached for an ice-cold bottle of beer. He took a long swig. The cool liquid slid down his throat but did little to soothe the tightness in his chest.

I missed you. What the hell kind of crazy thing was that to say?

The truth, a tiny voice whispered. A voice that had better shut up pretty damn quick.

He took another long drink and stared at the ballroom entrance where Jaycee had disappeared a few minutes ago. As if his thoughts had conjured her, she reappeared. Minus half her dress.

The once-floor-length hem now hit her midthigh. His gaze swept her bare legs and a fierce wave of possessiveness rolled through him. He had the sudden urge to stomp across the room, hoist her over his shoulder and carry her back to his hotel.

He would have, except for the all-important fact that he was over her. He'd exorcised this particular demon. Satisfied the lust. It was over. From here on out he was back to keeping his focus, to racing his heart out, to winning. He couldn't do that if he was hung up on Jaycee.

Talk about a conflict of interest and a surefire way to kill his season.

Rory watched as she made her way around the tables. He entertained a quick vision of his arms closing around her, the white linen from a nearby tablecloth covering all major body parts, before he gave himself a mental kick in the ass. Yep, he'd kill his season all right. And probably get arrested.

"Hey, there." Cody's voice cut into his thoughts, and Rory turned to see his brother approach with an older gentleman next to him. "This is Arthur Jenkins. He's with Adrenaline Solutions."

"The Internet service provider," Rory recognized. "I've been using you guys for years. You're fast."

"So are you," the man told him. "Which is why we're thinking of coming on board with Xtreme. If you do as well as everyone expects you to do this season, that is. We're contemplating a new marketing campaign that, obviously, hinges on speed. Which means we need the fastest driver out there for it to be really effective. Our stock prices have taken a few hits lately, what with the influx of competition, and we want to reverse the situation before it becomes a trend. A win at Daytona would get us off to a good start."

"This is our year," Cody told the man. "We've won twice at Daytona and last year we placed second. We're the favorite to win. And we will," Cody vowed. "We're bringing our best game to the table, make no mistake about that. The new car handles like a dream and there's no one better than Rory behind the wheel. Isn't that right, bro?"

Anxiety coiled in the pit of Rory's stomach and his muscles tightened as the weight of Cody's gaze hit him. He had the crazy urge to turn, to walk away and forget Adrenaline and Xtreme and his dad. To chuck it all, walk over to Jaycee, pull her into his arms and simply hold her.

Rory leveled a stare at the would-be sponsor. "Have your checkbook handy in Daytona, Mr. Jenkins. You'll need it."

Arthur Jenkins smiled. Cody grinned. Rory took another sip of his beer.

His gaze shifted back to Jaycee and he steeled himself against the jealousy that clawed at his gut. No, he didn't miss her. Even if he had volunteered to fly halfway across the country for this awards ceremony on the off-chance that she would be there with Schilling. He'd come because that's what winning drivers did: schmoozed with sponsors at every available opportunity and kept their name out there.

It was all about business. About winning.

That's what he told himself as he watched her smile at Martin Schilling. And maybe, just maybe, if he drank enough tonight, he might actually start to believe it.

"Are you trying to land this entire race team in the unemployment line?" Riley demanded when Jaycee picked up her cell phone the next morning.

At least she thought it was morning. The drapes were drawn and the hotel room was pitch-black. Her head pounded and the smell of cream cheese clung to her, making her stomach churn.

Cream cheese?

"I don't know what you're talking about." She forced herself upright and her stomach pitched.

"I'm talking about *USA Today*."

"Uh-huh." She drew a deep breath and stumbled toward the window.

"The sports section."

"Yeah." She caught the curtain with one finger and sunlight blinded her. Yep, it was morning.

"Front page," Riley blurted. "I'm so pissed I don't know where to start. I take that back. Let's start with you telling me what you're doing in freakin' North Carolina."

Jaycee closed her eyes as the past night rolled through her and she remembered. "I had a date with Martin Schilling."

"The engineer?"

"Yes. He helped with some engine adjustments free of charge," she added, "in exchange for a date with me."

"So in addition to ruining our lives, you're also selling yourself in exchange for engine pointers?"

"I'm not selling anything. We're just friends. I needed help on the engine—which you refused to let me pay him for—and he needed an escort for the most boring awards ceremony in the history of ceremonies."

"I didn't refuse. We didn't have the money."

"Exactly. So I bartered."

"What about the dress? I distinctly remember that it actually had a bottom half when Danielle picked it out, but in this picture, that part is missing."

"I accidentally stepped on my hem. It ripped. I didn't have an extra formal with me and I didn't want to call it a night, so I improvised."

She'd been determined to walk back into the ballroom, her head held high, and prove to Rory—and herself—that she didn't care about him. A great plan, when she'd thought about it. But as she'd sat there next to Martin, it hadn't seemed that great. Rory had kept staring at her and she'd tried not to stare at him, and so she'd had a little bit more wine. Before she'd known it, she'd drunk half a bottle. Martin had been busy celebrating his award and so he'd drank the other half and they'd both ended up tanked. The last she'd seen of him, he'd been trying to proposition the wife of one of the team owners.

He hadn't been joking when he'd told her he had a habit of picking the wrong women.

"What about your shoes?" Riley's voice drew her back to the here and now. "I'm staring at a picture of you barefoot."

"I needed to get comfortable, so I sort of slipped them off." While Martin had been putting the moves on Mrs. Team Owner, Jaycee had decided to have some more wine.

"I see one hooked over the arm of the candelabra."

"I sort of slipped them off and then plopped them on the table so I wouldn't forget them when I finished."

"Finished doing what?"

She swallowed as the memory swam in her head. "Arm wrestling." Okay, so she'd decided to have more wine and a little fun.

"That explains the next picture. At first I thought you were fighting over a crab claw."

"I would never do something so unladylike as to fight over a crab claw."

"No, but judging by this next picture, you're more than happy to go at it over a piece of chocolate-covered cheesecake."

"It was really good cheesecake."

"This isn't funny, Jaycee. Aaron Jansen is ready to

bail right now. *Today*. He says that if you can't make a serious commitment, he's through wasting his time."

"I have made a serious commitment. I've done everything. I'm killing myself with this diet. I can't even remember the last time that I watched Letterman or drank a cup of coffee. What does he want? Blood?"

"Money. And money comes from selling more of his product. And he only sells more product if consumers relate to you. And consumers only relate to you if you walk the walk and talk the talk."

"You can't tell me you've never craved a piece of cheesecake."

"I have, but I've never crawled across a banquet table and accosted a pastry chef."

"I didn't accost anyone. I just wanted another piece and he wouldn't give it to me."

"We'll be lucky if he doesn't press charges."

"He was a race fan."

"Obviously not one of yours, or he would have handed over the extra piece of cake. You have to control yourself. This isn't *Monday Night Raw*."

"I have been controlling myself."

"Then what happened last night?"

Everything. "Nothing. Listen, I'm sorry. Tell Aaron that I'm committed and last night was just a big misunderstanding."

"One that happened to be witnessed by every news crew in the country. You were supposed to keep a low profile until the interview with Trick Donovan. Now, when you go live on his show, the makeover will seem like some glam job for Daytona. . ." Riley launched into a half-hour-long tirade that ended with Jaycee popping several Tylenol and smelling an individual packet of Folgers.

"You have to walk the straight and narrow for the next two weeks or this team is out," Riley finally finished. "I can't believe you would do something so stupid. You're just like Ace," she muttered. "Always thinking about yourself."

Jaycee wanted to tell Riley she was wrong, but the words stuck in her throat. Last night she *had* been thinking about herself. How lonely she was. And how sad. And how upset. And how mad. Over Rory. But Riley wouldn't understand. She didn't give a flip about Jaycee's personal problems. All she cared about was getting her share of the money.

"Why?" she heard herself ask.

"Excuse me?"

"Why do you need the money so badly?"

"Because I never had the luxury of being self-involved. My mother's sick," her half sister added after a long moment. The voice on the other end of the phone was quiet, hesitant. "She has a lot of medical bills."

Jaycee had contemplated Riley's motivation too many times to count, but she'd never figured it for an act of kindness. Sadistic torture, yes. Perhaps personal revenge: she'd stuck around to make Jaycee's life miserable. But that wasn't the case at all.

"I've got money in the bank."

"Enough to sponsor a race team?"

"My father didn't pay me that much." No, Ace had paid her the bare minimum. But she'd driven for him anyway, because she'd known that one day the team would be hers.

She'd been wrong.

"I'm not loaded, but I've got enough to help out with your mom," she added.

Silence settled over the line for several long moments. "If you want to help, just get with the program," her sister finally said. "No more cake and no more wine."

"I swear."

"I'll do my best to calm down Aaron, but I can't make any promises. In the meantime, get your butt back home. We've got a busy schedule."

"I fly out at noon."

"I'll pick you up at the airport. And Jaycee," Riley said after a long moment, "thanks."

The soft word echoed in Jaycee's ears and sent a burst of warmth through her.

But then she opened the drapes and nearly blinded herself, and she was back to having the worst morning of her life.

The worst morning of Jaycee's life turned into the worst week. NASCAR news had a way of going mainstream, and the pictures showed up everywhere, including Letterman.

Not that Jaycee discovered this bit of information by watching Letterman. No way. She'd given her word and she meant to keep it. Savannah had been the one to catch the show that had featured one of Letterman's infamous lists, this one entitled "Top Ten Reasons the U.S. should reinstate prohibition."

Jaycee had barely made the count at number nine: *So Jaycee Anderson wouldn't have to take a Breathalyzer at Daytona*. The top slot had been a tie between Britney Spears and the star of the VH1 reality show, *I Love New York*. But the fact that she'd made the countdown at all had driven Aaron mad. He'd delivered an ultimatum: if things didn't die down by the time Daytona rolled around, he was pulling out after the first race. Even Jaycee agreeing to daily hypnosis sessions with The Reinforcers from Image Nation wasn't enough to soothe his ruffled feathers.

Jaycee knew this was it. No more wasted chances. She was banking on the fact that a good finish would stall for more time, during which she intended to prove herself and make him the happiest sponsor in NASCAR history. She spent her days playing goddess at various meet and greets and even a local golf tournament, and her evenings helping Savannah adjust both the main car and the backup that would be used in Daytona.

Her nights? She still spent those tossing and turning and trying not to think about Rory and the fact that she was hopelessly, desperately in love with him.

Chapter Twenty-five

He missed her.

Rory came to that conclusion over the next two weeks as he prepped for a win at Daytona and tried to forget Jaycee completely.

It should have been easy. Out of sight, out of mind. That's what he'd been banking on. He'd been busy with sponsor commitments and all the other prerace stuff. Too busy to make his usual Monday morning workouts at Chucky's. And he hadn't caught even a glimpse of her around the track.

Until now.

He stared at the familiar pink race car idling a few stalls ahead of his own. She wore her now-signature pink racing suit, her helmet in hand as she went over some changes with Savannah.

As if she felt his attention, she turned. Her eyes locked with his and it felt like a sucker punch to his gut. The breath rushed from his lungs and a sense of expectancy gripped him, along with a twinge of hope.

Because he missed her. All of her. The talking, the sharing. It was a truth that had nothing to do with the hot, incredible sex they'd had, and everything to do with the days leading up to the sex. The talking and sharing and laughing. They'd become friends again, and he'd liked it.

Too damned much.

She'd liked it, too. He could see it in the sudden shift in her expression. Her game face had slipped away and for a few frantic heartbeats, she was all woman. Soft and vulnerable and lonely.

Before he could stop himself, he pushed his hand into the air and waved. It was a simple gesture. Just a quick acknowledgment from one driver to the next. One that she couldn't ignore.

He waited for her to wave back or flip him off or something. Anything.

Her expression shuttered and she turned back to her crew chief. Rory was left to wonder if he'd just imagined the fierce longing in her gaze. Even more, he was left to wonder why he cared one way or another.

He *didn't*. Not any more than she did. If she could just forget him, he could do the same.

"Come on, buddy," Cody told him. "This is it. The moment of truth. Give her a spin and let's see how she does."

The car would do great. Rory already knew it, because she'd *been* doing great. The specs were perfect. The wind-tunnel tests had been extremely promising. The problem? The missing ingredient for a win on Sunday? A dedicated driver.

He shook away that thought. He was right here. Ready. Committed. Focused.

He watched Jaycee disappear through the window of the pink Chevy and roar out of the pit stall.

"Rory?" It was Cody's voice again, followed by a hand on his shoulder. "Daylight's burning, buddy."

Rory turned and climbed through the window of his

own car. He slipped on his HANS device and connected his earpiece. His attention fixed on the gauges in front of him.

He flipped a switch and the car roared to life. He idled for a few seconds as his crew went through some last-minute prep and then he heard his spotter's voice over the earpiece.

"Everything A-OK, buddy?"

No. The truth pulled at the edges of his brain. His world was caving in and he couldn't seem to get a deep breath. His stomach knotted.

"Rory?" It was Cody's voice through the line this time. "You ready?"

"Yeah." He forced himself to say the one word. His throat burned as he accelerated. The engine roared. The tires squealed. And then he was flying around the track, suddenly desperate to distract himself from the truth that ate away inside of him.

You want her. You need her. You—

"Yes!" Cody's excited voice rushed over the earpiece. "Way to go, bro. That's the fastest lap time we've logged in three years! I knew you had it in you. How's she doing?"

"Running like a champ. Plenty of power and she's handling pretty good in the turns."

"Good. Let's go a few more before we talk adjustments."

Rory muttered a response and held tight as the wheel vibrated beneath him. He hit the next turn, his gloves gripping and sliding. He leveled the car out and nosed up behind a familiar red, white and blue Chevy being driven by Linc Adams.

The draft sucked him in, pulling him closer as the first car punched through the air, making space for both of them. He was just about to go for a slingshot move when he saw a pink blur in the corner of his eye. She was on the opposite side of the racetrack, just beyond Turn Three.

"Debris to the left," his spotter warned and he steered to the right, losing the car in front of him and the draft as he edged to the side. The pink blur kept going, staying in his peripheral vision as they both kept time on opposite sides of the track. Anxiety rushed through him, along with desperation, and he picked up his speed, swerved back behind the red, white and blue car. He ran in close and plotted a pass.

"You're up on the next turn." The spotter's voice sounded in his helmet, guiding him as he hit his points and kept moving.

Racing.

Running.

He leveled the car out and saw Jaycee up ahead. A knife twisted in his gut. He knew no matter how fast he went, or how far, he couldn't catch her.

He *had* to. Desperation welled and he urged the car faster. But he wasn't running away from his own damnable feelings this time. No, Rory was running *to* something.

To her.

The realization hit him as he turned abruptly to the left and felt himself get sucked in by the air flowing off the car in front of him. He shot past Linc and moved into the lead. And then Rory was the one punching through the air, leading the way down the superspeedway. He narrowed the distance to her, giving it his all. He wasn't sure what he would do when he caught her, just that he had to get there.

With each turn, he gained on the bright pink Chevy

until he sat maybe three car lengths behind. One more lap and he would nose up behind her. Relief washed through him.

Followed by a rush of pure terror as Jaycee hit the next turn a little too sharply. Her back end was loose and she started to spin.

"Go right! *Go right!*"

The spotter's voice barely pushed past the thunder of Rory's heartbeat as he watched the woman he loved—the only woman he'd ever loved—careen across the track, headed straight for the nearest wall.

Shit!

Jaycee fought for control, but her car had been running loose all afternoon and it was a no-win situation. She slammed into the wall, the crash jarring every bone in her body. Everything shook, from her toes to her teeth, and just like that, it was over.

Her head swam for a few moments before she finally got her bearings. Savannah's desperate voice came over the earpiece, but Jaycee was too focused on the flames licking at her front end. She unstrapped herself and struggled through the window.

She was halfway out when she felt the strong hands on her upper arms.

Rory pulled her free and helped her get her helmet off. And then he hauled her close and hugged her tight. In the distance, she heard Savannah's voice over the earpiece and the commotion as crew members started toward where she stood next to the smoking car.

She closed her eyes against a rush of hot tears. A crazy reaction. She'd crashed many times and she'd always walked away. This time, too.

At the same time, the moment felt different.

Because of Rory.

He was here, and he was holding her, and she wanted him to keep holding her. Her hands snaked around his waist and she held on, and so did he. His arms were tight, possessive, as if he wasn't going to let her go.

Not now. Not ever.

The thought was like a dousing of ice water and she stiffened.

"Stop." She struggled free of his embrace, her chest heaving, her arms hanging like dead weight at her sides. The ground trembled and she fought to keep her footing as she stumbled away from him. She needed to catch her breath. To breathe. To forget. "Just stop it."

"What are you talking about?"

She shook her head. "Stop acting like you like me."

"I *don't* like you."

"I know you don't. This is all just—"

"I *love* you." The words were deep, gruff, heartfelt. They sliced through the distance to her and snatched the oxygen out of her lungs.

He *loved* her?

She felt a split second of elation before reality snatched her back to the moment. He couldn't. He didn't. *No!* Her throat burned and a vise tightened around her heart. A few feet away, a fire-and-rescue team pulled up to her car and started going through the usual motions. The track officials had already called a caution and sent the other cars back to pit road to clear the track. One of the rescue paramedics started toward her, but she held up a hand and shook her head. She turned the other way. "I have to get out of here."

"Jaycee?" Rory was on her before she could take a step, mindless of their growing audience. Strong, warm hands cradled her face as he searched her gaze. "Didn't you hear me? I said I love you. I've always loved you. Back when we were kids. And now. *Always*."

"Is everything—," one of the officials began, but Rory flashed him a look and the man backed off.

He pulled Jaycee several feet away out of earshot and faced her. They stood near the edge of the raceway, smack-dab in the middle of the blazing sunshine, surrounded by dozens of rescue workers and crew members. But when he stared down at her, his gaze so blue and bold that she had the sudden urge to dive in headfirst, it felt as if they were the only two people on earth.

"I was an asshole." His voice was deep, compelling, regretful. "I never should have turned away from you that time you kissed me so long ago. I threw our friendship away and I hurt you, and I'm sorry. And I'm even more sorry that I haven't called you these past two weeks." He shook his head and raked a hand through his hair. "I should have told you how I felt. I would have, except I didn't really realize it myself. But when I saw you slam into that wall . . ." Anguish glittered hot and bright in his gaze. "Baby, I love you. I—"

"Don't!" Jaycee felt a rush of pure joy, followed by a wave of fear unlike anything she'd ever felt before.

Because *she* loved *him*, too. With all of her heart and soul. Yes, she loved him. And like every other person in her past, he didn't love her back. He loved the new and improved Jaycee, maybe. But while she'd turned herself into a goddess on the outside, deep down she was still the same grease monkey she'd always been. She still hated the color pink and detested floor-length dresses and she would be happy if she never, ever saw another waxing specialist.

No, he didn't love *her*. He loved the ultrafeminine

woman she was pretending to be. The woman she would have to keep pretending to be if she wanted to keep his love.

"This isn't me," she blurted. "It's an image put together by Riley and Image Nation to keep my sponsor happy. But the crazy thing is, it isn't working, because I'm not good at all of this. I'm awkward and uptight and wrong. All wrong." There. She'd said it. Now he would walk. Hell, he would run.

"Marry me," he said.

His deep, husky words stalled her heart for a long moment. Pure happiness rolled through her, but her panic multiplied. "Didn't you hear me? It's a charade. I'm a fake. I hate yoga. And I can't stand bean sprouts. And I've never made spaghetti in my entire life. I just got lucky that it turned out okay despite the burned meatballs."

A grin played at his lips. "Actually, you didn't get so lucky."

Her eyes narrowed. "But you said it was good."

"I didn't want to hurt your feelings, Trixie."

Warmth blossomed in her chest and she stiffened. "You mean you didn't want to hurt the new Jaycee's feelings. The one who dresses up and looks pretty. That's not me." She shook her head and blinked against a sudden rush of tears. She was not going to cry. Because Jaycee Anderson didn't cry. Never. *Ever.* "It's all an act." She waved an arm. "So take a hike."

He stiffened, as if all the more determined to hold his ground. "I can't do that."

"Sure you can." She held tight to the anger and resentment that churned inside of her. A lifetime of it. "You did it once, you can do it again."

"I didn't want to," he admitted. "I had to." Sincerity gleamed in his gaze and suddenly she didn't feel half as angry as she felt sad. For herself. And for him. Because he'd spent his life living another person's dream.

She knew what that was like. She'd buried her own hopes back then so that she could crawl into the driver's seat for Ace.

But she'd stayed in racing for herself. Because she was good at it. And, most importantly, because she liked it. Regardless of the reason, this had become her dream as much as it had been her father's.

But Rory was different. He didn't love racing as she did. He loved the fact that he was carrying on the family tradition. Because he didn't want to defy his dad.

"I needed to focus on my career and you were too much of a distraction. You made me think about other things besides the driving."

"Like walking away?" She kept pushing, determined to show him the real woman—hard and rough around the edges—behind the goddess facade.

"Like working on my mom's old Harley." A wistful smile touched his lips. "You were always talking about how I should open up my own motorcycle shop."

"We were kids. We talked about a lot of things."

"But you made me want to really do it. You made me believe I could." He shook his head. "Until my dad took it away. He was so mad . . . I didn't want to piss him off anymore. He was all I had, so I did what he wanted. I drove, which meant I couldn't afford to think about anything else. So I cut you out of my life." His voice softened. "But not because there was anything wrong with *you*."

The moment he said the words, a memory stirred

and she heard her father's voice. *You're doing it wrong again, Jaycee. Don't do it like that. Do it like this. Drive like this. Talk like this. Be like this.*

Be like me.

Suddenly, Jaycee felt the hard shell around her heart break a little. "I wasn't good enough for him." The words slid past her defenses before she could snatch them back.

"That wasn't you." He stepped toward her, closing the small distance she'd gained. But he didn't touch her this time. Not with his hands. Instead, his gaze caught and held hers. "It was *him*, baby. He didn't know how to be a father. Not to Riley, and sure as hell not to you. This sport was the only thing he knew how to do. The one thing he was good at, and so he did it at the expense of everything else. It was wrong to push you so hard. And it was wrong of him to abandon your sister. And keeping the two of you apart? That was criminal. But he was the one responsible. He did it." His voice softened. "You're not him, Jaycee."

She wanted so much to believe Rory, to throw herself into his arms and take what he offered: love and maybe marriage and . . . And what? A house in the suburbs? A couple of dogs? His and hers minivans? Kids?

Everything. She could see the answer in the brightness of his eyes and the fierce expression on his face. He wanted it all. With her.

She wanted it, too. But she couldn't shake the *what if?* that swirled deep inside of her. A question that wouldn't be answered until later, until she settled down and had her own family. Maybe she would do exactly what Ace had done. Maybe not.

Jaycee wasn't willing to bank on a maybe. She

wouldn't risk hurting her own children the way Ace had hurt her.

He'd hurt Riley the same way. As much as Jaycee had fought the truth, she'd always known deep down that Ace had indeed walked out on Riley and Riley's mother. She'd known it from the moment she'd learned of Riley's existence. But admitting it meant declaring to the world, and to herself, that she came from one cold, heartless bastard. A man who could turn his back on his child with no thought to the consequences. A man who didn't know how to love. A man incapable of it.

Her father.

Her blood.

Herself.

"I—I don't trust you." She pulled away from him, her heart pounding and her hands trembling.

She started toward the fire-and-rescue team without looking back.

Chapter Twenty-six

"That was great!" Cody pulled off his headset and clapped Rory on the back as soon as he climbed out of the race car. "Based on the stats, you just had the fastest lap clocked at this speedway in the past five years." Cody's grin quickly turned into a frown. "Before you decided to stop for Jaycee Anderson." His brow furrowed. "What in the hell were you thinking?"

But he hadn't been thinking. He'd been feeling. The love. The fear. The worry.

"Uh-oh," Cody said. "Please tell me this isn't what I think it is."

Rory just shook his head. Jaycee *loved* him. He knew it now. The knowledge should have made him feel like a million bucks, but it just made his chest ache that much more. He loved her and couldn't have her, and suddenly everything else meant nothing. Not his car. Or his dad. Or winning. It all meant zip without Jaycee.

"You do that tomorrow and we're home free," Cody went on, heeding the warning in Rory's eyes and changing the subject back to the track test. He led Rory over to a metal table where a row of computer screens had been set up. He motioned to the calculations displayed on the monitors. "You do this during the race and you'll go all the way, bud."

Cody patted Rory on the back. His eyes danced with excitement, but there was something else as well. Envy. "Smile, bro. Daytona is as good as yours."

Rory shook his head. "No."

"Don't be crazy. This is it. I can feel it. This is your year, buddy. You've been waiting a lifetime for this."

But he hadn't. He'd been waiting a lifetime for Jaycee. She was what haunted his thoughts night after night. A win was fleeting. Here today, gone tomorrow. But Jaycee . . . She was there in his head, in his heart. When he was with her, he didn't feel the restlessness. Or the anxiety. Or the damned certainty that something was missing.

Because *she* was the something missing in his life.

"It's not my year," he told his brother. "It's *your* year."

"What are you talking about? Hold up!" Cody shook his head as Rory started to walk past him. Disbelief gleamed in his familiar blue eyes, along with a spark of excitement. "Did you hit your head climbing out of the car?"

"No."

"Then what's this about?"

"It's about you driving this car. You should be out there on the track, not back here. You don't belong back here. You were meant to drive, Cody. And not on the short tracks. You're better than that. I know it. You know it. It's high time that dad knows it. You stood up to him once, you can do it again."

"He'll never let me drive for him."

"We'll see about that." Rory left Cody staring after him and walked over to Word Canyon, who stood several feet away talking to one of the tire crew. "We need to talk," he told the old man.

"I'm sorry," Aaron said. "I can't very well stay on board now that every team member and NASCAR official within hearing distance already knows about the makeover."

They stood in the garage, the team frantically assessing the damaged car while Jaycee and Riley stood off to the side with the sponsor.

"I didn't think anyone could hear me," Jaycee explained.

But someone had. Maybe the guys from fire and rescue. The other team members who'd held back while she'd faced off with Rory. Regardless, someone had heard, and in the three hours since the incident, the rumors had spread.

"After Daytona," he told her, "we're out." He turned. "Good luck," he said as an afterthought. And then he left the garage.

Riley looked as sick as Jaycee suddenly felt. She looked ready to throw up or cry. She'd done both when Jaycee had walked into the garage after the crash.

Because she'd known then about Aaron's decision? Or because she cared about Jaycee?

Not the latter, a voice whispered. The same voice that had told her that Rory could never love the real woman beneath the facade. A voice that sounded so much like her father.

She stared across the few feet that separated her from her sister. Her flesh and blood. Riley was nothing like the cold, heartless man who'd fathered her. She was here, right in the middle of a sport she hated, to make enough money to pay her mother's medical bills.

It was selfless and so unlike Ace, and it totally disproved Jaycee's chip-off-the-old-block theory. Riley had turned out different. Which meant that maybe, just maybe, Jaycee had as well.

Did that mean Rory was right?

Hope flowered in her chest and this time she didn't try to squash it. She held tight and asked the one question of her sister that had haunted her since the crash. "You were scared, weren't you? When I hit the wall?"

Riley looked as if she wanted to say something, but then she shook her head. She started rummaging in her purse for her cosmetics bag. "Does it matter?"

"Actually, it does," Jaycee pressed.

Riley pulled out a tube of lipstick. Halfway to her lips, her hand faltered. "I never liked you. . ." The words were soft and quiet and cutting.

Jaycee stiffened, suddenly wishing she'd kept her mouth shut. *Told you so.*

"Never," Riley went on. Her gaze found Jaycee's. "I didn't want to like you. Because *he* liked you." When Jaycee started to open her mouth, Riley waved a hand at her. "I know it wasn't *Leave It to Beaver* for you either, but I still resented you. You had him and I didn't." She laughed, a bitter sound. "Crazy, huh? I hated him and, at the same time, I wanted him there." She shook her head again. "But that never happened and so I hated you, too. Before I met you."

Jaycee's heart pounded. "And now?"

A smile tugged at Riley's lips. "It's easy for me to still hate you sometimes. You're so stubborn." She shook her head. "But you're sweet, too, in a really stubborn, infuriating way. And determined. I admire you, Jaycee. For all your faults, you're one tough chick." She shook her head. "When I saw you crash, I realized that I might never get the chance to tell you that, and it made me feel bad. That probably sounds stupid. I know you don't really like *me* that much. I'm bossy and overbearing and a little stubborn myself."

Jaycee grinned. "One tough chick."

Riley's gaze met Jaycee's and she smiled. "I guess I am. My mom certainly thinks so. She couldn't function without me."

"I'd like to meet her sometime."

"You might regret that decision. She can be a little draining. But then you know mothers." After a pause, her pain-filled gaze snagged with Jaycee's. "I didn't mean . . ." She shook her head. "I wasn't thinking."

"It's okay. While I don't have my own firsthand experience when it comes to moms, I've seen enough television to get the gist. They can be as much a pain as any father."

"Amen." Riley licked her lips. "I'm sorry about your mother." Sincerity gleamed in her eyes, along with compassion and concern.

A bubbling warmth swept through Jaycee. If she'd had any lingering doubts about the power of genetics, one look into her sister's eyes was enough to change her mind. Riley was as far from Ace as anyone could get. And so was Jaycee. They cared about people. They cared about each other.

"Do you ever wonder why he did it?" Riley finally asked.

"More times than I can count," Jaycee admitted.

"He probably thought we'd kill each other."

"Or . . . maybe he had a change of heart." It was the last thing Jaycee had meant to say. At the same time, she couldn't help but voice the slim possibility. Not because of loyalty to her father, but because of loyalty to herself. And Riley.

Her older sister leveled a stare at her. "You really think that's what happened?"

"Probably not." She shrugged. "But people do change. Just look at me. I'm in a pink racing suit and I haven't bitched about it in over fifteen minutes. That's got to be some kind of record."

"True enough." Riley smiled. "So"—she shrugged—"which one of us gets to break the news to everyone? We could wait, but I think it would be better if we went ahead and told the crew now. That way they can put out feelers and consider their options. Being without a sponsor . . ."

People do change. The notion stuck in Jaycee's head, overriding her sister's comments. Maybe Ace had changed. Maybe he'd regretted keeping his daughters apart and the will had been his way of making up for it, dragging them together in a forced alliance. Maybe not. And Jaycee would never know, because there would be no second chances with Ace, no opportunity to ask him questions or ease the hurt that a lifetime with him had caused.

Either way, she had a second chance with her sister. A chance to get to know Riley. To get to know herself.

"We could tell them," Jaycee said, "or we could hold off and go with Plan B. We still have a race to win."

"It won't matter."

"No, but the interview with Trick Donovan might." If Jaycee played her cards right. "I'm not ready to give up just yet." In that one little way she was like Ace, and that was okay. Because Jaycee had finally made peace with her past.

She stared at her sister, at the cosmetics bag clutched

in Riley's manicured hands, and wondered if she would ever be as comfortable with a tube of lipstick. Only time would tell.

"What about you?" Jaycee asked Riley. "You going to cut your losses and go back home, or are you going to stay and fight for our season?"

Indecision played across Riley's face as she seemed to think. Finally, she shrugged. "I'm not sure. We've lost our sponsor and I'm almost out of Ritzy Red. Things couldn't get much worse." Her gaze met Jaycee's. "What are you going to do?"

"Start trusting myself."

She'd lied when she told Rory that she didn't trust him. It was herself she'd had doubts about. She realized that truth in a crystalline moment as she stared at the demolished race car that sat a few feet away. While she could physically put herself on the line every Sunday, she hadn't been able to do it emotionally. That's why she'd turned away from Rory. Not because she'd really believed that he loved her image. He'd seen past it. He always had.

Yeah, and he turned his back.

For his own reasons.

Just as Ace had pushed her, demoralized her, for his own selfish reasons. He'd spent so much time telling her she wasn't good enough, deep down she'd started to think that maybe he was right. When Rory had walked away, it had confirmed it.

But it wasn't true.

It had never been true.

Ace had been wrong to push her, just as Rory had been wrong to walk away. But Rory had come back.

I love you.

He did, she realized. She wasn't drop-dead gorgeous

and she didn't know her chartreuse from her lime green, but neither did a lot of other women. She wasn't a bona fide goddess, but she wasn't 100 percent grease monkey, either. She was a little of both. She had a big mouth and bad attitude. But Rory had come for her. He loved her anyway, and she loved him.

Just as important, she loved herself. And it was time to start showing it.

"I have an idea."

She spent the next few minutes explaining to Riley what she was thinking. "It's a long shot," she finally finished, "but it just might work."

Riley thought it over. "Okay, genius. What do we do first?"

"I never thought I'd actually say this," Jaycee grinned, "but let's go shopping."

Chapter Twenty-seven

The next morning dawned bright and sunny, ideal conditions for the first qualifying race for the Daytona 500. The first- and second-fastest drivers had already locked in their positions during the previous week—Linc Adams and Mackenzie Briggs—and now it was up to the rest of the drivers to secure their spots in this Super Bowl of NASCAR.

It was early in the morning, but the speedway already buzzed with excitement. The parking lot overflowed with vehicles. There were people everywhere, overflowing the tents, the motor-home lots. The ones with credentials filled pit road, watching the different crews go through their race prep until the area went hot. Then everyone except crew members and those with Hot Pass credentials would be forced to leave. Folks would crowd the stands and the moment of truth would be upon each and every driver.

Except for Jaycee. For her, the moment of truth was right now.

She stood in the yellow tent where *Life in The Fast Lane* was being broadcast to millions of race fans the world over, her sister next to her.

"How much longer?" Riley asked the assistant who

flitted around Jaycee, checking her microphone hookup and adjusting wires. "She has a driver's meeting in an hour."

"Mr. Donovan's just about ready. He's got Linc Adams in the hot seat right now, but then it'll be Jaycee's turn."

"Hot seat, huh?" Riley's gaze met Jaycee's. "You sure you want to go through with this?"

Jaycee tamped down the last niggling doubt and nodded. "How do I look?"

"Perfect."

Jaycee smiled and turned toward the mirror that stood a few feet away. She eyed her reflection, her gaze going from her simple ponytail pulled up beneath a pink Race Chicks cap, to the matching pink T-shirt that had GIRL POWER spelled out in rhinestones. She wore a pair of simple boot-cut jeans, loose enough so that she didn't worry over her circulation, but fitted enough to be flattering. A pair of low canvas wedges completed the look.

It was casual yet feminine. A cross between a goddess and a grease monkey. She wore a minimal amount of makeup and zero hair products. Danielle would surely have a fit—not that Jaycee cared. She was no longer desperate to please Aaron or Image Nation. She certainly wouldn't win any fashion awards, but Riley had given her stamp of approval. Even more, Jaycee herself liked it. She felt at ease in the casual but flattering clothes. Pretty. Confident.

Until the assistant tugged on her arm.

"You're on."

Jaycee turned toward Riley, who smiled and said, "Go give 'em hell."

Jaycee nodded, summoned her courage and walked

toward the stage to give Trick and his viewing audience their first look at the real Jaycee Anderson.

Trick asked the usual questions, speculating about the race and the season ahead. He even touched on the rumors that Jaycee had been undergoing a makeover with Image Nation. Jaycee smiled and answered every question as openly and honestly as possible, without making Aaron look pushy. This wasn't about retaliating against Revved & Ready. It was about moving forward, about showing the public who and what she was as a person as well as a driver. She ended with the all-important fact that she was actively looking for a new sponsor because after the race on Sunday, she would be losing hers due to a conflict of interest.

"That's tough, but I'm sure someone out there will step up and get behind Race Chicks."

"I hope you're right."

Trick smiled. "Good luck in the race today," he said, signaling the close of the interview. "Any parting words for your fans?"

"Actually, I would like to say something to one in particular." She drew a shaky breath, gathered her courage and stared directly into the camera. "I love you, Rory. I always have and I always will, and if you still want a relationship, then I'm definitely interested. I'll wait for you here after the broadcast."

It wasn't the most romantic speech, but it left no doubt that, while Jaycee Anderson might not be a goddess, she was very much a woman.

"Rory?" Trick eyed her. "Rory Canyon?"

She smiled. "The one and only. *My* one and only."

Rory normally stopped to sign autographs for everyone, but he couldn't waste a minute. He had to get to

Jaycee before she gave up waiting for him and disappeared into the chaos of qualifying day. If that happened, he would have to wait until later that afternoon to see if what Cody had told him had been the truth: Jaycee Anderson had just declared her love on national television.

He picked up his stride, dodging past signs, darting around stunned fans until he reached the familiar yellow tent.

"Jaycee!" He called her name as she was about to round the tent and head toward pit road. Her familiar caramel-colored eyes locked with his and the disappointment she'd obviously been feeling because he was late faded into a gleam of pure excitement.

He reached her in a few swift strides. Before he could drag some much needed air into his lungs, he hauled her close and kissed her. Hard and hot and hungry, at first. Then slow and sweet and promising. He finally pulled away and stared down at her. His heart pounded and his blood rushed and he felt more excited than he'd ever felt at the start of any race. Affirmation that Rory Canyon wasn't half as interested in driving as he'd always pretended to be. He'd done it because of his father.

No more.

A crowd had gathered around them. People hooted and hollered. Cameras and cell phones flashed. Video cameras rolled. But Rory didn't care about any of it. His attention riveted on the woman standing in front of him.

"It's about time you showed up." She licked her lips. "I love you."

The words sang through his head and he smiled. "I know."

"You were watching?"

"Actually, I wasn't. Cody was. I was busy with a press conference about some recent changes to the Xtreme driving team. My dad's giving Cody a shot behind the wheel since I'll be retiring after this year."

"*What?*"

"You heard me." His expression grew serious. "I love driving, but it's not my real passion."

"The motorcycles?"

He nodded. "I've always wanted to open up my own shop. I've got the means to do it, so there's no reason not to go after it. I've even got some part-time help lined up." He'd called several of his foster boys just that morning and offered them jobs, including Mike. He'd offered not only to pay the boy a decent wage, but to donate a percentage to a college fund *and* foot the bill for violin lessons. Mike's mother hadn't been able to refuse the generous offer, particularly with Mike so excited at the prospect of working with Rory, and so she'd finally agreed.

"What about the race on Sunday?" Jaycee asked.

"I'll start the season and stay with it while Cody races a second Xtreme car. He's gained some notoriety on the short tracks, so he's already on everyone's radar. Once he proves to the sponsors that he can make the transition, he'll step into the lead and I'll bow out."

"And your dad agreed to this?"

"He will. I'm leaving Sprint and none of my brothers want to leave Busch or the Truck series. And neither Ian nor Jared want to race both. Which means Xtreme will have to go outside the family to find a driver for Sprint. My dad would sooner gnaw off an arm, so he agreed to talk about it over Sunday dinner."

He grinned. "He invited Cody and Cheryl and the girls."

"I'm assuming that's a good thing."

"Probably not. I'm sure he and Cheryl will go at it. She's not exactly the ideal Himanist wife. But at least they're going to give it a try. It's a start. In the meantime"—he stared down at her—"you've got a race on your hands, because I plan on going out on top."

"We'll see about that." She lowered her lashes and her gaze darkened. "You know I like being on top."

His memory stirred. "If I seem to recall, you like being on top, and on the bottom, and in front, and behind."

Sincerity gleamed in her gaze. "I like it any way, every way, because it's with you."

He drew her close and held her tight. "I love you, Jaycee. *You.* Whether you're wearing overalls or a dress. Whether you're cussing me out or cooking me dinner. I love everything about you."

"Even the morning breath?"

"Maybe I can pass on that." She pinched him and he grinned before the expression faded and he stared deep into her eyes again. "I want you to come home with me, Jaycee. I want us to get married and make babies and grow old together."

"I will. I do." She hugged him fiercely for a long moment before she pulled back. A wicked light danced in her gaze as she stared up at him. "On one condition."

"And what's that?"

Her gaze twinkled with all of the love and affection he felt overflowing his own heart. "I always get to drive. Someone needs to teach you how to handle that Mustang."

A smile tugged at his lips. "How about we *both* get to drive?"

"Now that's an offer I can't refuse." Then Jaycee Anderson leaned up on her tiptoes, pressed her lips to his, and sealed the deal.

Epilogue

"Hello race fans! This is Trick Donovan doing a special radio broadcast live from Daytona on XM radio. We're in the Winner's Circle with Rory Canyon and Jaycee Anderson. Jaycee, how does it feel to win your first race at Daytona?"

"It feels great, but I couldn't have done it without my crew. And my sister. And special thanks to Martin Schilling, whom I am not dating. We're just friends."

"I guess Jaycee's seen the tabloids, too, folks. You heard it here first. Jaycee and Martin. Just friends. Rory? What are your thoughts?"

"I actually thought it was serious at first. I have a jealous streak."

"Not the tabloid reports on Jaycee and Schilling. The race. Care to tell us what you were thinking when Jaycee zoomed past you in the last two seconds and took the lead?"

"Just that it couldn't have happened to a better woman."

"That's 'driver,'" Jaycee corrected. "A better driver."

"Not to me, baby. Not to me."

"You guys aren't going to kiss now, are you? Okay, yeah, well, I guess kissing's okay. It's the Winner's Circle, after all. Well, folks, there you have it. Final thoughts on a groundbreaking race from NASCAR's hottest couple. This is Trick Donovan signing off. Until next time. . ."

> *Trouble in Mudbug*
>
> by JANA DeLeon
>
> COMING FEBRUARY 2009!
>
> Read ahead for a peek.

"I still can't believe she's gone," Maryse Robicheaux told her best friend, Sabine, as she stared down at the woman in the coffin.

Of course, the pink suit was a dead giveaway—so to speak—that the wearer was no longer with them. For the miserable five years and thirty-two days she'd had to deal with her soon-to-be-ex and now-departed mother-in-law, Maryse had never once seen her wear a color other than black. Now she sorta resembled the Stay Puft Marshmallow Man dressed in Pepto-Bismol.

"I can't believe it, either," Sabine whispered. "I didn't even think it was possible. I was certain her existence represented the rise of the Antichrist."

Maryse jabbed her friend with her elbow. "For Pete's sake, we're at the woman's funeral. Show some respect."

Sabine let out a sigh. "Sorry, Maryse, but the woman gave you holy hell and that son of hers was even worse. I don't even understand why you wanted to come."

Maryse stared at the casket again and shook her head. "I don't know. I just felt compelled to. I can't really explain it."

Looking down at Helena, Maryse still didn't have an answer for why she was there. If she'd come for some sort of closure, it hadn't happened. But then, what had she expected—a dead woman to pop up out of the coffin and apologize for bringing the most useless man in the world into existence, then making Maryse's life even more miserable by being the biggest bitch on the face of the earth?

It wasn't likely when you considered that Helena Henry had never apologized for anything in her entire life. It had never been necessary. When you had a pocketbook the size of the Atchafalaya Basin, people tended to overlook bad behavior.

"I think they're ready to start," Sabine whispered, gesturing to the minister who had entered the chapel through a side door. "We need to take a seat."

Maryse nodded but remained glued to her place in front of the coffin, not yet able to tear herself away from the uncustomary pink dress and the awful-but-now-dead woman who wore it. "Just a minute more."

There had to be some reason she'd come. Some reason other than just to ensure that Helena's reign of terror was over, but nothing came to her except the memory of Helena's gardenia perfume.

"Where's Hank?" Sabine asked. "Surely he wouldn't miss his own mother's funeral. That would be major bad karma, even for Hank. I know he's a lousy human being and all, but really."

Maryse sighed as Sabine's words chased away a wistful vision of her wayward husband, Hank, in a coffin right alongside Helena. If her best friend had even an inkling of her thoughts, she'd besiege her with a regime of crystal cleansing and incense until Maryse went insane, and she was saving the insanity plea to use later in life and on a much bigger problem than a worthless man.

"Hank is a lot of things," Maryse said, "but he's not a complete fool. He's wanted for at least twenty different offenses in Mudbug. This is the first place the cops would look for him. There's probably one behind that skirt under the coffin."

Sabine stared at the blue velvet curtain for a moment, then pulled a piece of it to the side and leaned down a bit.

Sarcasm was completely lost on Sabine.

Maryse rolled her eyes and turned away from the Pink Polyester Antichrist and pointed to a pew in the back. "He'll turn up for the reading of the will," she whispered as the music began to play and they took a seat in the back of the chapel. "Even I would bet on that one."

Sabine smirked. "Then he'll work a deal with the local cops through Judge Warner and everything will be swept under the rug as usual."

"Yeah, probably. The only thing different is maybe I'll finally get my divorce."

Sabine's eyes widened. "I hadn't even thought of that but you're right. When Hank appears, you can have him served." She reached over and squeezed Maryse's hand. "Oh, thank God, Maryse. You can finally be free."

Maryse nodded, as the song leader's voice filtered through her head. What a mess she'd made of her life. She hadn't even been married to Hank thirty days before he disappeared, leaving her holding the bag while the various and numerous bookies and collection agents came calling. That was five years ago, and despite the efforts of four different private investigators and several angry friends, she hadn't seen Hank Henry ever since. Oh, but she'd seen Helena.

The pastor began to read the standard funeral Bible verses, meant to comfort those in attendance that the person they loved had moved on to a better place. Maryse smirked at the irony. Mudbug was the better place now that Helena was gone. She cast her gaze once more to Helena, lying peacefully in her coffin.

That's when Helena moved.

Maryse straightened in her pew, blinked once to clear her vision, and stared hard at Helena Henry. Surely it was a trick of the lights. Dead people didn't move. Embalming and all that other icky stuff that happened at funeral homes took care of that, right?

Maryse had just about convinced herself that it was a trick of lights and shadows when Helena opened her eyes and raised her head. Maryse sucked in a breath and clenched her eyes shut, certain she was having a nervous breakdown that had been five years in the making. She waited several seconds, then slowly opened her eyes, silently praying that her mind was done playing tricks on her.

Apparently, it wasn't.

Helena sat bolt upright in the coffin, looking around the chapel, a confused expression on her boldly painted face. Panicked, Maryse scanned the other attendees. Why wasn't anyone screaming or pointing or running for the door? God knows, she hadn't been to many funerals, but she didn't remember the dead person sitting up being a part of any of them.

She felt a squeeze on her hand and Sabine whispered, "Are you all right? You got really pale all of a sudden."

Maryse started to answer, but then sucked in a breath as Helena crawled out of the coffin and stood in front of it gazing up at the pastor. "Don't you see that?" Maryse asked and pointed to the front of the chapel. "Don't you see what's happening?" Maryse tore her gaze from Helena and looked at Sabine.

Her friend cast a look to the front of the chapel exactly where Maryse was pointing, then looked back at her with concern, but no fear, no terror…nothing to indicate that she saw anything at all wrong with the service.

"See what?" Sabine asked. "Do we need to leave? You don't look well."

Maryse looked back to the front of the chapel. That's when Helena turned to the pastor and started to yell.

"What the hell is going on here, Pastor Bob? For Christ's sake, I'm Catholic." Helena ranted. "What are all these people doing here, and why did someone dress me like a hooker and shove me in a coffin? If this is some sort of weird Baptist ceremony, I don't want any part of it." Helena paused for a moment, but the pastor continued as if she'd never said a word.

Maryse stared, not blinking, not breathing, her eyes growing wider and wider until she felt as if they would pop.

Helena turned from the pastor and stared out at the attendees. "I'll have you all arrested, is what I'll do. Damn it, someone drugged me and put me in that coffin. I didn't get there by myself! What are you—some kind of weird cult? I'll see every one of you assholes in jail, especially you, Harold." Helena stepped over to the nearest pew and reached for her husband, Harold, but her hands passed completely through him.

Helena stopped for a moment, then tried to touch Harold once more, but the result was exactly the same. Helena frowned and looked down at herself, then back at the coffin. Maryse followed her gaze and that's when she realized Helena's body was still lying there—placid as ever.

Helena stared at herself for what seemed like eons, her eyes wide, her expression shocked. The pastor asked everyone to rise for prayer, and Maryse rose in a daze to stand alongside Sabine, but she couldn't bring herself to bow her head. Her eyes were glued on the spectacle at the front of the chapel. The spectacle that apparently no one else could see.

Helena tore her gaze from the coffin and began to walk slowly down the aisle, yelling as she went and waving her hands in front of people's faces. But no one so much as flinched. As she approached the back, Maryse's heart began to race and her head pounded with the rush of blood. She knew she should sit down, but she couldn't move, couldn't breathe.

All of a sudden, Helena ceased yelling and stopped in her tracks about ten feet from Maryse's pew. Her expression changed from shocked to worried, then sad. Maryse tried to maintain her composure, but the breath she'd been holding came out with a whoosh. Helena looked toward the source of the noise and locked eyes with Maryse.

Maryse held in a cry as Helena moved toward her. A wave of dizziness washed over her, and her head began to swim. One step, two steps, then right in front of her.

And that's when everything went dark.

Gemma Halliday

MAYHEM *in* HIGH HEELS

Maddie Springer is finally walking down the aisle with the man of her dreams. And she's got the perfect wedding planner to pull it all off in style. Well, perfect, that is, until the woman winds up dead — murdered in buttercream frosting. Suddenly Maddie's dream wedding melts faster than an ice sculpture at an outdoor buffet. And when her groom-to-be is made the detective in charge of the case, there goes any chance of a honeymoon. Unless, of course, Maddie can find the murderer before her big day.

With the help of her fellow fashionista friends, Maddie vows to unveil the cold-blooded killer. Is it the powerful ex-husband, the hot young boy toy, a secret lover from the past, or a billionaire bridezilla on the warpath? As the wedding day grows closer, tempers flare, old flames return, and Maddie's race to the altar turns into a race against time.

ISBN 13: 978-0-8439-6109-6

✂ ☐ **YES!**

Sign me up for the Love Spell Book Club and send my FREE BOOKS! If I choose to stay in the club, I will pay only $8.50* each month, a savings of $6.48!

NAME: _____

ADDRESS: _____

TELEPHONE: _____

EMAIL: _____

☐ I want to pay by credit card.

☐ **VISA**　　☐ **MasterCard**　　☐ **DISCOVER**

ACCOUNT #: _____

EXPIRATION DATE: _____

SIGNATURE: _____

Mail this page along with $2.00 shipping and handling to:

Love Spell Book Club
PO Box 6640
Wayne, PA 19087

Or fax (must include credit card information) to:
610-995-9274

You can also sign up online at www.dorchesterpub.com.

*Plus $2.00 for shipping. Offer open to residents of the U.S. and Canada only. Canadian residents please call 1-800-481-9191 for pricing information. If under 18, a parent or guardian must sign. Terms, prices and conditions subject to change. Subscription subject to acceptance. Dorchester Publishing reserves the right to reject any order or cancel any subscription.